Dominant Impressions: Essays on the Canadian Short Story

REAPPRAISALS:
CANADIAN
WRITERS

Dominant Impressions: Essays on the Canadian Short Story

Edited by
Gerald Lynch and
Angela Arnold Robbeson

University of Ottawa Press

REAPPRAISALS
Canadian Writers

GERALD LYNCH
General Editor

Canadian Cataloguing in Publication Data

Main entry under title:
  Dominant impressions: essays on the Canadian short story

(Reappraisals, Canadian writers; 22)
Includes bibliographical references.
ISBN 0-7766-0505-4

  1. Short stories, Canadian (English)—History and criticism.
I. Lynch, Gerald, 1953–   II. Arnold Robbeson, Angela, 1967–
III. Series.

PS8187.D65 1999   C813'.0109   C99–901330–0
PR9192.52.D65 1999

University of Ottawa Press gratefully acknowledges the support extended to its publishing programme by the Canada Council and the University of Ottawa.
  We are grateful to the Faculty of Arts Research and Publication Committee and the University Research Fund of the University of Ottawa for generously provided funds.
  We acknowledge the financial support of the Government of Canada through the Book Publishing Industry Development Program for this project.

UNIVERSITY OF OTTAWA
UNIVERSITÉ D'OTTAWA

Cover design: Robert Dolbec

"All rights reserved. No part of this publication may be reproduced or transmitted in any form or by any means, electronic or mechanical, including photocopy, recording, or any information storage and retrieval system, without permission in writing from the publisher."

ISBN 0-7766-0505-4
ISSN 1189-6787

© University of Ottawa Press, 1999
  542 King Edward, Ottawa, Ont. Canada   K1N 6N5
  press@uottawa.ca   http://www.uopress.uottawa.ca

Printed and bound in Canada

Contents

Introduction   1

It Almost Always Starts This Way
    BONNIE BURNARD   9

Of Kings and Cabbages: Short Stories by Early Canadian Women
    WANDA CAMPBELL   17

"The Thing Is Found to Be Symbolic": *Symboliste* Elements in the Early Short Stories of Gilbert Parker, Charles G. D. Roberts and Duncan Campbell Scott
    D.M.R. BENTLEY   27

Present but Unaccounted For: The Canadian Young Adult Short Story of the Nineteenth Century Comes of Age
    JEAN STRINGAM   53

"Just Above the Breadline": Social(ist) Realism in Canadian Short Stories of the 1930s
    JAMES DOYLE   65

The Language of the Law: The Cases of Morley Callaghan
    GARY BOIRE   75

Rediscovering the Popular Canadian Short Story
    ALLAN WEISS   87

"Love and Death": Romance and Reality in Margaret Laurence's *A Bird in the House*
    NORA FOSTER STOVEL   99

Oedipus and Anti-Oedipus, Myth and Counter-Myth: Sheila Watson's Short Fiction
    DEAN IRVINE   115

Mapping Munro: Reading the "Clues"
    ROBERT THACKER   127

Hands and Mirrors: Gender Reflections in the Short Stories of Alistair MacLeod and Timothy Findley
    LAURIE KRUK   137

"To make the necessary dream perpetual": Postrealist Heroes in Canadian Short Fiction
    DEBORAH BOWEN   151

The Canadian Short Story
    ALISTAIR MACLEOD   161

Introduction

CANADIAN CRITICS AND SCHOLARS, along with a growing number from around the world, have long recognized the high achievements of Canadian short story writers in this at-once oldest and newest of the genres. However, these critics have tended to view the Canadian short story as a recent phenomenon, as a product of the post-1960 rise of Canadian cultural nationalism. Or such well-intentioned critics focus exclusively on one kind of Canadian short story: the exquisitely crafted modern story, say, that highest achievement in prose fiction of concision, indirection, and unhappy endings. Or they focus yet more narrowly on contemporary fiction, the postmodern short story, like narcissistic children who see their older siblings as fumbling attempts toward this present perfection. *Dominant Impressions* intends to counter such mistaken views by addressing the question: What are some of the literary and cultural antecedents of the Canadian short story? The exploration of possible answers to this question, in terms of the new scholarship and criticism presented here, should help toward establishing a continuum of the Canadian short story from at least the mid-nineteenth century to the present.

Attempts at distinguishing among genres, let alone prose fictional forms, are most often productive only of categorizing ends. The many expert contributors to *Short Story Theory at a Crossroads* (1989), perhaps the single most useful text on the genre, can be said to arrive at a tautological definition of the short story as a story that is short. We don't intend this observation as a wholly facetious compliment. In these times of rampant genre confusion such elementary observations, if not this one especially, are often those of lasting usefulness. And genre theory can be a labyrinthine thicket indeed, covering ground that, at one end, categorizes compulsively with a neoclassical dedication to the rules and, at the other, would do away with the whole notion of identifiable genres. When the generic status of even the novel can be made to appear questionable, it is perhaps most sensible to adopt Alistair Fowler's conception of genre (derived from Wittgenstein by way of Dugald Stewart) as kinds of literary works that share a "family resemblance": "Literary genre seems just the sort of concept with blurred edges that is suited to such an approach. Representatives of a genre may then be regarded as making up a family whose septs and individual members are related in various ways, without necessarily having any single feature shared in common by all" (41). Familiarity and common sense tell us when we are reading short stories and, to turn a slightly different observation of Mavis Gallant's, as Canadian readers we know when we're reading Canadian stories: the author is Canadian or/and the setting is Canadian; Mordecai Richler is a Canadian writer, Montreal is a Canadian setting. Ergo, *The Street* is a book of Canadian short stories.

That said, it might nevertheless be observed that among prose narratives there are short stories, longer stories (novellas), and the longest (novels). It remains a fact for those theorizing the short story (*Short Story Theory at a Crossroads* provides ample testimony) that much of what is most lastingly productive was said with Aristotelian precision by Edgar Allan Poe in his mid-nineteenth-century review of Nathaniel Hawthorne's *Twice-Told Tales*. Working out of the same Romantic-*Symboliste* aesthetic that has made the lyric the dominant poetic form since, Poe asserted the primary point that short stories had to be short enough to be read in one sitting, else his chief aesthetic virtues of unity of effect and dominant impression are lost. Thus was first uttered the mantra of twentieth-century literature classrooms and creative writing workshops (especially those adhering to New Critical principles): every word of a short story must count toward the telltale tally. To this end—and Poe implies as much—short stories might better be composed backwards. Thus too the short story, and most obviously in its high-impact modern manifestation (the version most readers know, from Chekhov to Joyce to Norman Levine), has often been said to be closer to poetry than to the traditional novel (which further lends credence to the concept of genre confusion).

Inarguably there is much to recommend these sketched first principles of short story construction and study, these strongest family features of the genre: those of brevity, concision, unity of impression and effect. But they do not tell the whole story of the Canadian short story.

It remains a pleonastic fact that short stories must first of all be *short* (though even this word is a relative adjective; and the historical variability of attention spans, not to say of posteriors, might well make us wonder just what duration Poe had in mind for a single sitting. Moreover, this qualifying of the genre's key term "short" supports Fowler's observation that, when it comes even to the most basic definitions of genre, "to begin is almost to end," because even with as supposedly distinct a genre as tragedy, "the common features are few and indistinct" [39]). But doubtless the time it takes to write a short story had as much to do with the form's popularity among nineteenth-century Canadian writers as the time it takes to read one. In this way, the two activities—time to write, time to read—are creatively related, attaching author to audience in the formation of a new genre and the making of literary culture. Or put concretely, in a pioneer country such as nineteenth-century Canada's especially, populated early on by besieged mothers and fathers beleaguered by trees, who apart from such a maverick as John Richardson could find the time to write novels? Interestingly, this lack of time as a result of domestic responsibilities was being given still in the mid-twentieth century by such Canadian women short story writers as Margaret Laurence and Alice Munro as the main pragmatic cause of their writing short stories instead of novels. Such considerations of length, especially as regards available time, may not be theoretically exciting, but they do remind us that the short story is a product of context and culture defined in the most inclusive way. As readers and critics—old and new, historian, historicist and post-structuralist—we ignore this ground of literature at the risks of falling into prejudice or receding into historical irrelevance.

In his landmark study of the Canadian and New Zealand short story, *Dreams of Speech and Violence* (1987), W. H. New argues that the short story is the marginal genre. In historically marginal cultures such as Canada's and New Zealand's, writers have found the marginal form accommodating of their situations and ambitions. Canadian and New Zealand writers use the short story, perhaps all unconsciously, as a kind of cultural-political protest, subversively, and with a sophisticated irony that remains mostly lost upon the central, dominant, financially rewarding, self-regarding cultures in which they need to succeed (America's and Australia's). New's theory has about it the ring of truth. Tested in pseudo-scientific fashion, it can be proven elsewhere. Ireland's writers, working on the margins of *the* dominant English literature culture, have thrived not only in the form of the short story but also in what many of them still consider the colonizer's language. The Americans dominated the form—with Poe, Hawthorne, and Melville—when in their so-called Renaissance they were defining and asserting their culture's value as against the British; in other words, when as a culture they were feeling most marginal. And consider: the British have been lacking in great short story writers (with D. H. Lawrence being the most notable exception).

Foregoing further definitions, then, and without distinguishing among such mini-forms as the sketch, the anecdote, the tale, the short story, and so on, we might simply observe the enduring centrality of the short story in Canada's literary history. Our first internationally acclaimed author was a writer of short stories: Thomas Chandler Haliburton, a colonial man whose *Clockmaker*—the Sam Slick stories—testifies to a keen, not to say an anxious, awareness of his position on the margins of two great cultures. Moreover, the first series of his *Clockmaker* forms a story cycle, and this form, the story cycle, has come increasingly to dominate the genre of the short story in Canada. The comic-satiric sketch and story at which Haliburton excelled continued to flourish through the nineteenth century, and by far the most important nineteenth-century magazines for its dissemination were the highly influential *The Week* (1883–96) and *Grip* (1873–94). Although primarily an organ of social and political culture, *The Week* regularly published short fiction and the literary journalism of Sara Jeannette Duncan in her "Saunterings" column. *Grip* published a great number of parodies, sketches, and satires of the kind that would later win Stephen Leacock international acclaim (in fact, Leacock published his first comic piece in *Grip* while still a student at the University of Toronto). And the work of some other of the prolific writers of comic stories, such as James McCarroll (pseudonym Terry Finnegan), is recently being recovered and valued for its contribution to the development of the Canadian short story.

The romantic short story also flourished in a popular magazine culture that included such publications as Montreal's long-lived *Literary Garland* (1838–51), Susanna and Dunbar Moodie's *Victoria Magazine* (1847–48) out of Belleville, Halifax's *Mayflower* (1851–52), Toronto's *Anglo-American Magazine and Canadian Journal* (1852–55), [*Rose-Belford's*] *Canadian Monthly and National Review* (1872–82), *New Dominion Monthly* (1867–79), and *Canadian Illustrated News* (1869–83), to name but the most successful. Short stories were contributed to these publications regularly by such writers as Eliza Lanesford Cushing, Harriet Vaughan Cheney, Susanna Moodie and Catharine Parr Traill, May Agnes Fleming, Rosanna Mullins Leprohon, Ethelwyn Wetherald, Susan Frances Harrison, Agnes Maude Machar, Louisa Murray, and Joanna Wood, to name but the more prolific and those who are becoming better known. The short stories in these periodicals, pioneering a somewhat alternate Canadian literary culture, were written predominantly by such women who thrived on the margins of patriarchal society. Their stories are not "merely" sketches, or effusive romances, or amateurish (and therefore dismissable) in any sense. They are fully realized short stories as accomplished and important in their historical-cultural contexts as any that came before or afterwards. Failure to appreciate this work in its own terms is the (our) genuine failure of imagination.

In 1896, at the beginnings of the modern story, Duncan Campbell Scott published his seminal story cycle, *In the Village of Viger*, comprising a virtuoso's gallery of nineteenth-century story forms, from folk tale to Gothic to local colour—and again with most being romantic rather than realistic in mode. At about the same time, Charles G. D. Roberts invented the so-called realistic animal story (with help from Ernest Thompson Seton); and Sara Jeannette Duncan continued publishing stories, many of which (such as the title story from her masterful *The Pool in the Desert*, 1903) are equal to those of Henry James in the niceties of their psychological realism and to those of William Dean Howells in their attention to the particularities of place.

Canada's next most famous writer after Haliburton is of course Stephen Leacock, and Leacock was not only a humorist too, like Haliburton, but in his fiction also a writer exclusively of sketches and short stories. After him, through the Modern period, the Canadian story continued to fare well in the hands of such practitioners as J. G. Sime (*Sister Woman*, 1919, a story cycle), D. C. Scott, and Raymond Knister (in 1928 Knister dedicated the first anthology of Canadian stories, which he edited, to Scott). Frederick Philip Grove's *Over Prairie Trails* (1922) remains a signal achievement of the period and genre (*Trails*, another story cycle, is mixed genre actually, what now is called creative non-fiction). Morley Callaghan performed his own version of a Hemingway pruning of prose even as he moved the modern Canadian story into an urban setting.

The mid-century saw a great number of writers who would go on to achieve international reputations as novelists, such as Robertson Davies and Margaret Laurence, first come to attention as writers of humorous sketches and psychologically realistic stories. They were able to do so in popular weekly supplements to newspapers such as the *Star Weekly*, in magazines such as *Maclean's* and *Saturday Night*, and in literary periodicals such as *Queen's Quarterly* and *Tamarack Review* (the latter of which was edited by Robert Weaver, a key figure in the development of the contemporary Canadian short story), which provided a venue for writers too numerous to name during what was both the heyday and swan song for short story writing and reading in Canada. Ironically, the well-crafted modern short story as well as the popular version were probably assisted in gaining this high point of reputation in the early- to mid-twentieth century by the falling off of literary attention spans (short stories *are* short), before the full occupation of an electronic mass media bent on rendering literary pursuits obsolete and drawing off the advertising revenue that was the lifeblood of magazines.

It needs to be said that many of those Canadian novelists who first found success in the short form are better in it than in the novel. Some of the causes of this irrational development from good short story writer to middling novelist may be the same as those given for the attraction of the short story in the nineteenth century: constraints of time, the relative risk involved as compared to the time spent on a novel, market considerations given inflated importance by publishers' delusions about what readers want. Whatever the reasons—and they would include mistaken perceptions of aesthetic merit and the megalomaniacal tendencies of modern life—the novel early became and remains the form in which fiction writers feel they must prove themselves. And publishers do encourage them to think so: both Laurence and Munro had to resist pressure from their American publishers to turn story cycles into novels. Although it is critically cockeyed to see the short story as the apprentice work of future novelists, readers might well wonder about the kind of novels that will be (and are being) written by writers who have not learned to hone their prose and trim their tales in the discipline of the short story. One palpable observation: novels have certainly been getting bigger and baggier at the end of the twentieth century, reverting to the dimensions of their nineteenth-century ascendancy, when minute representationalism was understandable given the unavailability of photographic and cinematic versions of events. But if literary attention spans have been dwindling, and they have, we might well wonder: Are these all-new jumbo narratives being read at all? Or are such tomes not perhaps being bought and displayed as quaint cultural kitsch, like man-size hookah pipes in the smoke-free home?

Regardless, many of Canada's most accomplished novelists do continue to write short stories that are among the best being published anywhere (and the names Atwood, Shields, and Vanderhaeghe come readily to mind). The form would seem to hold an enduring attraction for Canadian writers indeed, even if very few collections of short stories are published any more by Canada's major commercial publishers, and by fewer and fewer of our literary publishers. Everyone wants a novel, it must seem, and publishers' declarations that story collections do not sell, and therefore cannot be successfully published, become self-fulfilling prophecy. New's theory of marginality helps explain the traditional (and to some extent) lasting appeal of the short story for Canadian writers. What then might its weakening, assisted by (im)purely commercial marketing interests, portend? That Canada's is no longer a marginal culture? That the concept of a marginal culture no longer applies in our netted world? Or that, as a distinct culture, we are drifting closer to the expanding American centre, that place where incisive irony bewilders and where literary fiction, like all else, is successful or not in terms exclusively pecuniary and megalomaniacal—that place where the title of Alice Munro's masterful cycle of stories, *Who Do You Think You Are?*, was changed to *The Beggar Maid*, because the American publisher found the original idiom too mystifyingly Canadian. Tellingly, Munro's original title points to the question of identity, the revised one to somewhere else.

To the end of recognizing and outlining a continuum of the Canadian short story, the following essays present new criticism and research on such subjects as the distinctive cultural contexts of some important nineteenth-century women writers; the shaping influence of *fin-de-siècle symboliste* aesthetics; and the determining role played in the lives of earlier Canadian readers by the nineteenth-century young adult short story. Essays dealing with the early twentieth century consider the heretofore overlooked importance of social(ist) realism in the short fiction of the Depression years; the legal vocabulary of Morley Callaghan's short fiction (Callaghan having been a lawyer who never practised law); and, in an essay parallelling the one on the nineteenth-century young adult story, compelling findings on the wide influence of the popular (that is, general-interest magazine) short story of this century. Thus the ground will have been prepared (the way contextualized) for four essays that assess the short fiction of five of Canada's most popular and respected writers—Margaret Laurence, Sheila Watson, Alice Munro, Alistair MacLeod, and Timothy Findley—and one that examines the concept of the hero in contemporary Canadian short fiction.

Essentially, then, this volume offers essays toward a long overdue historical and cultural re-contextualizing of the Canadian short story based on new scholarship and criticism. Its coverage is wide-ranging and our ambitions for it doubtlessly overreaching. As one unavoidable consequence of our determination to reach back to the beginnings of the Canadian short story, many subjects and short story writers could not be mentioned or are only touched upon. It is hoped that our repeated use of the word "toward" will eventually be justified by the publication of other individual essays, collections, and monograph studies widening the range and describing particular features of the extensive ground outlined here and waiting to be mapped. And finally, in recognition of the fact that there could be no scholarship or criticism without short stories and their authors, we give first place to an essay by one of Canada's finest short story writers of the younger generation, Bonnie Burnard, a meditation that gives us privileged insight into the prismatic relation between fiction and reality in one short story; and we conclude the book with an essay by Alistair MacLeod—the Canadian short story writer's short story writer—on his view of the tradition in which he writes.

In closing, the editors thank our colleagues in the Department of English at the University of Ottawa for their generous advice and assistance, particularly Glenn Clever, Frank Tierney, Seymour Mayne, John Moss, Camille La Bossière, David Staines, Klaus Peter Stich, Gwendolyn Guth, Linda Morra, Jonathan Meakin, and Chair Keith Wilson. For commentaries on the symposium papers that began *Dominant Impressions*, we thank Sandra Campbell of the University of Ottawa and Tracy Ware of Queen's University. And we are grateful to the Faculty of Arts Research and Publication Committee and the University Research Fund of the University of Ottawa for generously provided funds.

SECONDARY WORKS CITED

Fowler, Alistair. *Kinds of Literature: An Introduction to the Theory of Genres and Modes.* Cambridge: Harvard UP, 1982.
Lohafer, Susan, and Jo Ellyn Clarey, eds. *Short Story Theory at a Crossroads.* Baton Rouge: Lousiana State UP, 1989.
New, W. H. *Dreams of Speech and Violence: The Art of the Short Story in Canada and New Zealand.* Toronto: U of Toronto P, 1989.

It Almost Always Starts This Way

BONNIE BURNARD

I GUESS I BELIEVE THAT the only thing the writing of a short story really requires is an altered state of mind.

Achieving an altered state of mind has never been much of a problem for me; there are those with my best interests at heart who would argue that it has occasionally been far too easy. I cannot remember a time when this was not true, although I do remember when I learned that this inclination would have to be managed.

When I was perhaps eleven, on Friday nights my best friend and I used to go uptown in our small town to the Kineto theatre to watch whatever mindless Hollywood pap was on offer that week. On one of these nights, near the end of a long forgotten movie, there was a scene in a very large, very impressive parliament. After some crucial and startling dialogue, all of the men in the parliament stood up and began to applaud and shout. Sitting in my seat in the Kineto theatre beside my best friend, I too began to applaud, whole-heartedly. I have no idea what stopped me from standing and shouting as well; restraint, I like to think. My best friend turned to me in the dark of the hushed theatre and said, "Okay, that's it."

Of course you get used to living a certain way inside your head. And you get used to pretending to be alive primarily and vigorously in the here and now, which I sometimes think of as passing. And if you're very lucky, you get to realize, to make real, some of the people and phrases and thoughts and images that give birth to themselves inside your head; you get to write a bit of fiction. But how do you discover the stories that will hold these people and phrases and thoughts and images? With me, it almost always starts in reality. It almost always starts with a true story, true events and places.

For a while, I have been aware of a horseshoe cluster of stories sort of parked in the side yard of my brain waiting to be written. I'm going to use those potential stories to try to examine how I write, how I make a story. This exercise spooks me not a little; I am afraid of losing the stories if I approach them analytically, with cold blood as it were. Analysis of a raw story can be a clumsy, rough, ham-handed thing. But perhaps the very best potential stories are tough and patient and kind of loyal; perhaps the ones that slip away have no grips, no natural adhesion. And who wants them?

So here is a true story, or a cluster of true stories. After my first collection was published I was sent on a reading tour in British Columbia. I was two days in Vancouver and then I was driven by a woman, a librarian I think, to White Rock, for an evening reading. It was February. It was raining. The plan was that I would spend the night in White Rock and then the librarian would pick me up in the morning and deliver me to Mission for the next gig.

I was tired and, not being much of a public performer, anxious to get to a place where I wouldn't have to talk to anyone for a while. The hotel chosen for me was down by the shore in White Rock, with only the train tracks between it and the lapping water. The building was frame, painted white I think; even from outside in the parking lot the wood seemed thin, insubstantial. I was escorted into the lobby where I registered. My hair had got wet running across the parking lot and was quickly becoming extremely curly, which can sometimes set me off. Anyway, the librarian wished me a good night's sleep, said she'd pick me up at eight and left to go to her own warm home somewhere. I climbed the stairs.

The room was small with a low ceiling, it was dingy and damp. The lock on the door was one of those push locks that can easily be sprung with a credit card. The carpet was worn but still thick enough in places to host a substantial life system and the spread on the bed was ready to be ripped into dusters. But what's it matter, I thought, checking the sheets, which were clean. What's it matter when you're really tired. So I undressed, showered in the mouldy shower, put on my nightie and got into bed. This mattress isn't too bad, I thought. This is going to be fine, I thought.

In a few minutes I heard the first rumbling. Someone across the hall, someone a good size, was drunk or angry or both. He began to mutter things, loudly. Questions mostly. Although I couldn't hear the specific words, I could easily enough recognize that lift at the end of a sentence that implies that something is wanted in response to the words that have been said. I turned over, assuming he'd wear himself down in due time.

He didn't, but I was soon distracted. Lying there watching the rain stream down the window, having lived a life exhibiting no patience whatsoever with people who snuff and sniffle and fuss around about such things, I found myself suddenly sneezing repeatedly with something like gale force. And my head, as my mother used to say, had filled up. It was the mould. Of course it wasn't just in the shower, it was everywhere it could get a foothold. Why wouldn't it be? I got up to get the box of tissues from the bathroom and when I climbed back into bed the sheets felt damp to me, as they hadn't before. I was cold. A train was approaching. And the guy next door was becoming extremely impatient with his absent friend or wife or brother, really fed up. By this time it was perhaps midnight. The train rolled on by, the window panes quivered. I tried to dream; I tried to put my brain to sleep by offering it the images it likes best. I sneezed some more. Eventually the box of tissues was empty. I got up and switched on the bathroom light: one-thirty. I took the roll of toilet paper off its thing. Enough, I thought.

I got dressed, stuffed my toothbrush and nightie into my satchel, went down to the front desk and asked for a cab. The desk clerk, a dark haired man, let's say medium build with a tattoo on his neck, asked in a tone of voice more belligerent than concerned if something was wrong with the room. I unrolled some toilet paper, blew my nose and reassured him that everything was fine, I just needed a cab please. I didn't hand over the key. I had already determined on the way down the stairs that if morning ever came I would be in the lobby to meet the librarian at eight, rested and discreet. I would not let on that I had changed hotels. I certainly didn't want her to think I thought I was too good for this one.

The cab driver seemed to be about my age, maybe forty-five. As I approached the car he leaned way over and opened the back door for me from the inside, asked me, Where to? I said could he please take me to another hotel, something inland a bit. I sneezed. I unrolled some toilet paper. Hmmm, he said, with his long right arm draped across the back of the seat. He began to drive slowly up the hill away from the shore. The rain streamed down my window like syrup.

He wanted to know where I was visiting from. And what did I do for a living? I usually lie in circumstances like this but for some reason, fatigue maybe, I told the truth. And then the next question came, as it always does: So what kind of thing do you write? Regretting my brief moment of truthfulness, I lied.

By this time he had cruised around downtown White Rock and we finally pulled into the lit-up parking lot of a promising looking motel; this one white for sure, one storey high, stretched out wide into the dark on either side. Buddy of mine runs this, he said, I'll see if he's got anything left. He shuffled through the rain and ducked under the overhang and just as he was about to pull the screen door open, his buddy came out to meet him, to stand with him under the overhang. They stood side by side, looking directly ahead out into the rain, bending over their cupped hands to light their cigarettes. One of them, my driver, was long and lanky with arms held tight to his sides; his buddy was squat and solid, bigger in his movements. Not tonight, I heard. Last one went a half hour ago. So there were no rooms. But we were going to stay put until the cigarettes got smoked, the talk would last as long as the cigarettes. There was quiet and then I heard: There's the place out-of-town. And then the response: Yeah, well. And just before I opened the car door to indicate my impatience: Says she's a writer.

Back on the road again, we drove past what was called our last chance. No vacancy there either. I checked my watch: two-fifteen. It occurred to me that there are worse things than spending the night sneezing in a damp bed listening to an angry drunk, but instead of saying could you take me back to where I came from, I asked about the place out-of-town. Just how far out was it? Oh not that far, I was told, but people don't like it much. Why don't people like it? I asked. Aware that a visitor can sometimes have a hard time understanding how a place works, he was patient. It's been bought by East Indians, he said. It used to be owned by my buddy's aunt and her husband but they had to pack it in and there aren't many buyers for a place out-of-town. I'm very tired, I said. Please take me there.

The lights were on in the small front office. I asked the cab driver to wait and when I went inside I was met at the counter by a young man, a young husband, who had been sitting in an armchair with a paperback novel, the title of which I couldn't read. He'd been sleeping a bit from the look of his puffy face. But he was happy to see me. Yes, he had some rooms. I paid him and was given a key.

This motel, which not too recently had been painted a medium, minty green, disappeared lengthwise back into the dripping trees. It was two storeys high with a long narrow balcony. After we drove around to one of the staircases and I paid the driver and got out, he said through his open window that maybe he should walk me up. I said no, that was all right.

In the morning, I called another cab. By eight I was back where I began. I'd slept well, considering. The librarian was none the wiser.

When I started writing this down, perhaps an hour ago, it was my intention to tell this anecdote to you truthfully. But in this first telling it has already begun to attract to itself small helpful lies. Rereading, I see that these lies appear more in connection with the detail than in the hard facts or in the order of events. And maybe they are not lies at all but only honest attempts at precision, precision mattering more than truth.

So I guess this is how a story begins to design itself. Of course if I were to try to turn this material into publishable fiction, I would have to be receptive to whatever lies turned up; I would have to trust these lies. And each fact would have to earn its keep because I don't like to make room in my fiction for useless facts. And in the interest of shape, the order of events might have to change into a different kind of order altogether. The shape of the story could be modelled on anything, an unexpected stand of spruce, a wet city street cutting into a hill, a sinking ship. I don't allow myself to think too directly about this shape business.

And I would have to try to guess whose story this wants to be. I mentioned earlier that I thought there was a cluster of stories here and, from this initial contemplative distance, that's still how I see it. If I went in closer to the material, the stories would begin to break off, or break away. Each character would become a potential nucleus, ready to draw some of the material to itself. It would likely be at this point in the process that I would begin to hear a narrative voice, a tone or narrative attitude.

The first potential nucleus is the librarian. I am certain that she wouldn't be a vehicle for me, for my thoughts, she wouldn't be me at all. She would be a true, unrelated "she," a true other. Anything would be possible. She could be relentlessly rude to the writer; she could hate her job, hate fiction in particular. She could have had an abortion the week before, the father already a family man, rough luck. She could have breast cancer, lots of women do. Or she could be a sincerely pleasant person who wants only good things for everyone around her, which might get on the writer's nerves a bit. She could be a talker, a careless driver. She could be the cause of an accident between an innocent logging truck and an old Lincoln, before she gets rid of the writer or after.

There is the desk clerk. That tattoo on his neck. Perhaps he served some time in prison. Maybe the navy. Not likely. But he would be rough trade, or appear to be. Maybe he would have a male lover who comes to work with him, who hangs around in the back, who is beautiful and slow-witted and bone lazy. Maybe they met in Jasper and the entire story has to move in flashback to Jasper. The mountains would be stunning, and described that way, without apology. Lots of light on the snow and the rock, blue-white light and blue-black shadows. Maybe someone in Jasper was dying of AIDS and a promise had to be broken, maybe he had to be abandoned to his family, his mother useless, beyond consolation, his father, a small man, utterly defeated by sadness. Three deaths then, in the mountains.

There is the guy next door, the drunk who mutters the angry questions. Is he a failed something? Has he fallen? Not necessarily. He could be simply a perpetual non-achiever. Perhaps he first got angry when he was twelve and has just stayed angry. Of course it would be connected to poverty. Family history. Stupid bad luck. There would be no woman waiting, hoping for a final turnaround. He might go downstairs for some company and be approached by the lazy, bored queen, who would intend no harm, it would be just some kind of campy, "Hi there, big fella." But the drunk would drag the queen out into the parking lot and break three of his ribs. An ambulance would come, and the cops. No, one cop. One cop is more interesting than two.

There is the East Indian, who would be well aware of the attitudes around him. He would not start out stoic and brave and later cave in to frustration. No. He would be only a young husband trying to help his wife, who is an ordinary, gently funny woman and quite unused to disdain let alone hatred, come to terms with what they have done to themselves, what they have allowed in the name of hope. One night he would listen quietly to the heartbeat of his child through the thick wall of his wife's flesh and he would want badly to say something to this child. He would decide that he has left behind him all his real words, his natural, spontaneous words. Then the story could jump twenty years. They could have a house, kids, jobs, a faith, money, great sex, a dental plan, friends, respect, some joy. Why not? Could this be made valid, credible, interesting? Could this happen in a piece of serious fiction?

There is the cab driver. The lean, lanky man who keeps his arms close to his sides. Is this where the edge is, in this character? Could he return to her room? Could she let him in? Could they make extraordinarily gentle love in some kind of absolute, terrifying silence, a silence that begins as omission and soon becomes commission? Not one word spoken, no dialogue? Could the East Indian, fully awake to nuance and the sound of a car on gravel, stand in the rain at the dark corner of the front office and watch the window of number 17 for a sign, listen for a sound that was meant to be heard by someone like him? Could this be any of his business?

Lastly, there is the storyteller, the narrative "I." I could either keep that first person voice or give the narrative "I" a good hard push over into the realm of "she." "She" is usually quite a bit more fun, more malleable; "I" is annoyingly susceptible to earnestness and would have to put up a very good argument to be allowed to stay in the story. Whichever of these voices did stay, something would have to be exposed, exposed or hidden. There would have to be a discovery, a cost or risk, a break or a healing that would be hard to identify in the beginning and that could only be discovered by writing, one word, one sentence, one draft after another. This is where courage comes in; not nerve or perseverance but courage.

And what makes any of this Canadian?

Perhaps the bad hotel?

The challenge of an altogether new kind of weather; the need to adapt to an entirely different world within the same country?

Certainly the woman wanting it both ways, wanting both a decent room and not to be seen making a big deal about it.

The underexpressed fear of strangers?

The immigrant family, understood so superficially?

The quiet?

The water?

I don't really know what makes any of this Canadian. I guess I'd have to say I don't think it's my business right now. Maybe after the stories get written I'll know more.

Of Kings and Cabbages: Short Stories by Early Canadian Women

WANDA CAMPBELL

IN *DREAMS OF SPEECH AND VIOLENCE*, W. H. New argues that "the short story is one of the most central of [Canada's] cultural adaptations of literary form" (24) and it is a form in which women writers have always been active. However, Janice Kulyk Keefer warns against an "essentialist explanation" (170) for what has been described as the "dominance" of women writers in the field (Gadpaille vii). In "Shaping a Vehicle for Her Use: Women and the Short Story," Gail Scott suggests that women have been attracted to the form for economic reasons, but also because as a genre with few firmly established conventions, it provides "space to play" (187). Historically, the short story, as it was being developed by such authors as Nathaniel Hawthorne and Edgar Allan Poe, received a great boost with the rise of the lady's books, largely created by and for women. In 1839, Sarah Hale, the editor of *Godey's Lady's Book* advised her contributors:

> We want short, racy, spirited essays; stories and sketches that embody pages of narrative and sentiment in a single paragraph, and by a few bold touches paint rather than describe, the characters they exhibit for the instruction and entertainment of our readers. Such stories may be called *too short*, but that usually implies they are very popular. (Qtd. in Pattee 71)

Recently published collections such as *Aspiring Women*, edited by Lorraine McMullen and Sandra Campbell, reveal that dozens of Canadian women were publishing short stories in the latter half of the nineteenth century. The work of three women born within a dozen years of each other, Isabella Valancy Crawford, Susan Frances Harrison, and Sara Jeannette Duncan, reveals the shift from romance to realism that was occurring in the Canadian short story. Despite differences, the stories of these women are all distinguished by an intense interest in language, identity, and the role of women, particularly in relation to marriage and motherhood. In her introduction to *Stories by Canadian Women*, Rosemary Sullivan writes, "Though the authors attack subjects women write of today they do so by covert excursion rather than by candid assaults" (xi).

Many of Crawford's prose pieces can best be described as fairy tales complete with elfin monarchs, and critics agree that she was a better poet than prose writer; however, her desire to earn a living from her writing resulted not only in formula fiction, but in some "local colour" stories described by Penny Petrone as "regional idylls" (12). Catherine Ross points out that "in the poetry and prose alike, her characteristic mode of perception is romance" (47), but two of the stories she wrote in the last years of her life, "In the Breast of a Maple" and "Extradited," offer increasing realism, both historical and psychological. The local colourists had discovered that "there were unexplored social areas in America where the bare truth was stranger than any romance" (Pattee 269).

According to Elizabeth Waterston, it is not *Malcolm's Katie* but "In the Breast of a Maple" that is the "real feminine epic in Crawford's repertoire" (68). At the heart of the story is Marie de Meury, an axe-wielding "Amazon" who triumphs through the strength of her arm as well as her spirit. The story opens when Monsieur Dalmas, the wealthy and devious landowner, comes upon her chopping down a tree. The vision of her knee as it "moved under her clinging woolen skirt, showing itself boldly like that joint in the statue of the Venus de Milo" is one Dalmas clearly finds erotic (60), but he concludes that "an adorable woman with an axe in her hand is an anomaly" (59). He has come in search of his son Jean who is in love with Lucille, Marie's sister, a romance that takes backstage to Marie's aggressive refusal of Dalmas's advances. In fact, the pining Lucille, described by Crawford as ghost-like, transparent, and a "charming little phantom," is almost invisible beside her sturdy sister, "a large strong rose born to bloom in, rejoice in, and perfume the cold dry, still Canadian air" (63). In contrast to Dalmas, who is "caricatured throughout the tale with small animal images" (Petrone 64) including a snipe, kid, rabbit, and squirrel, Marie is compared with figures from classical mythology including Diana, Hebe, and Mercury.

Marie finds her father's lost wallet in the breast of the maple and in it the receipt that proves their financial independence. His treachery revealed, Dalmas vanishes like "an ugly, little, yellow fog" (64). Rachel Blau DuPlessis writes that in the nineteenth century the only endings for women were marriage or death; accepting a man turned the female hero into a heroine and brought the story to an end (8). Crawford proves herself capable of writing beyond the ending in allowing at least one of the female characters to defy heroically the romance resolution, and ride into the sunset astride the tree she herself has conquered. The names of her oxen, Solon and Plutarch, reveal that though she has been impoverished by Dalmas' deception, Marie is not without education, and it is the combination of physical and intellectual vigour that allows her to earn a living from the Canadian landscape, as symbolized by the maple tree.

Another surprising portrait of a lady appears in the story "Extradited" (67–78), published in the Toronto *Globe* in 1886. This time it is the woman, despite her education and cultural pretensions, who is compared with an animal, a serpent, and a bird of prey. Motherhood brings out the worst in this angel in the house. "Her conjugal love," writes Crawford, "was a compound of vanity and jealousy; her maternal affection an agreement of rapacity and animal instinct" (69). Though she appears to be successful as a housewife, she is a failure as a human being. Deeply jealous of her uneducated husband's friendship with the fugitive he has hired to clear their fields, she decides it is her duty to turn him in for a reward. Throughout the story Crawford cleverly contrasts prim with primitive, proving that the true capacity for love lies in the latter. Waterston draws attention to Crawford's iconic use of colour in this story. Red is associated with the life-giving sun, the red flannel shirt of the hired man, the frock of the lively baby. As the faithful Joe is crushed under the logs of the spring drive, the American detective who has come at Bess's bidding to extradite him comments that he has been extradited after all. Because Joe gives up his life saving her child, Bess receives no reward and must be contented with "regarding herself as an unrewarded and unrecognized heroine of duty" (78), terms dripping with irony. This story is memorable because Crawford's characterization of Bess is neither simple nor stereotypical.

V. S. Pritchett defines the short story as a hybrid that "owes much to the poet on the one hand and the newspaper reporter on the other" (854). Susan Frances Harrison was both, and her stories, like those of Crawford, combine lyric and documentary elements. In the memorable title story of her 1886 collection *Crowded Out! and Other Sketches*, a Canadian goes to England to market his writing only to find himself "crowded out," but in "The Idyl of the Island," the Englishman comes to Canada: "There lies mid-way between parallels 48 and 49 of latitude, and degrees 89 and 90 of longitude, in the northern hemisphere of the New World, serenely anchored on an ever-rippling and excited surface, an exquisitely lovely island" (12). The Englishman who comes upon this island at five o'clock on a July morning finds a young Canadian woman sleeping on a bed of moss, a perfect "union of art and nature" (13). The cry of the loon, described variously as weird, unearthly, maniacal, and melancholy, awakens her. She welcomes the stranger ashore to try his hand at the "genuine Canadian experience" of camping out. While making a fire and cooking breakfast, the man falls in love with the object of his gaze. The reader discovers halfway through the story that the man's name is Amherst, later to be known as Admiral Amherst. This choice of name is significant, as it was the Englishman Jeffrey Amherst who made a conquest first of the island of Cape Breton at Louisbourg and then the island of Montreal to become Governor General of British North America between 1760 and 1763. The subtle pattern of military imagery is repeated in the tent, the description of the stones of the campfire as "fortifications" (16), Amherst's kiss as an "involuntary salute" (18), and the Othello-like description of the island's "too lovely occupant" (19).

Discovering he has been misled by the absence of visible signs of conquest, flags or wedding rings, the Admiral-to-be makes a hasty retreat, nearly overturning the boat of his adversary, the woman's plump and pleasant husband returning from fishing. The question of the woman's happiness remains unanswered. According to Sullivan, "Harrison does not mount an attack on the rigidities of the institution of marriage, but grieves instead for one of its unfortunate victims" (xi). The story is narrated in the first person, not by either of the central characters, but rather by a friend of the Admiral who unsuccessfully attempts to bring about a romantic resolution. The Admiral will not attempt further contact, preferring, like Roberts, rather to remember than see. Harrison chooses to call the story an "idyl" and indeed it does contain pastoral and descriptive elements, but there is nothing idyllic about the conclusion. Marie de Meury finds her independence in the Canadian wilderness, but the independence gained by the unnamed Canadian with the red-brown hair is only temporary. MacMillan reads the story as an allegory of "the imprisoned poet-princess longing for escape" (114). There is no island, however wild and self-reliant, that is not subject to conquest.

The image of female imprisonment becomes literal in "The Story of Delle Josephine Boulanger," which like many of Harrison's fictions, makes use of the French Canadian setting that Duncan Campbell Scott was later to exploit in his short stories. "I may say here," wrote Harrison in 1895, "that I really was the first writer in Canada to attract general attention to the local colour, so to speak, of the French" (qtd. by MacMillan 107). As Carole Gerson points out, "Several of the pieces in *Crowded Out! and Other Sketches* strikingly illustrate an imaginative relationship between English Canada and Quebec in which the Lower Province serves as a looking-glass for the Upper, where fears and desires can be clothed and confronted in tangible, outer forms" (128). In "The Story of Delle Josephine Boulanger," the division is explored along linguistic and gender lines, with an Englishman encountering a French woman in the tiny village of Bonheur du Roi, or Bonneroy. From the opening sentence, Harrison foregrounds language. "Delle Josephine Boulanger, Miss Josephine Baker; Miss Josephine Baker, Delle Josephine Boulanger. What a difference it makes, the language! What a transformation!" (85). Patricia Yaeger cites the portrayal of a bilingual heroine as a central emancipatory strategy in nineteenth-century women's writing (35ff.) and the invention of a female discourse that escapes the "dictatorship of patriarchal speech" (Showalter 253) has long interested feminist critics. Throughout Harrison's story the man and the woman struggle to communicate. "Our conversation always came to a sudden stop when one of us lapsed into the mother tongue. As long as a sort of common macaronic was kept to we managed to understand one another" (92). This verse form combining the classical and the vernacular seems appropriate to describe the dialogue between genders as well as nationalities. The male narrator attributes many characteristics stereotypically applied to women to the French, garrulousness, vanity, vim and gesture in telling tales, and strange behaviour. He also places special emphasis on Delle Boulanger's mouth with its "yellow tusks of eye-teeth, and the blackened stumps and shrunken gums" (87) as a threatening and fearful site.

What first attracts the Englishman who has come to sketch the nearby falls of Montmorenci to Delle Boulanger is the red hat in her window, the only bit of "local colour" in the snowbound landscape. Harrison's self-reflexive use of this term applied in the 1880s to short stories distinguished by dialect and authentic rustic detail alerts us to the metafictional emphasis to follow. The impact of the milliner's artistry is extraordinary.

> It was a triumph in lobster-colour... made of shirred scarlet satin with large bows of satin ribbon of the same intense colour and adorned with a bird of paradise. I can see it now and can recall the images it suggested to my mind at the time. These were of cardinals and kings, of sealing-wax and wafers, of tropic moons and tangled marshes, of hell and judgement and the conventional Zamiel. (86)

The fact that the hat is scarlet may be an allusion to Hawthorne's novel in which the scarlet letter is a symbol of guilt. The narrator discovers that Delle Boulanger carries a secret guilt that is eroding her sanity, a guilt that relates to her failure at the maternal task, allowing a baby in her care to slip away to her death on the hilly streets of Quebec City. One way in which the "insanity" manifests itself is in Delle Boulanger donning the scarlet hat and holding a conversation with herself in the mirror. Whether or not Harrison was familiar with Mary Coleridge's poem "The Other Side of a Mirror" (1882) upon which Sandra Gilbert and Susan Gubar base their image of the female artist as the queen in the looking glass, this is an intriguing connection. In her discussion of "Crowded Out!" MacMillan expresses regret that Harrison "did not feel confident enough to present the situation of the female artist" (120), but that appears to be the subtext of this story. It is worth noting that Harrison's first choice of pseudonyms at the age of sixteen was Medusa, a myth that speaks to the power of the female gaze and the necessary deflection of the polished shield.

Delle Boulanger, obsessed by the memory of Baby Catherine who died in her care, and surrounded by images of death including a memorial wreath made of human hair, and the entombing snow, dons, like Miss Havisham, her most festive and ghastly apparel and converses with her double, in a language the English*man* cannot understand. It is in this posture that death finds her. In nineteenth-century fictions, death "comes for a female character when she has a jumbled, distorted inappropriate relation to the 'social script' of plot designed to contain her legally, economically and sexually" (DuPlessis 15). After her death, the Englishman and the priest who knows nothing of her inner life, find boxes and boxes of white quilled ribbon. "If you have any imagination," says the narrator at one point, you can fancy your "Franklin" stove is an English hearth. A similar imaginative leap allows the reader to interpret these preparations for the coffin and shroud of Baby Catherine as authorial products. The rows and rows of ribbons as white as paper are quilled, embroidered into cylindrical folds, but also penned. The fact that each box includes a written dedication to Catherine, makes the parallel explicit. These are the tame and socially acceptable results of Delle Boulanger's artistry, in contrast to the flamboyant hat, which despite the Englishman's original desire to buy it as a "souvenir" is *not* for sale. Once again, red is associated with life, in particular the life of the imagination. The narrator's description of the hat shifts as the story progresses. It begins as an "extraordinary" and "wonderful" triumph and ends as "the nightmare in red, a kind of mute scarlet 'Raven'" (90). Harrison's tribute to Poe is appropriate here, as she was certainly influenced by his concept of the short story, especially with regard to a unity of effect carefully constructed through extravagant and thrilling details. And yet Harrison was to insist, "I am a realist, a modern of the moderns" (MacMillan 133).

In the end, the narrator escapes the tomb of snow that buries Delle Boulanger, but he is so haunted by the power of her art that his own is destroyed. "My sketch of the frost bound Montmorenci was never finished, and indeed my winter sketching fell through altogether after that unhappy visit to Bonneroy" (97). In particular, he feels so threatened by the colour that symbolizes the dead woman's secret and wild self, that he takes a "strong dislike to scarlet in the gowns or head-gear of [his] wife and daughter" (97). Though her "rhapsodizing" has been silenced, Delle Boulanger endures in the narrator, who feels compelled to tell her story.

The short stories of Crawford and Harrison prepare the way for the work of Sara Jeannette Duncan, described by Sullivan as "the bravest and most powerful" of the three (xii). Influenced by Henry James and William Dean Howells, Duncan advocated realism but not without reservations. In "Criticism and Fiction," an essay in which he notes that short stories "by the women seem faithfuler and more realistic than those of the men" (64), Howells declares that "realism is nothing more and nothing less than the truthful treatment of material" (38). But, as both Gerson and Misao Dean point out, Duncan favoured a kind of truth that made room for transcendence: "The ordinary detail of humdrum life and circumstance, pen-painted by an artist with sympathies keen enough to detect the mysterious throbbing of the life that is inner and under, fascinates us like our own photographs" (qtd. in Gerson 60).

One of Duncan's lesser known short stories, "The Heir Apparent," first published in *Harper's Monthly Magazine* in March of 1905 and anthologized in Campbell and McMullen's *New Women: Short Stories by Canadian Women, 1900–1920*, illustrates Duncan's desire to preserve a place for the ideal in the real. Gone are the improbable plots, the extravagant and melodramatic details, and the larger-than-life characters. Instead, Duncan offers three women sitting on a Toronto veranda, "watching the electric cars flash up and down," and discussing a handsome young man. There is indeed a love story between the young American Ida Chamier and the Englishman Randal Cope, but the exchange of flash and smile between them is limited to a few lines: "It happened then, just then—the story and a moment's silence followed it" (87). Similarly, the "happily ever after" is dismissed in one prosaic sentence: "The younger Copes live in Westminster near the Colonial Office, where Randal has got a 'job'—his wife delights, I think maliciously, to dwell upon it under that unlovely term" (95). The rest of the narrative is taken up with speculations about whether the young man will live up to his heritage as the son of poet and scholar Margaret Cope and the grandson of "classicist, dialectician, all but artist" Charles Randal (83). The story opens with Ida's aunt proclaiming that she likes "the shape of his head" (82), but the remainder of the story proves to the Canadian narrator that there is, in fact, little in it. She is so disappointed with his article about Canada—a railway station built of bricks when she had hoped for a marble palace—that she flings the journal across the room.

McMullen and Campbell draw attention to the political allegory in "The Heir Apparent," which extends Duncan's "allegorical method in her creation of characters" (Dean 48) with Jamesian results. The three North

Americans have an affinity for the "*al fresco* life" defined by Ida's aunt as "this emancipation all about you, this sitting on verandas in the public of the moon, these airs of the forest in the city streets" (84–85), but they each must wrestle with tradition in their own way. The Americans see Randal Cope as an opportunity, a Prince Charming they refuse to admit is actually quite ordinary. To them he is the heir apparent, an heir whose claim cannot be set aside, but to the Canadian narrator he is the heir in appearances only.

Because Cope is "out here" on an "imperialistic mission" of writing about Canada (84), the narrator asks whether he has been "penetrated by our national anthem?" (86). Duncan's reference is to "The Maple Leaf Forever," written by Scarborough school teacher Alexander Muir in 1867 and popular until well after the English lyrics of "O Canada" appeared in 1908. The young American knows two lines, but the Englishman has never heard of it, asserting that the maple seems "to have more leaves than rhymes" (86) as if to say there is still more nature than art on the Atlantic's "still half-hostile farther shore" (83). Yet, as the narrator points out, those that are not maples are chestnuts (86). The Englishman is the one with the stale imagination and Latin verses that lose their wit in translation. Duncan's story is primarily an indoor story about the human heart, but there are moments when the outside enters in: "The rain struck softly on the trees and murmured over the grass. The quiet breath of it came into the room" (91). Like Crawford before her, but with more realism and subtlety, Duncan uses the maple as a symbol of what is fresh in the Canadian experience.

Duncan was influenced by realism, but rejected "the poverty of the merely material" (Dean 55) she associated with the United States and Britain. In 1887 she wrote in the *Montreal Star*:

> No theory of realism, however admirable its aims and useful its effect, can destroy our *ad valorem* notion of nature. A cabbage is a very essential vegetable to certain salads, but we do not prostrate ourselves adoringly before the cabbage bed in everyday life, and it is a little puzzling to know why we should be required to do so in art galleries and book stores, however perfect the representations there of cabbages, vegetable or human. If we do it is certainly purely the art which we admire, not the nature. And so we take the liberty of thinking that literature should at its best be true not only to the object upon and about which it constructs itself, but faithful also to the delicate attractions and repulsions which enter so intimately into the highest art. (2)

Whether inspired by kings or cabbages, romance or realism, these early Canadian women wrote vitally of the fibre of human relationships. Carol Shields maintains that if there is a feminine voice in literature it is not in form, but in tone and topic. From Moodie to Munro, she writes, women's stories are about the "struggle of the feminine spirit to survive" (85).

WORKS CITED

Campbell, Sandra, and Lorraine McMullen, eds. *New Women: Short Stories by Canadian Women, 1900–1920.* Ottawa: U of Ottawa P, 1991.
Crawford, Isabella Valancy. *Selected Stories of Isabella Valancy Crawford.* Ed. Penny Petrone. Ottawa: U of Ottawa P, 1975.
Dean, Misao. *A Different Point of View: Sara Jeannette Duncan.* Montreal: McGill-Queen's UP, 1991.
Duncan, Sara Jeannette. "Bric-a-Brac." *Montreal Star* (December 5, 1887): 2.
———. "The Heir Apparent." *New Women: Short Stories by Canadian Women 1900-1920.* Eds. Sandra Campbell and Lorraine McMullen. Ottawa: U of Ottawa P, 1991. 82–95.
DuPlessis, Rachel Blau. *Writing Beyond the Ending.* Bloomington: Indiana UP, 1985.
Gadpaille, Michelle. *The Canadian Short Story.* Toronto: Oxford UP, 1988.
Gerson, Carole. *A Purer Taste: The Writing and Reading of Fiction in Nineteenth-Century Canada.* Toronto: U of Toronto P, 1989.
Gilbert, Sandra, and Susan Gubar. *The Madwoman in the Attic: The Woman Writer and the Nineteenth-Century Literary Imagination.* New Haven, Conn.: Yale UP, 1979.
Harrison, Susan Frances. "The Idyl of the Island." 1886. *Short Stories by Canadian Women.* Toronto: Oxford UP, 1984. 12–19.
———. "The Story of Delle Josephine Boulanger." 1886. *Aspiring Women: Short Stories by Canadian Women, 1880–1900.* Eds. Loraine McMullen and Sandra Campbell. Ottawa: U of Ottawa P, 1993. 85–97.
———. (Seranus). *Crowded Out! and Other Sketches.* Ottawa: Evening Journal Office, 1886.
Howells, William Dean. *Criticism and Fiction and Other Essays.* Eds. Clara Marburg Kirk and Rudolf Kirk. New York: New York UP, 1959.
Kulyk Keefer, Janice. "Gender, Language, Genre." *Language in Her Eye: Writing and Gender.* Toronto: Coach House, 1990. 164–172.
MacMillan, Carrie. "Susan Frances Harrison ('Seranus'): Paths Through the Ancient Forest." *Silenced Sextet: Six Nineteenth-Century Canadian Women Novelists.* Montreal: McGill-Queen's UP, 1992. 107–136.
McMullen, Lorraine, and Sandra Campbell, eds. *Aspiring Women: Short Stories by Canadian Women, 1880–1900.* Ottawa: U of Ottawa P, 1993.
New, W. H. *Dreams of Speech and Violence: The Art of the Short Story in Canada and New Zealand.* Toronto: U of Toronto P, 1987.
Pattee, Fred Lewis. *The Development of the American Short Story: An Historical Survey.* New York: Biblo and Tannen, 1966.
Petrone, Penny, ed. *Selected Stories of Isabella Valancy Crawford.* Ottawa: U of Ottawa P, 1975.
Pritchett, V. S. "Short Stories." *The Art of Short Fiction.* Ed. Gary Geddes. Toronto: HarperCollins, 1993. 854–855.
Ross, Catherine Sheldrick. "I.V. Crawford's Prose Fiction." *Canadian Literature* 81 (Summer 1979): 47–58.

Scott, Gail. "Shaping a Vehicle for Her Use: Women and the Short Story." *in the feminine: women and words*. Edmonton: Longspoon, 1985. 184–191.
Shields, Carol. "Is There a Feminine Voice in Literature?" *How Stories Mean*. Eds. John Metcalf and J. R. Struthers. Erin, Ont.: Porcupine's Quill, 1993. 84–86.
Showalter, Elaine. *The New Feminist Criticism: Essays on Women, Literature and Theory.* New York: Pantheon, 1985.
Sullivan, Rosemary. "Introduction." *Short Stories by Canadian Women*. Toronto: Oxford UP, 1984.
Waterston, Elizabeth. "Crawford, Tennyson, and the Domestic Idyll." *Isabella Valancy Crawford Symposium*. Ottawa: U of Ottawa P, 1979. 61–77.
Yaeger, Patricia. *Honey-Mad Women: Emancipatory Strategies in Women's Writing*. New York: Columbia UP, 1988.

"The Thing Is Found to Be Symbolic": *Symboliste* Elements in the Early Short Stories of Gilbert Parker, Charles G. D. Roberts, and Duncan Campbell Scott

D.M.R. BENTLEY

> It is a very simple matter. Find the idea in the thing in Nature and put the idea in the thing in Art, and the problem is solved.
>
> — Richard Hovey, "The Passing of Realism" (1895)

IN THE ESSAY ENTITLED "Modern Symbolism and Maurice Maeterlinck" that serves as the introduction to the first series of his translations of Maeterlinck's *Plays* (1894), Richard Hovey makes the bold but not untenable assertion that in their symbolic practices Bliss Carman, Gilbert Parker, and Charles G. D. Roberts are akin to "Mallarmé in France [and] Maeterlinck in Belgium." With an eye very likely on Mallarmé's *L'Après-midi d'un faune* (which he had recently used as a basis for "The Faun. A Fragment" in *Songs from Vagabondia* [1894]) as well as on the poems and plays of Maeterlinck, Hovey defines "[t]he symbolism of today" as a literary mode characterized by evocative suggestion rather than explicit statement:

> It by no means... involves a complete and consistent allegory. Its events, its personages, its sentences rather imply than definitely state an esoteric meaning. The story, whether romantic... or realistic..., lives for itself and produces no impression of being a masquerade of moralities; but behind every incident, almost behind every phrase, one is aware of a lurking universality, the adumbration of greater things. One is given an impression of the thing symbolized rather than a formulation. (5)

In Hovey's view, Parker's "The Stone" in *Pierre and His People* (1892) and Roberts's "The Young Ravens that Call upon Him" in the May 1894 number of *Lippincott's Monthly Magazine* are North American instances of a type of "symbolism [that is] suggestive rather than cut-and-dried": in Parker's work "the Man and the Stone exist primarily for their own simple terrific story" but "are lifted up at the same time into Titanic primitive types" and, similarly, Roberts's "tales of animals are symbolic... not with the artificial symbolism of 'Aesop's Fables'..., but by revealing in the simple truth of animal life a universal meaning. The symbol is not invented; the thing is found to be symbolic" (6–7). "[I]t promises well for the literature that is to be," adds Hovey, "that the strongest of the young writers of to-day have a tendency to myth-making" that reveals itself in their adherence to this modern "symbolic principle" (7, 8).

As motivated as they doubtless were by a desire to give European symbolism a local habitation and to publicize the names of some of his best literary friends (see Macdonald 157), Hovey's remarks are nevertheless valuable for the light that they shed on the early short stories of Parker, Roberts, and—to substitute a third short-story writer for a friend and collaborator—Duncan Campbell Scott. If not quite as strikingly as *Pierre and His People* and *Earth's Enigmas. A Book of Animal and Nature Life* (1896) (where "The Young Ravens that Call upon Him" was first published in book form), Scott's *In the Village of Viger* (1896) displays the *symboliste* "traits and methods" that Hovey admired (7), particularly the evocation of "esoteric meaning" and a reliance on "types." Nor should this be at all surprising, for *In the Village of Viger*, like *Pierre and His People, Earth's Enigmas* and, of course, Hovey's own preference for "primitive types" and naturally symbolic animals, participates in two of the discourses that shaped Canadian almost as much as American writing in the 1880s and '90s: (1) the discourse of anti-modernity that valorized pre- and undercivilized spaces as realms of emotional and spiritual intensity anterior or adjacent to the materialistic and artificial world of the modern city; and (2) the related discourse of therapeutics that encouraged writers to produce books set in such spaces that would medicine the minds and nervous systems of the victims of modernity (see Lears, and Bentley "Carman and Mind Cure"). Hovey's closing observation about his Canadian *confrères* carries the imprint of both discourses in its insistence that "[t]heir work is saner, fresher, and less morbid" than its British equivalents and that "[t]he clear air of the lakes and prairies of Canada blows through it" (8). A "romantic" or a "realistic" work set in the Northwest, the animal world, or a French-Canadian village, Hovey implies, would allow the reader to experience vicariously the health-giving properties of these environments. If such a work also contained evocations of "universal" and "esoteric" meaning, so much better (for) the reader.

Of the circumambient presence of these ideas in late nineteenth- and early twentieth-century Canadian literature there can be no doubt. As demonstrated elsewhere (see Bentley, "Carman and Mind Cure"), the *Vagabondia* volumes of Carman and Hovey (1894, 1896, 1901) are programmatically therapeutic, as are the collections of poems and essays that Carman published between Hovey's untimely death in 1900 and the First World War. By 1885–87 in "Heat" and "Among the Timothy," Archibald Lampman was offering poetic renditions of what the Canadian novelist James Macdonald Oxley was calling "wise idleness"—"quietly absorbing something through the eye or ear that for the time at least drowns the petty business and worries of life" (56)—as a cure for minds disturbed by the enervating conditions of modern life. "I confess that my design for instance in writing 'Among the Timothy' was not in the first place to describe a landscape," Lampman told Hamlin Garland in 1889, "but to describe the effect of a few hours spent among the summer fields on a mind in a troubled and despondent condition" (qtd. in Doyle 42).[1] That Scott, who wrote and published the first of the Viger stories in the late 1880s, shared his friend and mentor's faith in "wise idleness" as a cure for—to quote "Among the Timothy"—the "aching mood" induced by "blind gray streets [and] the jingle of the throng" (*Poems* 14)—becomes very clear in the second of the two poems that preface *In the Village of Viger*, where the reader is invited to see the stories that follow as a therapeutic equivalent of "a few hours spent among… summer fields":

> Whoever has from toil and stress
> Put into ports of idleness,
> And watched the gleaming thistledown
> Wheel in the soft air lazily blown…
> ....
> Might find perchance the wandering fire,
> Around St. Joseph's sparkling spire.
> And wearied with the fume and strife,
> The complex joys and ills of life,
> Might for an hour his worry staunch,
> In pleasant Viger by the Blanche.

As explicit as this about the therapeutic benefits of short fiction is Roberts's account of the emancipatory effects of the modern animal story at the conclusion of his Introduction to *The Kindred of the Wild. A Book of Animal Life* (1902): "It frees us for a little from the world of shop-worn utilities, and from the mean tenement of self of which we do well to grow weary. It helps us to return to nature, without requiring that we at the same time return to barbarism. It leads us back to the old kinship of earth… [t]he clear and candid life. … It has ever the more significance, it has ever the richer gift of refreshment and renewal, the more human the heart and spiritual the understanding which we bring to the intimacy of it" (29, and see Lucas vi). Parker is silent on the therapeutic aspect of his short stories, but his insistence in his introductory Note to *Pierre and His People* that, despite the impact of the railway and other manifestations of modernity on the Canadian west, life in "the far north... is much the same as it was a hundred years ago" (1: xv)[2] could well indicate his awareness of the regenerative properties ascribed to remote times and places by contemporary therapeutical discourse. Certainly, the extreme enthusiasm of W. H. Henley for the Pierre stories (see Adams 67–68) aligns them with the school of thought, soon to be espoused by Theodore Roosevelt, that strong doses of (masculine) strenuosity were needed to cure British and American culture of their (feminine) effeteness.[3]

Like their American and British counterparts, Canadian practitioners of literary mind cures may have disagreed about whether "wise idleness" (rest) or atavistic exertion (exercise) was the best prescription for the diseases of modernity, but none appears to have doubted that the writer and the reader's capacity to see beyond "things" to "greater things" was crucial to the efficacy of book therapy. In his Introduction to the Imperial Edition of *Pierre and His People*, Parker claims that the text from the Bible that he quotes in the opening short story—"*Free among the Dead like unto them that are wounded and lie in the grave, that are out of remembrance*" (1: 24; Psalm 88.5)—"became in a sense, the text for all the stories which came after" and describes the collection's unifying subject-matter as characters "wounded by Fate" and "The soul of goodness in things evil" (1: x–xi). In the prefatory poem to *In the Village of Viger*, "the wandering fire"—the Will-o'-the-wisp that distracts people from their workaday world—may be glimpsed "Around St. Joseph's sparkling spire." And in the Introductory to *The Kindred of the Wild*, the modern animal story brings its richest gifts of "refreshment and renewal" to those who have the most "humane... heart and spiritual... understanding." To the extent that they invoke orthodox Christianity as an interpretive context, all of these statements are somewhat misleading, for situations and occurrences abound in the short stories of Parker, Scott, and Roberts that clearly intimate the existence of occult forces in the human and natural worlds and impress upon the reader a disquieting (and presumably, enriching) sense of the mystery of the universe. As discussions of each collection will quickly show, superstition, the supernatural, and an emphasis on the uncanny are common features of *Pierre and His People*, *In the Village of Viger*, and *Earth's Enigmas* (which Roberts initially considered calling "Riddles of the Earth" [*Collected Letters* 183]). "As the visible world is measured, mapped, tested, weighed," wrote Andrew Lang in 1905, readers increasingly turn to literature to feel "the stirring of ancient dread in their veins" (qtd. in Lears 172, and see Bentley, "UnCannyda"). What more efficacious prescription for the rationalism, materialism, and "spiritual blindness" (Lears 173) of modern life than a dose of the immaterial, the inexplicable, and the affecting?

As Parker constructs "the Far North" in his Note to *Pierre and His People* and his Introduction to his *Works*, it is a veritable pharmacopoeia for the anaemia of modern life—a hinterland of "adventure," "isolation and pathetic loneliness," "poignant mystery, solitude, and primitive incident" salubriously remote from "cities... towns" and "the fertile field of civilization" (1: xv; 3: vii–ix). "In these... stories it was Mr. Parker's good fortune to be first in an unoccupied field," wrote Carman in 1894; in "[t]he unknown vastness of the Canadian Northwest... [a] region stretching far away into the land of perpetual night and everlasting snow, touched with the glamour of uncivilized romance and the mysticism of an earlier race, he found... a canvas large enough for the elemental scenes he wished to portray" (qtd. in Adams 61).[4] Since Parker's main interest lay less in local colour and Jamesian portraiture than in types and archetypes, or, in his terms, "reincarnat[ions] [of] the everlasting human ego and its scena" (2: ix), the settings and characters of the short stories in *Pierre and His People* are usually presented through minimalist description and portentous allusions that invite the reader to consider their "symbolic" or "universal" significance. Encouraging this movement from "the thing" to "the greater thing" are anonymous and omniscient narrators who not only enter minds and appear simultaneously at different places but also—and this is crucial to the evocation of "mystery" in the stories—contrive to be both knowledgeable and reticent about the hidden forces that appear to be shaping the "primitive incident[s]" and "elemental scenes" that they are describing. The result of this is that—to adapt an observation by James L. Kugel in *The Techniques of Strangeness in Symbolist Poetry*—many of the short stories in *Pierre and His People* exude "a certain aura of mystery... due to missing information which, it is implied, is necessary for full comprehension. In other words, the [narrator] creates... strangeness by not telling everything, or, more precisely, by implying that not everything has been told" (38).

A good case in point is "The Patrol of the Cypress Hills," the story that begins the collection and sets the tone of what is to follow in a variety of ways, including the incorporation of the text from Psalm 88.5 that seemed to Parker "to suggest the lives and the ends of the workers of the pioneer world" (Works 1: x). Despite the geographical specificity of its title, the setting of "The Patrol of the Cypress Hills" is more suggestive than precise: the frontier is a realm of "breadth... vastness, and... pure air"; the "[s]now is hospitable-clean... restful and silent"; the "sun [comes] up like a great flower expanding. First the yellow, then the purple, then the red, and then a mighty shield of roses" (1: 7, 13, 23). The principal character, the Kiplingesque Sergeant Fones of the Northwest Mounted Police, is "part of the great machine of Order" and, according to his commandant "'the best soldier on the patrol,'" but he is also described by the narrator as a "little Bismarck" and, when mounted on his "stout bronco," likened by an Irish private to "the Devil and Death" (1: 8, 7, 11). Moreover, he is the subject of numerous unanswered questions: "But what of Sergeant Fones?... But was Sergeant Fones such a one?... What was Sergeant Fones' country? No one knew. Where had he come from? No one asked him more than once" (1: 6, 7, 8). Compounding these ambiguities and uncertainties are allusions to the myth of the Minotaur (1: 12–13), gestures toward the parable of the prodigal son (1: 23), references to "unknown" and "unreckoned forces" (1: 19, 20), and a series of puzzling parallels or coincidences ("And Sergeant Fones in the barracks said just then... 'Exactly'... What did it mean?" [1: 19–20]) whose cumulative effect is to surround the characters and events of the story with an "aura" of mystery and foreboding and, more than this, to suggest that they are fulfilling some unknown and unknowable design.

When Sergeant Fones is finally found dead on Christmas Day, "[m]otionless, stern, erect... upon his horse, beside a stunted larch tree" with "[t]he bridle rein... still in [his] frigid fingers, and a smile upon his face" (1: 23), the reader shares the bafflement of the narrator and the other characters, not merely because of the enigmatic nature of the Sergeant's death and smile, but also because Parker has thwarted any single or straightforward interpretation of his fate by presenting him as neither a simple, allegorical figure with a specific meaning nor as a complex, rounded character with justifying motivations. If intentions can be judged by results, then the purpose of "The Patrol of the Cypress Hills" is to suggest that the events and relationships of human life are indeed governed by "unseen" and "unreckoned forces." In the pensive and incomplete "'I felt sometimes'" that one of the characters utters "silently" to herself over the dead body of Sergeant Fones may perhaps be read a metonymy of the gnomonic qualities of a story that leaves the reader with an abiding sense that there is much in human nature that cannot be expressed in words, explained in rational terms, or reduced to materialistic laws of cause and effect.

Many of the qualities of "The Patrol of the Cypress Hills" are also present in the story that Hovey praises for its mythopoeic presentation of "Titanic primitive types." In the opening paragraphs of "The Stone," the reader is quickly inducted into a realm where human beings—in this case the inhabitants of a small settlement named Purple Hill—live in the shadow of "portentous" "Nature" in the form of a "mighty and wonderful" Stone that, according to "Indian legends" to which "white men pay little heed," "one whom they called The Man Who Sleeps" will one day dislodge from its "jutting crag" to crush those who have "dared [to] cumber his playground" in the village below (*Works* 1: 205–207). From the outset, the narrator prepares the way for the inevitable fulfillment of the Indian legend by emphasizing the strange logic of The Stone's relationship to the villagers: the terrain seems to have been designed to facilitate the prophesied catastrophe ("the hill hollow[s] and narrow[s] from The Stone to the village, as if giants had made... [a] path" [1: 205]); The Stone itself is uncanny in its appearance and apparent behaviour ("[a]t times... it... [seems] to rest on nothing. ... But if one look[s] long, especially in summer, when the air throb[s], it evidently rock[s] upon... [its] toe" [1: 205–206]); the "first man"—later The Man—who settled in the valley had "a strange feeling" about The Stone, and his daughter goes "mad, and g[ives] birth to a dead child" at the thought that it "would hurtle down the hill at her great moment and destroy her and her child" (1: 206–207). As to what force or power has created this portentous situation, the narrator offers only alternatives: "Nature," "God or Fate" (1: 207).

Of one thing, however, the narrator is certain: the destruction of the village is a consequence of the selfishness, cruelty, unjustness, and evil of its inhabitants, whose most heinous sins of omission and commission include the acts that drive The Man into exile in "a rude hut" near The Stone and, finally, provoke him to enact his revenge: the death of his sick wife by starvation "because none... remembered... her and her needs"; the "lynching" of his only son for a crime that someone else was found to have committed; and the attempted murder of Pierre by dropping him over "the edge of a hill" (1: 207–209). As Pierre wakens from "the crashing gloom which succeeded [his] fall," he is confronted by "a being whose appearance [is] awesome and massive—an outlawed god" who has grown in his long exile to resemble not just a "Titan" and a "god" but also an Old Testament prophet and the immense Stone with which he had come to be identified. "Indeed, The Stone seemed more a thing of life...: The Man was sculptured rock. His white hair was chiselled on his broad brow, his face was a solemn pathos petrified, his lips were curled with an iron contempt, and incalculable anger" (1: 209).

In the nights following his rescue, Pierre first hears and then watches as The Man chips away at the "toe" of The Stone with the "eagerness of an avenging giant" (1: 210). Initially resolving to be the "cynical and approving spectator of an act of exquisite retaliation," Pierre gradually comes to harbour doubts about the justice of destroying the entire village: "had all those people hovering about those lights below done him harm?... [A] few—and they were women—would not have followed his tumbril to his death with cries of execration. The rest would have done so,—most of them did so,—not because he was a criminal, but because he was a victim, and because human nature as it is thirsts inordinately at times for blood and sacrifice—a living strain of the old barbaric instinct" (1: 211–212). As he continues to think "now doubtfully, now savagely, now with irony" about what is about to occur, Pierre suddenly sees the "fitness" for his situation of Abraham's final plea to God in Genesis 18.32 to spare the city of Sodom: "'*Oh, let not the Lord be angry, and I will yet speak but this once: Peradventure ten righteous shall be found there*'" (1: 212). To this, The Man's reply is a Jehovistic "'I will not spare it for ten's sake'" and a resolute "'*Now!*'" (1: 212). With the moon temporarily behind a cloud, "a monster spr[ings] from its pedestal upon Purple Hill, and, with a sound of thunder and an awful speed, race[s] upon the village below. The boulder of the hillside crumble[s] after it" (1: 213). When "[t]he moon sh[ines] out again for an instant," Pierre sees "The Man st[anding] where the Stone had been but when he reache[s] the place The Man [is] gone. Forever!" (1: 213). Melodramatic though this is, it leaves the reader disquietened and querying. Has The Man fled the scene or jumped to his death? Was his destruction of the village just or unjust? Was its ultimate cause God, Fate, (human) Nature or some combination of the three? Which of Pierre's attitudes to the event— doubt, savageness, or irony—is most appropriate, and what ethical weight should be given to the references to the "tumbril[s]" of the Reign of Terror and the persistence of "the old barbaric instinct" in his analysis of the villagers' behaviour? It is not difficult to see why Hovey singled out "The Stone" for special mention: arguably more than any other story in *Pierre and His People*, it raises momentous questions and frustrates full comprehension, leaving the reader with something like the "strange feeling" that prompted The Man to pay his first visit to The Stone.

As their collective title suggests, the short stories in *Earth's Enigmas* are also designed to generate feelings of mystery and puzzlement in the reader. In a Prefatory Note to the 1903 edition of the collection, Roberts both confirms this intention and emphasizes it by referring to the non-rational aspects of the bulk of the volume's contents:

> Most of the stories in this collection attempt to present one or another of those problems of life or nature to which, as it appears to many of us, there is not adequate solution within sight. Others are the almost literal transcript of dreams which seemed to me to have a coherency, completeness, and symbolic significance sufficiently marked to justify me in setting them down.[5] The rest are scenes from that simple life of the Canadian backwoods and tide-country with which my earlier years made me familiar. ([5])

While the stories in Roberts's third category are not without interest as therapeutic conduits to a "simple life" remote from the vexing complexities of modernity,[6] those that show the clearest affinities with the *symboliste* mode are the "problem" and "dream" pieces. "The Young Ravens that Call upon Him" (which Hovey mentions) is here, as are the very similar "Do Seek Their Meat from God" (the first story in the collection) and the eerily supernatural "The Perdu," a story that Francis Sherman, probably primed by Roberts, pronounced "more symbolic than tales of realism are likely to be" (qtd. in Pomeroy 140). Almost half a century after their first appearance in book form in 1896, Roberts used Elsie Pomeroy's "almost autobiographical record" of his life and work (*Collected Letters* 629) to call attention to the "grim symbolism" of the "dream" stories in *Earth's Enigmas* and to lament the "explanatory conclusion" and "practical explanation" that were added to two of them—"The Stone Dog" and "In the Accident Ward"—to satisfy "the market" (Pomeroy 140–141). He also has Pomeroy proclaim "The Hill of Chastisement" probably the most powerful of the dream pieces (141), very likely because its "grim symbolism" is not divested of its affectiveness by rational explanation.

"The Hill of Chastisement" may well have been generated by a dream, as Roberts claimed, but this does not prevent it from also being the product of literary influences. Of these the most obvious are the macabre poems and short stories of Edgar Allan Poe,[7] whose influence Roberts would have felt both directly in any number of collections and anthologies and indirectly through the work of Dante Gabriel Rossetti and various other writers. Since "The Hill of Chastisement" was one of the stories added to *Earth's Enigmas* in 1903, some eight years after Roberts informed Carman on January 8, 1895 that he already had a copy of the first series of Hovey's translations of Maeterlinck's plays ("I have Dick's 'Maeterlinck.' Fine essay, admirable translation" [Boone, *Collected Letters* 190]), those other writers doubtless included the playwright whose work Hovey explicitly likens in his introductory essay to "Poe's ghastly tales" (11). A juxtaposition of excerpts from Hovey's translations of the opening and closing stage directions of two of Maeterlinck's most Poeian plays, *Les Aveugles* ("The Blind") and *L'Intruse* ("The Intruder"), with the equivalent parts of "The Hill of Chastisement" highlights their similarities:

> An ancient Norland forest, with an eternal look, under a sky of stars. In the centre, and in the deep of the night, a very old priest is sitting, wrapped in a great black cloak. The chest and the head, gently upturned and deathly motionless, rest against the trunk of a giant oak. ... The dumb, fixed eyes no longer look out from the visible side of Eternity and seem to bleed with immemorial sorrows and with tears. The hair, of a solemn whiteness, falls in stringy locks, stiff and few, over a face more illuminated and more weary than all that surrounds it in the watchful stillness of that melancholy wood.

•

The cave-mouth wherein I dwelt, doing night-long penance for my sin, was midway of the steep slope of the hill. The hill, naked and rocky, rose into a darkness of gray mist. Below, it fell steeply into the abyss, which was full of the blackness of a rolling smoke. ...

In the heart of the sanctuary, far withdrawn, sat an old man, a saint, in a glory of clear and pure light. ... He sat with grave head bowed continually over a book that shone like crystal, and his beard full to his feet.

•

Here suddenly a wail of fright is heard in the child's room, on the night; and this wail continues, with gradations of terror until the end of the scene. ...

At the moment a hurrying of headlong heavy steps is heard in the room on the left.—Then a deathly stillness.—They listen in a dumb terror, until the door opens slowly, and the light from the next room falls into that in which they are waiting. The Sister of Charity appears on the threshold, in the black garments of her order. ...

•

As I grasped my sanctuary, the air rang with loud laughter; the faces, coming out of the smoke, sprang wide-eyed and flaming close about me; a red flare shattered the darkness. Clutching importunately, I lifted up my eyes. My refuge was not a calvary. I was it clear. It was a reeking gibbet. (Maeterlinck, *Plays* 265, 258–259; Roberts, *Earth's Enigmas* [1903] 197–198, 202–203)

Different as they are in certain respects, these passages share a common vocabulary of elemental space, pervasive darkness, terrified illumination, and religious types ("The Priest" and "The Sister of Charity" [Maeterlinck, *Plays* 263, 211], "a saint" and a penitent). It is, of course, impossible to state with absolute certainty that "The Hill of Chastisement" is primarily indebted to "The Blind" and "The Intruder" rather than to Poe or, say, Rossetti,[8] but the many qualities that the story shares with the plays, not least the "mastertone [of]... terror—terror... of the churchyard" that Hovey sees as Maeterlinck's distinguishing "mood" (11), do conspire with the external evidence to make this a distinct possibility.

But what about the animal stories in *Earth's Enigmas*? Were they written, as Hovey also claims of the *symboliste* work of Carman and Parker, "without any communication from France of Belgium" (8)? At first glance the answer seems to be yes, for "Do Seek Their Meat from God" was published in *Harper's Monthly Magazine* in December 1892 and "The Young Ravens that Call upon Him" in *Lippincott's* in May 1894, the former eighteen months before and the latter a month after Carman, in his role as literary advisor to the Chicago publishing house of Stone and Kimball, persuaded Hovey to translate the first series of Maeterlinck's *Plays* in April 1894 (see Macdonald 155). Yet Roberts may have known *Les Aveugles* and *L'Intruse* in the original or in a translation that preceded Hovey's, for both plays had been available in French and English since the early 1890s[9] and, as indicated by Lampman's comments on "The Belgian Shakespeare" in his *At the Mermaid Inn* column for March 12, 1892 (34–35), their author's fame had spread to Canada well before the publication of "Do Seek Their Meat from God." Perhaps Roberts's attention was drawn to Maeterlinck's plays by Hovey in September and early October 1892 when, after returning from a year and a half in England and France, Hovey wrote and holidayed with Roberts and Carman in Windsor, Nova Scotia. "I like [Hovey] *immensely*," Roberts wrote on September 11, "we get on most excellently together. We are both getting lots of work done" (*Collected Letters* 152). It is quite possible that "Do Seek Their Meat from God" and "The Young Ravens that Call upon Him" (especially the latter) were written or at least revised at this time or later. Certainly, the Fall of 1892 was a productive time for Roberts in fiction as well as poetry: in early June he had complained of "*not* [having] turned the corner in short story writing yet" but by late October he was possessed of enough material and confidence to contemplate assembling the collection of stories that eventually became *Earth's Enigmas* (*Collected Letters* 149, and see 155 and 159). "I am much gratified by your praise of 'Do Seek Their Meat from God,'" he told James Elgin Wetherell on December 14. "I have a few more sketches of a somewhat similar scope and carefully finished; and these I hope to print soon in book form" (*Collected Letters* 161).

Whether by coincidence or indebtedness, the initial descriptions of "Do Seek Their Meat from God" and "The Young Ravens that Call upon Him" resonate strongly with the opening stage directions of "The Blind." In the play, the initial directions concerning the "ancient Norland forest" and the "very old priest" are followed by instructions that specify the location of "six old men" and "six women" "[o]n the right" and "[o]n the left" of a set consisting of "stones, stumps... dead leaves... an uprooted tree and fragments of rocks" (Maeterlinck, *Plays* 265). "Tall funereal trees,—yews, weeping willows, cypresses,—cover [the old men and the women] with their faithful shadows," continue the directions, and "[i]t is unusually oppressive, despite the moonlight that here and there struggles to pierce for an instant the glooms of the foliage" (266). A similarly gloomy and blasted setting appears briefly at the beginning of "The Young Ravens that Call upon Him" ("It was just before dawn, and a grayness was beginning to trouble the dark above the top of the mountains. ... The veil of cloud that hid the stars hung a hand-breadth above the naked summit. ... Just under the brow, on a splintered and creviced ledge, was the nest of the eagles" [*Earth's Enigmas* (1903) 56]), but much more similar is the scene that opens "Do Seek Their Meat from God":

> One side of the ravine was in darkness. The darkness was soft and rich, suggesting thick foliage. Along the crest of the slope tree-tops came into view—great pines and hemlocks of the ancient unviolated forest—revealed against the orange disk of a full moon just rising. The low rays slanting through the moveless tops lit strangely the upper portion of the opposite steep,—the western wall of the ravine, barren, unlike its fellow, bossed with great rocky projections, and harsh with stunted junipers. Out of the sluggish dark that lay along the ravine as in a trough, rose the brawl of a swollen, obstructed stream.
>
> Out of the shadowy hollow behind a long white rock, on the lower edge of that part of the steep which lay in the moonlight, came softly a great panther. In common daylight his coat would have shown a warm fulvous hue, but in the elvish decolorizing rays of that half hidden moon he seemed to wear a sort of spectral gray. He lifted his smooth round head to gaze on the increasing flame, which presently he greeted with a shrill cry. That terrible cry, at once plaintive and menacing, with an undertone like the first protestations of a saw beneath the file, was a summons to his mate, telling her that the hour had come when they should seek their prey. From the lair behind the rock, where the cubs were being suckled by their dam, came no immediate answer. Only a pair of crows, that had their nest in a giant fir-tree across the gulf, woke up and croaked harshly their indignation. These three summers they had built in the same spot, and had been nightly awakened to vent the same rasping complaints. (*Earth's Enigmas* [1963] 11–13)

As is the case with the stage directions to "The Blind," the interplay of darkness and moonlight plays a major part in what Hovey would call the "impression" (5) created by this description: at first the moon is a portentously "orange disk," then its "slanting" rays "strangely" light the "western wall of the ravine," and, finally, its "elvish decolorizing rays" turn the panther's coat "a sort of spectral gray." As in "The Blind," Roberts's setting is elemental, apparently blighted, and shadowed by trees that, if not exactly "funereal," are certainly ominous in their appearances and associations—"great pines and hemlocks" "stunted junipers" and "a giant fir-tree." To judge by its lighting and *flora*, Roberts's "ancient unviolated forest" could easily be an adaptation of Maeterlinck's "ancient Norland forest." Of course, Roberts's characters are not people but animals (or, as Misao Dean calls them "(m)animals"), though even here the tone of terror and foreboding so central to Maeterlinck's plays has its equivalent: the cry of the panther is "shrill, terrible,... plaintive and menacing," and it is ominously answered by "a pair of crows"—two corbies, so to say—that have been nesting in "the same spot" for, in the words of Pierre in "The Patrol of the Cypress Hills"—"the magic number" of "three summers" (Parker, *Works* 1: 17). As Sherman observes of "The Perdu," "Do Seek Their Meat from God" is "more symbolic than tales of realism are likely to be." "It is one of Roberts's most notable contributions to Literature," Hovey would maintain, for in it "[t]he problem of the struggle for existence, of the preying of life on life, is treated with an inexorable fidelity to fact, a Catholic sympathy, a sense of universality and mystery, and a calm acceptance that reaches the level of 'pathos' in the highest Greek usage of the word" (qtd. in Pomeroy 107).

As any reader of Roberts's short stories well knows, the portents that darken the beginnings of "The Young Ravens that Call upon Him" and "Do Seek Their Meat from God" are amply fulfilled: in the former, the eagle kills a newborn lamb to feed its starving young, leaving its distraught mother remote from her flock and susceptible to a similar fate; and, in the latter, the panthers attempt to kill a small boy to feed their starving cubs but are shot by the boy's father, who later finds the "rapidly decaying" bodies of their cubs in their lair (*Earth's Enigmas* [1903] 27). As any reader of Roberts's short stories also well knows, such plot lines are unsentimentally Darwinian and Spencerian in their depiction of the struggle for survival and the survival of the fittest. But "The Young Ravens that Call upon Him," "Do Seek Their Meat from God," and other stories like them in *Earth's Enigmas* and subsequent collections do not merely provide their readers with a simple evolutionary explanation of occurrences in the human and natural worlds; rather—to quote Roberts's Prefatory Note to *Earth's Enigmas* again, this time with some interpretive inflections—they strive "to present one or another of those *problems* of life or nature to which, as it appears to many of us, there is no adequate solutions *within* sight." Both "The Young Ravens that Call upon Him" and "Do Seek Their Meat from God" have biblical titles[10] that work with the spatial and temporal patterns and coincidences of the stories to suggest that the solution to their enigmas, the answer to such questions as why did the ewe drop her lamb where and when she did and what made the father, despite his selfish instincts, heed the cries of the child that turns out to be his own, may lie *out of sight*, beyond full human comprehension in an "immaterial reality" whose intellectual or theological expression is such terms as Fate and God and whose emotional or "poetic expression" (or so Hovey argues) is "modern symbolism" (4–5).[11]

Although the animal stories of *Earth's Enigmas* differ from the pastoral tales of *In the Village of Viger* in offering vicarious atavism rather than "wise idleness" as a cure for the ills of modernity, the dream pieces and Canadian "scenes" that constitute the remainder of the collection have a considerable amount in common with Scott's short stories. Perhaps the most striking commonality lies in the geographical settings and contingent spiritual assumptions that are present in "The Perdu" and the village of Viger. By Roberts's own description, "a mystic psychological thing" (*Collected Letters* 144), "The Perdu" is set somewhere in French Canada beside the "narrow, tideless, windless, backwater" of its title, a stretch of river whose name seems to strangers to have a certain "occult appropriateness" and whose remoteness from "modern noises" and "the stream of modern ideas" has encouraged the persistence in the local people of "superstitions," "strange and not-to-be understood" mysteries, and a "sense of unseen but thrilling influences" (*Earth's Enigmas* [1903] 124–136). Akin to fantastic realism in its accreditation of two radically different epistemes, the story centres on a couple of visionary children, one of whom, Reuben, learns the ways of the modern world while the other, Celia, remains by the Perdu and, fulfilling the couple's earlier vision of "'a pale green hand'" sinking in the water (140), drowns as he is returning to marry her. None of Scott's stories is quite as uncanny as "The Perdu" but *In the Village of Viger* is, of course, also set in a part of French Canada where "modern noises and... ideas," though increasingly perceptible, have yet to alter the local ways ("on still nights... you c[an] hear the rumbles of... street-cars and the faint tinkle of their bells" and the time is coming for "Viger to be named in the city papers" [(1996) 3]), and, as a result, many of the village's inhabitants, particularly the elderly, retain such "pre-modern" characteristics as a belief in ghosts and a capacity for second sight.[12] Indeed, the further the reader travels into the collection (and, thus, away from modernity), the more the stories demand an acceptance of the irrational and the inexplicable: in "Sedan," Paul Latulipe knows without being told that the French have been defeated at the battle of 1870 for which the story is named ([1996] 37–38): in "The Tragedy of the Seigniory," Louis Bois is "as superstitious as an old wife" and gradually comes to believe that a dog is a human "spirit in canine form" ([1996] 57, 59); and in the final paragraphs of the final story, Paul Farlotte, an eccentric school teacher who lives in a cottage that has "the air of having been secured from the inroads of time" and is frequently "greeted with visions of things that had been, or that would be, and s[ees] figures where, for other eyes, hung only impalpable air" ([1996] 79, 81), learns from a "vision" of his mother's death in France:

> He saw a garden much like his own, flooded with the clear sunlight[;] in the shade of an arbor an old woman in a white cap was leaning back in a wheeled chair, her eyes were closed, she seemed asleep. A young woman was seated beside her holding her hand. Suddenly the old woman smiled, a childish smile, as if she were well pleased. "Paul," she murmured, "Paul, Paul." A moment later her companion started up with a cry; but she did not

move, she was silent and tranquil. Then the young woman fell on her knees and wept, hiding her face. But the aged face was expressably calm in the shadow, with the smile lingering upon it, fixed by the deeper sleep into which she hadfallen

....

Later in the day he told Marie that his mother had died that morning, and she wondered how he knew. ([1996] 89)

When Hovey wrote in "Modern Symbolism and Maurice Maeterlinck" that "[i]t would be interesting to trace the connection between English Pre-Raphaelitism and the new movement" (8) he was probably not thinking of "The Perdu" and certainly not of "Paul Farlotte," but both short stories would have confirmed the line of descent that he suggests, Roberts's with the debt of its "orange lilies" and "nameless spell" (126, 132) to such poems as "The Wind" and "The Blue Closet" in William Morris's *The Defence of Guenevere, and Other Poems* (1858)[13] and Scott's with its echoes of the vision in which the artist Chiaro is visited by his own soul in the form of a beautiful woman at the climax of Rossetti's "Hand and Soul" (1850).[14]

When viewed chronologically on the basis of their publication in magazines and newspapers between 1887 and 1893, the stories in *In the Village of Viger* not only show the increasing emphasis on supernatural themes that is discernible in the sequence of the collection, but also suggest that, like Hovey and Roberts, Scott may have felt the impact of Maeterlinck at the time of the meteoric rise to fame that Lampman recorded in *At the Mermaid Inn* early in March 1892. All of the *Viger* stories published in *Scribner's Magazine* in October 1887 and March 1891—"The Desjardins," "Josephine Labrosse," "The Little Milliner," and "the Wooing of Monsieur Cuerrier"— depict a world of realistic material and psychological causes and effects, but those published in *Scribner's* in October 1893—"The Bobolink," "The Pedler," and "Sedan"—contain events and characters that are *symboliste* as well as supernatural. Two further stories in the collection—"The Tragedy of the Seigniory" and "Paul Farlotte"—anticipate and fulfil this movement from realism to spiritualism: the former was first published in April 1892 in the Boston periodical *Two Tales*, and the latter did not appear prior to its publication in 1896 in the Viger collection itself (see Groening 501–502). It is in two of the short stories first published in 1892—"The Bobolink" and "The Pedler"—that Scott first employs the two hallmarks of the *symboliste* mode—evocative suggestion and character types—that three years later would stamp his poetic masterpiece, "The Piper of Arll," as an unmistakable product of Hovey's modern "symbolic principle."

Perhaps reflecting the direct influence of *Les Aveugles*, the central characters of both "The Bobolink" and "The Pedler" are blind and mysterious. In "The Bobolink," the questions of "the little blind daughter of... Moreau" often leave the "old man" who calls her " 'my little fairy' " at a loss for words and "mystefied" and, in "The Pedler," the "inscrutable" "green spectacles" of the blind pedlar who once brought his "magical baskets" to Viger every spring are as much a source of consternation to the villagers as his furious behaviour when by accident they are removed during a wind storm ([1996] 76–78). At the conclusion of "The Pedler," its central character disappears with the storm, leaving suspicions that he was a thief or the Devil and providing a basis for "tradition" and fantasy since "there are yet people in Viger who, when the dust blows,... see the figure of the enraged pedler, large upon the hills, striding violently along the fringes of the storm" ([1996] 74, 78). Consistent with the medicinal purposes of *In the Village of Viger*, this is more quaint and distracting than uncanny or terrifying. By the same token, the decision of the old man and the blind girl to release their caged bird at the conclusion of "The Bobolink" leaves the reader, like the old man himself, pensive and saddened by the evidence of change and loss rather than shocked or deeply troubled by the enigmas of life and death:

> "He's gone," she said, " ... Where did he go, Uncle?"
>
> "He flew right through that maple-tree, and now he's over the fields, and now he's out of sight."
>
> "And didn't he even once look back?"
>
> "No, never once."
>
> They stood there together for a moment, the old man gazing after the departed bird, the little girl setting her brown, sightless eyes on the invisible distance. Then, taking the empty cage, they went back to the cabin. From that day their friendship was not untinged by regret; some delicate mist of sorrow seemed to have blurred the glass of memory. Though he could not tell why, old Etienne that evening felt anew his loneliness, as he watched a long sunset of red and gold that lingered after the footsteps of the August day, and cast a great color into his silent cabin above the Blanche. ([1996] 54)

Whether or not "The Pedler" and "The Bobolink" were written under the influence of *Les Aveugles*, they certainly reflect a sensibility that would find the essays in Maeterlinck's *Le Trésor des humbles* (1896) congenial and inspirational (see Bentley "Duncan Campbell Scott and Maurice Maeterlinck") and, in 1904, would praise their author to Pelham Edgar as "*the* modern Mystic" who is constantly "endeavouring to awaken the wonder-element in a modern way" by "expressing the almost unknowable things which we all feel" (Scott, *More Letters* 24; emphasis added).

In the final analysis, it may not be possible to locate precisely the points of intersection and the sets of parallels that enmesh the *symboliste* aspects of the early short stories of Parker, Roberts, and Scott. Perhaps, as Hovey argues, the Canadian writers arrived at "the symbolic principle... without any communication with France of Belgium." Perhaps the (social) landscape and (intellectual) climate in Canada in the 1890s did, indeed, generate independent manifestations of "modern symbolism." Such views have their appeal, but against them stands a good deal of evidence that, thanks in part to Hovey himself, the work of the French and Belgian *symbolistes*, particularly Maeterlinck, was far from unavailable or unknown to Canadian writers from the early '90s onwards. There may not be conclusive proof that the stories of Roberts and Scott were written under the influence of *Les Aveugles* and *L'Intruse*, but there is certainly enough internal and circumstantial evidence to allow this to stand as a plausible hypothesis. But what about Parker's stories? Published as they were in periodicals and book form in the very early '90s, are they at least an independent manifestation of "modern symbolism," or do they, too, reflect the work of Maeterlinck, and was Parker himself, like Hovey, a channel though which *symbolisme* reached Canadian writers? Some support for this second proposition can be gleaned from the fact that Parker was living in London, writing the Pierre stories, and attempting to embark on a career as a playwright at precisely the time of Maeterlinck's rise to prominence in the English-speaking world. A fervent admirer of one of the presiding doyens of British theatre in the '90s, Herbert Beerbohm Tree, Parker was unlikely to have missed the opportunity of seeing the production of Gérard Harry's translation of *L'Intruse* that opened at the Haymarket Theatre with Tree in the leading rôle on January 27, 1892. Nor did he. "Mr. Tree's playing of the Grandfather in 'L'Intruse,'" he recalled in 1895, was "subtle,... poetic... fanciful and deep... for here came out" the "eerie quality" that is "entirely his own" ("Herbert Beerbohm Tree" 121, 118). Since Parker wrote quickly and had an eager publisher in W. H. Henley, "The Stone" could easily have been written between the end of January and its appearance in Henley's *National Observer* on February 20, 1892. (Parker would later recall that he sent an earlier story, "Antoine and Angelique," to Henley "almost before the ink was dry" and that "The Stone" "brought a telegram of congratulations" [*Works* 1: xi].) To secure the net of influence with such tight knots is not essential, however, since the Henley circle within which Parker moved included several artists and writers, such as James McNeill Whistler, William Butler Yeats, and Henley himself, who had produced works imbued or consistent with the *symboliste* aesthetic by the early '90s. *Pierre and His People* may not be of the same stature as *The Wanderings of Oisin* (1889) and *The Countess Cathleen* (1892), but it resembles Yeats's early work in its application to local and resonantly national subjects and settings of an increasingly international mode of writing, a set of "traits and methods" with roots, not only in France and Belgium, but also, like the French and Belgian *symbolistes* themselves, in Poe, the Pre-Raphaelites, and American and British transcendentalism.

On the other side of the Atlantic, it was the local and national elements in Parker's work that assured his quick rise to prominence in Canada. In a letter to Carman on March 19, 1892, several months before the appearance of *Pierre and His People* and probably on the basis of the five Pierre stories (including "The Patrol of Cypress Hills") that were published in *The Independent* between January 1891 and March 1892 (see Adams 230), Roberts told Carman of his liking for "Parker's work" and within the year he was asking his cousin for Parker's address in England and wondering whether he could be persuaded to review *Songs of the Common Day*, and *Ave: an Ode for the Shelley Centenary* (1893) in a British periodical (*Collected Letters* 144, 159, 163).[15] When Parker paid a brief visit to Canada in the late Fall and early Winter of 1892 to spend time with his family in Belleville and to gather material for more Canadian stories and "'a novel on Quebec,'" he was warmly received in Ottawa, Montreal, and Quebec by John Bourinot, William Van Horne, and James MacPherson LeMoine (see Adams 72–74). Among those who met him in Ottawa was Scott, who reported in his *At the Mermaid Inn* column for January 7, 1893 that "*Pierre and His People* ha[d] gone into its second edition" and that Parker was sure to meet similar success with a forthcoming novel (*Mrs. Falchion* [1893]) and stage production (*The Wedding Day* [n.d.]) (227). Neither Roberts nor Scott appears to have been as enthusiastic about the other's fiction as about Parker's but they certainly knew one another's short stories both before and after their appearance in book form and may well have been engaged in a process of mutual influence: perhaps it was the presence of Scott's "The Tragedy of the Seigniory" in one of the copies of *Two Tales* that Carman sent him in May 1892 that prompted Roberts to send a story to the Boston periodical (see *Collected Letters* 148) and perhaps it was the presence of two of Roberts's poems, "Her Fan" and "Her Glove Box," in the May 18 and July 13, 1895 issues of *The Truth* (New York) that led to the appearance there on December 14 of the same year of "The Piper of Arll." The famous line that led from Roberts's *Orion, and Other Poems* (1880), through Lampman and Scott, to John Masefield is surely more sensuous and tangled than it might first appear.

These days it is extremely unfashionable to attend to the sorts of literary-historical issues raised by the relationships among the short stories of Parker, Roberts, and Scott and between this ensemble of short fiction and the *symboliste* movement. To cast an eye over the lines and intersections and parallels that connect and divide the French, Belgian, English, American, and Canadian practitioners of Hovey's "modern symbolism" is not only to perceive part of the web that constitutes Canadian literature, but also to uncover some of the Canadian tendrils of the root-system from which Anglo-American modernism was already beginning to grow as the nineteenth century waned into the twentieth. *Pierre and His People, Earth's Enigmas,* and *In the Village of Viger* are all minor works, but individually and collectively they grow in richness if not in stature with an awareness of the background, functions, and presentiments of their symbolic practices.

NOTES

I am grateful to the taxpayers of Canada and Ontario through the Social Sciences and Humanities Research Council of Canada and the University of Western Ontario for their generous support of my research and teaching and to Jonathan Stover and J. M. Zezulka for valuable discussions of ideas contained in this essay.

1. The two fairy stories, "Hans Fingerhut's Frog Lesson" and "The Fairy Fountain," that Lampman wrote in the mid- to late 1880s are also therapeutic in nature, as are several of his other "nature" poems. In a letter of January 25, 1892 concerning "Comfort of the Fields," which eventually appeared in *Lyrics of Earth* (1895), Carman told Lampman that "it comes with tender, enduring, and most intimate solace; taking on itself the office of hands that are no longer near to soothe. It is a very sweet and wise thing and has fallen on my heart with abundance of relief beyond the requital of words. May the dear wood-gods give you ten-fold reward... for this gentle service rendered to an unworthy fellow vagrant" (Lampman Papers).

2. It is just possible that this statement was in Scott's mind when he concluded the opening verse paragraph of "At Gull Lake: August 1810" (1935) with the lines "All proceeds in the flow of Time / As a hundred years ago" (*Selected Poetry* 96).

3. In his Introduction to *The Lane that Had No Turning* (1899) in the Imperial Edition of his *Works,* Parker contrasts the "almost domestic simplicity" of the later stories, a quality "in keeping with the happily simple and uncomplicated life of French Canada," to the "more strenuous episodes of the Pierre series" (9: ix). Many of Carman and Hovey's *Vagabondia* poems offer vicarious strenuosity as a mental medicine, as do most of the pieces in *The Rough Rider, and Other Poems* (1909), which Carman dedicated to Roosevelt.

4. Carman's comment that the Canadian Northwest "furnished [Parker] with good hunting, only to be equalled in... Kipling's India" (qtd. in Adams 61) brings into view the imperialistic dimension of Parker's claim in the Introduction to *Pierre and His People* in the Imperial (!) Edition that "what *Pierre* did was to open up a field which had not been opened before, but which other authors have exploited since with success and distinction. *Pierre* was the pioneer of the Far North in fiction" (1: xiii). For a discussion of a much earlier instance of the imperial and literary

appropriation of the Canadian Northwest, see the chapter on Henry Kelsey's "Now Reader Read... " in Bentley, *Mimic Fires* 13–24.

5. One of the "dream" pieces in *Earth's Enigmas*, "The Stone Dog," is also one of Roberts's earliest stories (see Pomeroy 140). In a letter of January 31, 1892, Roberts tells Carman that he has "taken to writing in dreams once more" because "the Muse ha[s] deserted [his] waking hours" (Boone, *Collected Letters* 144).

6. There is a good deal of evidence to indicate that for several years beginning in the summer of 1890, Roberts suffered from bouts of weariness and depression of the sort usually attributed at the time to the effects of modernity but, in his case, apparently the result of domestic tension and excessively hard work on such projects as *The Canadian Guide-Book* (1891). "Now th[at] book is done," he told Carman on May 7, 1891, "I am setting myself to rest and recuperate for a week or two" (*Collected Letters* 133). In subsequent letters to various writers he appears to have diagnosed himself as a victim of the "nervous exhaustion" or "neurasthenia" that one of the principal theorists of the mind-cure movement, Dr. George Miller Beard, ascribed to modern American civilization. See, for example, his letter of August 8, 1891 to William Morton Paine: "Your last letter came while I was away in the wilds, with birch and paddle, trying to recuperate. As I was utterly used up, very nervous and miserable in every way, I went quite out of reach of all work. ... [F]or the last twelve months I had been dull and oppressed (with a sort of nervous prostration, the after effect of *Grippe*). ... Thank you for being interested in my poor guide-book, written in the midst of great depression" (*Collected Letters* 134, and see also 139, 144–145, and 153). On May 20, 1893, he would describe his recent stay with Hovey's parents in Washington, D. C. as "sick leave" and on October 10 of the same year he would write that he was "feeling better, but... still far from being out of the wood[s]" (*Collected Letters* 173, 186).

7. Roberts may have been thinking of Poe's well-known formal strictures when writing to Carman in April 1892 of the "absolute unity of effect" and the "*unity* complete in all respects" that he felt he had achieved in "A Tragedy of the Tides," a short story published in *The Independent* on May 26, 1892 and in *Current Literature* in July 1900 (*Collected Letters* 146).

8. Rossetti's "The Orchard Pit" and "St. Agnes of Intercession" had been available since 1886 in the two volumes of his *Collected Works*.

9. Roberts's first reference to Hovey is in a letter to Carman on May 24, 1892: "Glad to hear of Hovey. Shall do him up one of these days in 'Modern Instances' " (*Collected Letters* 148). None of the "Modern Instances" columns that Roberts published in the *Dominion Illustrated* in February, April, May, and August 1892 deals with Hovey, but in "The Genius of Richard Hovey" in the commemorative issue of *The Criterion* that was published shortly after Hovey's death he provides an astute and generous assessment of his friend's work.

10. Mary Vielé's translations of *Les Aveugles* and *L'Intruse* were published in 1891 in Washington, D. C., where Hovey was born in 1861 and his parents still lived. (Roberts, in fact, stayed with them during his "sick leave" in April and May 1893 [see *Collected Letters* 168–174].) The one translation of a Maeterlinck play other than Hovey's that almost certainly came to Roberts's attention, albeit after the publication of "Do Seek Their Meat from God," was that of *Les Aveugles* by Charlotte Porter

and Helen A. Clarke in the 1893 volume of *Poet-Lore* (Boston). Among the contents of the four issues of the magazine in which Porter and Clarke's translation appeared are two vignettes, "In Great Eliza's Golden Time" and "The Mistress of the Red Lamp," by Archibald MacMechan, a correspondent of Roberts since at least the Fall of 1892. By 1893 the two were exchanging poems, short stories, and encouraging comments: on May 30, Roberts thanked MacMechan for sending him a lyric that he "like[d] greatly" and for his "kind words of the 'Perdu'" and on November 24 he thanked him "for sending... *Poet-Lore*, with that thoroughly exquisite pastel," adding that "Carman thinks it the best English pastel he has seen" (*Collected Letters* 173, 177). (The *OED* cites the April 22, 1893 number of *The Critic* (New York) for the use of "pastel" as a literary term: "The French pastel is really a little study [without a definite beginning or end] of a trifling topic which lacks complexity, and needs little more than a moderate space.") In addition to anticipating Hovey's "The Blind" both technically and chronologically, Porter and Clarke's "The Sightless" is prefaced by an essay by Charlotte Porter that not only conveys a sense of Maeterlinck's importance for many of his contemporaries (his "work... stands... at the doorsill of that change in world insight and impulse which means a new era"), but also provides an astute analysis of the *symboliste* mode ("the worn literary words of the past... [are] symbols fresh-minted for new offices and strange effects" such as the use of "suggestion" to awaken the "inward intelligence" of the audience) (151–154).

11. The former alludes to Job 38.41 ("Who provideth for the raven his food? when his young ones cry unto God, they wander for lack of meat") and the latter to Psalm 104.21 ("The young lions roar after their prey, and seek their meat from God"). See also Job 38.39 ("Wilt thou hunt the prey for the lion, or fill the appetite of the young lions...?"), Psalm 147.9 ("He giveth to the beast his food, and to the young ravens which cry"), and Luke 12.24 ("Consider the ravens: for they neither sow nor reap; which neither have storehouse nor barn; and God feedeth them: how much more are ye better than the fowls?"). It is not fortuitous that most of these quotations raise large question about the relationship among humans, animals, and God.

12. Hovey's distinction in "Modern Symbolism and Maurice Maeterlinck" between "the natural,... the ethical, [and]... the poetic mind" (4) reflects his Delsartean or unitrinian belief that human beings consist of three components—body, mind, and spirit—that need to be brought into harmony to assure well-being (see Macdonald 62–79 and 75–78, and Bentley "Carman and Mind Cure"). See Gerald Lynch, "The One and the Many: English-Canadian Short Story Cycles" (97–98) for an excellent discussion of the formal characteristics and setting in *In the Village of Viger* and the same author's "'In the Meantime': Duncan Campbell Scott's *In the Village of Viger*" for another excellent discussion of the work as a cycle and as a reflection of Scott's attitudes to progress and community.

13. Roberts recommended "The Wind" to Carman in a letter of October 25, 1884 and, a month later, endorsed his cousin's opinion of "The Gilliflower of Gold" ("[i]t is splendid") and "Concerning Geffray Teste Noire" ("[a] curious and to me very touching though confused thing") (*Collected Letters* 47). Almost needless to say, the "pale green hand" that emerges from the water in "The Perdu" echoes the

"arm / Clothed in white samite" that takes Excalibur in Tennyson's *Morte d'Arthur* (1842) (*Poems* 592).

14. Chiaro's soul appears to him in a pulsing "light" and dressed in "green and gray raiment, fashioned to that time." After she has finished likening his career to a "garden," he falls "slowly to his knees. ... The air brooded in sunshine, and though the turmoil was great outside, the air within was at peace. But when he looked in her eyes, he wept." As he works later to fulfill his soul's instructions, Chiaro's face "gr[ows] solemn with knowledge" and, "[h]aving finished,... [he] lay[s] back where he s[its] and slips into a sleep that is death" (Rossetti, *Works* 553–555).

15. In his letter of November 30, 1892, Roberts also asks for the address of William Sharp (*Collected Letters* 159), a writer and editor with whom he had corresponded since the late '80s and to whom Hovey would pay the compliment in "Modern Symbolism and Maurice Maeterlinck" of linking his *Vistas* (1894) with Oscar Wilde's *Salomé* (1893) as English manifestations of the *symboliste* mode. (Of course, Roberts made much of the fact that he caroused with Wilde during his visit to Fredericton in October 1882 [see Pomeroy 42–43]). On January 7, 1895, Carman responded to Hovey's suggestion that *Vistas* and *Salomé* "might perhaps not have been written had the authors been less familiar with the contemporary literature of the Continent" (8) with his own assessment of Maeterlinck: "Yes, I see Sharp's indebtedness to Maeterlinck. ... But Maeterlinck himself does not get me yet. It is trying to make literature without the use of the adjective. One Stevensonian adjective, one Meredithian phrase gives more effect, more shiver than all of *The Intruder*. This method of iteration omits the use of surprise in getting its effect. A child could drill me into madness by asking questions, but I only find Maeterlinck tiresome. It does not take hold. But, mind you, this is only a first opinion. I will have to try him again and tell you how he works" (*Letters* 83, and see 91). Sharp's review of Gérard Harry's *The Princess Maleine* and *The Intruder* in the March 19, 1892 number of *The Academy* (London) reveals a thorough knowledge of Maeterlinck's works, influences, and critical history in Belgium, France, and England. "A new method is coming into literature," Sharp asserts, "and Maeterlinck is one of those who deserve honour as pioneers in a difficult path" (271). An earlier review by Sharp, "Ruysbroeck and Maeterlinck" in the March 16, 1892 number of *The Academy*, discusses both Maeterlinck's translation of *Les Ornamentes des noces spirituelles* by Ruysbroeck L'Admirable and *Ruysbroeck and the Mystics*, a translation of Maeterlinck's work by Jane T. Stoddart, whose "An Interview with M. Maurice Maeterlinck" precedes Roberts's "Three Good Things" in the May 1895 number of *The Bookman* (New York). See also Helen A. Clarke's "Maeterlinck and Sharp."

WORKS CITED

Adams, John Coldwell. *Seated with the Mighty: A Biography of Sir Gilbert Parker.* Ottawa: Borealis, 1979.

At the Mermaid Inn: Wilfred Campbell, Archibald Lampman, Duncan Campbell Scott in The Globe 1892–93. Ed. Barrie Davies. Literature of Canada: Poetry and Prose in Reprint. Toronto: U of Toronto P, 1979.

Beard, George Miller. *American Nervousness, Its Causes and Consequences: A Supplement to Nervous Exhaustion (Neurasthenia).* New York: G. P. Putnam's Sons, 1881.

Bentley, D.M.R. "Carman and Mind Cure: Theory and Technique." In *Bliss Carman: A Reappraisal.* Ed. Gerald Lynch. Reappraisals: Canadian Writers 16. Ottawa: U of Ottawa P, 1990. 85–110.

———. "Duncan Campbell Scott and Maurice Maeterlinck." *Studies in Canadian Literature* 21:2 (1996): 104–119.

———. *Mimic Fires: Accounts of Early Long Poems on Canada.* Kingston and Montreal: McGill-Queen's UP, 1994.

———. "UnCannyda." *Canadian Poetry: Studies, Documents, Reviews* 37 (Fall/Winter, 1995): 1–16.

Bithell, Jethro. *Life and Writings of Maurice Maeterlinck.* 1913. Port Washington, N. Y.: Kennikat, 1972.

Boone, Laurel, Ed. *The Collected Letters of Charles G. D. Roberts.* Fredericton, N. B.: Goose Lane, 1989.

Carman, Bliss. *Letters.* Ed. H. Pearson Gundy. Kingston and Montreal: McGill-Queen's UP, 1981.

———. *The Rough Rider, and Other Poems.* New York: Kennerly, 1909.

Carman, Bliss, and Richard Hovey. *Songs from Vagabondia.* Boston: Copeland and Day, 1894.

C[larke], Helen A. "Maeterlinck and Sharp." *Poet-Lore* 7 (1895): 157–161.

Dean, Misao. "Political Science: Realism in Roberts's Animal Stories." *Studies in Canadian Literature* 21:1 (1996): 1–16.

Doyle, James. "Archibald Lampman and Hamlin Garland." *Canadian Poetry: Studies, Documents, Reviews* 16 (Spring/Summer, 1985): 38–46.

Groening, Laura. "Duncan Campbell Scott: an Annotated Bibliography." In *The Annotated Bibliography of Canada's Major Authors.* Vol. 8. Eds. Robert Lecker and Jack David. Toronto: ECW Press, 1994. 469–576.

Hovey, Richard. "Impressions of Maurice Maeterlinck and the Theatre de L'Oeuvre." *Poet-Lore* 7 (1895): 446–50.

———. "Modern Symbolism and Maurice Maeterlinck." In *Plays.* By Maurice Maeterlinck. Trans. Richard Hovey. 1894, 1896. Chicago and New York: Herbert S. Stone, 1902. New York: Kraus Reprint, 1972.

———. "The Passing of Realism." *The Independent* 47 (August 22, 1895): 1125.

Kugel, James L. *The Techniques of Strangeness in Symbolist Poetry.* New Haven and London: Yale UP, 1971.

Lampman, Archibald. Papers. W. A. C. Bennett Library, Burnaby, B. C.

———. *Poems.* Ed. Duncan Campbell Scott. Toronto: George N. Morang, 1900.

Lears, T. J. Jackson. *No Place of Grace: Antimodernism in American Culture, 1880–1920.* N. Y.: Pantheon Books, 1981.

Lucas, Alec. Introduction. *The Last Barrier, and Other Stories.* By Charles G. D. Roberts. Ed. Alec Lucas. New Canadian Library 7. Toronto: McClelland and Stewart, 1958. v–x.

Lynch, Gerald. "'In the Meantime': Duncan Campbell Scott's *In the Village of Viger.*" *Studies in Canadian Literature* 17:2 (1993): 70–91.

———. "The One and the Many: English-Canadian Short Story Cycles." *Canadian Literature* 130 (Autumn 1991): 91–104.

Macdonald, Allan Houston. *Richard Hovey, Man and Craftsman.* Durham, N. C.: Duke UP, 1957.

MacMechan, Archibald. "In Great Eliza's Golden Time." *Poet-Lore* 5 (1893):431–432.

———. "The Mistress of the Red Lamp." *Poet-Lore* 5 (1893): 488–490.

Maeterlinck, Maurice. "Alladine and Palomides." Trans. Charlotte Porter and Helen A. Clarke. *Poet-Lore* 7 (1895): 281–301.

———. *Les Aveugles.* Bruxelles: Paul Lacomblez, 1890.

———. *Pelléas and Mélisande.* Trans. Erving Winslow. New York and Boston: Thomas Y. Crowell, 1894.

———. *Pelleas and Melisande and The Sightless.* Trans. Laurence Alma Tadema. The Scott Library. London: W. Scott, [1895].

———. *Plays* [First Series: "Princess Maleine," "The Intruder," "The Blind," "The Seven Princesses"; Second Series: "Alladine and Palomides," "Pelléas and Mélisande," "Home," "The Death of Tintagiles"]. Trans. Richard Hovey. 2 vols. Chicago: Stone and Kimball, 1894, 1896. The Green Tree Library. Chicago and New York: Herbert S. Stone, 1902. New York: Klaus Reprint, 1972.

———. *The Princess Maleine.* Trans. Gérard Harry. London: Heinemann, 1890.

———. *The Princess Maleine, a Drama in Five Acts; and The Intruder, a Drama in One Act.* Trans. Gérard Harry and William Wilson. New York: J. W. Lovell, 1892.

———. *Blind. The Intruder.* Trans. Mary Vielé. Washington, D. C.: W. H. Morrison, 1891.

———. "The Seven Princesses." Trans. Charlotte Porter and Helen A. Clarke. *Poet-Lore* 6 (1894): 29–32, 87–93, 150–161.

———. "The Sightless." Trans. Charlotte Porter and Helen A. Clarke. *Poet-Lore* 5 (1893): 159–163, 218–221, 273–277, 442–452.

Morris, William. 1858. *The Defence of Guenevere.* London: Scolar Press, 1979.

Oxley, J. Macdonald. "Busy People." *Man, a Canadian Home Magazine* (Ottawa) 1 (December 1885): 55–57.

Parker, Gilbert. "Herbert Beerbohm Tree. A Study." *Lippincott's Monthly Magazine* 55 (January 1895): 117–122.

———. *Pierre and His People.* London: Methuen, 1892.

———. *Works.* Imperial Edition. 23 vols. New York: Charles Scribner's Sons, 1912.

Pomeroy, E. M. *Sir Charles G. D. Roberts: A Biography.* Toronto: Ryerson, 1943.

Porter, Charlotte. "Maurice Maeterlinck: Dramatist of a New Method." *Poet-Lore* 5 (1893): 151–159.

Roberts, Charles G. D. *The Canadian Guide-Book: The Tourist's and Sportsman's Guide to Eastern Canada and Newfoundland.* London: William Heinemann, 1892.

———. *Earth's Enigmas. A Book of Animal and Nature Life.* Boston: Lamson, Wolffe, 1896.

———. *Earth's Enigmas.* Boston: L. C. Page, 1903.

———. "The Genius of Richard Hovey." *The Criterion* 23 (April 1900): 9–10.

———. *The Kindred of the Wild. A Book of Animal Life.* 1902. Boston: L. C. Page, 1935.

Rossetti, Dante Gabriel. *Collected Works.* Ed. William M. Rossetti. 2 vols. London: Ellis, 1886.

———. *Works.* Ed. William M. Rossetti. London: Ellis, 1911.

Scott, Duncan Campbell. *At the Mermaid Inn:* see *At the Mermaid Inn*

———. *In the Village of Viger.* 1896. Intro. Tracy Ware. New Canadian Library. Toronto: McClelland and Stewart, 1996.

———. *More Letters.* Ed. Arthur S. Bourinot. Ottawa: Arthur S. Bourinot, 1960.

———. *Selected Poetry.* Ed. Glenn Clever. Ottawa: Tecumseh, 1974.

Sharp, William. Rev. *The Princess Maleine and The Intruder.* By Maurice Maeterlinck. Trans. Gérard Harry. *The Academy* 41 (March 19, 1892): 270–272.

———."Ruysbroeck and Maeterlinck." Rev. *Les Ornamentes des noces spirituelles.* By Ruysbroeck L'Admirable. Trans. Maurice Maeterlinck; and *Ruysbroeck and the Mystics.* By Maurice Maeterlinck. Trans. Jane T. Stoddart. *The Academy* 47 (March 16, 1895): 232–233.

———. *Vistas.* Green Tree Library. Chicago: Stone and Kimball, 1894.

Stoddart, Jane T. "An Interview with M. Maurice Maeterlinck." *The Bookman.* New York (May 1, 1895): 246–248.

Tennyson, Alfred Lord. *Poems.* Ed. Christopher Ricks. Annotated English Poets. London: Longman, 1969.

Present But Unaccounted For: The Canadian Young Adult Short Story of the Nineteenth Century Comes of Age

JEAN STRINGAM

Those of us given to celebrating age milestones in adolescent literature will want to take special note of the following announcement: "The Canadian Young Adult Short Story Turns 123 Years Old in 1999." Some would have adolescent literature be a postmodernist occurrence dating from *The Outsiders* by S. E. Hinton (1967) or, more expansively, a half-century-old endeavour beginning with *Seventeenth Summer* by Maureen Daly (1942), but this would be to ignore the hundreds of stories written by Canadians, and about Canada and Canadians, the first of which began to appear in 1876 and thereafter in the most popular and influential of the U. S. children's magazines. Judging from the overwhelming number of adolescent protagonists in these stories who are specifically described by their authors as being between the ages of fourteen and eighteen, the target market was undoubtedly the Young Adult. Caroline Hunt's article in the Spring 1996 *Children's Literature Association Quarterly* (4–11) is correct in asserting that Young Adult literature has been neglected by theorists; but in no respect can it be said to come into existence in the twentieth century.

The four periodicals selected as the focus of this paper, *St. Nicholas: A Magazine for Boys and Girls* (1870–1943), *Harper's Young People* (1879–1899), *Golden Days for Boys and Girls* (1880–1907), and *Youth's Companion* (1882–1928), contain numerous short stories by Canadian authors still recognized today for their contributions in adult literature: Charles G. D. Roberts, Sara Jeannette Duncan, E. W. Thomson, and Marjorie L. C. Pickthall. Other Canadian authors publishing in these periodicals, such as L. M. Montgomery, Norman Duncan, and Marshall Saunders, continue to be applauded as setting the standard in children's literature on an international level. But beyond these well-known names exists the works of lesser-known or entirely forgotten authors whose hundreds of stories form the formidable bulk of texts that need and deserve to be evaluated as a genre, as an art, and as an ethos of an age.

Canadians were favoured with wide publication in these journals, and the realistic animal stories of writers such as Charles G. D. Roberts and Ernest Thompson Seton brought an international reputation to their authors as well as to their Canadian subjects. Since these stories have been treated with critical vigour by a number of theorists, this paper will not consider them even though they comprise a very large portion of the periodical literature. Rather, I will consider broad issues such as class considerations, gender differentiation, and nineteenth-century racial stereotypes. Using R. Gordon Moyles' research published in *Canadian Children's Literature* (1995) as a base, this paper will sample approximately forty years of the Young Adult short story beginning in 1876 with Mrs. C. E. Groser's "A Summer Ride in Labrador," published in *St. Nicholas*, and ending in 1914 when World War I forcibly altered the existing social structures.

Mrs. Groser's story may never need to see the light of day again, but I begin with it because, after all, it *is* the first story published by a Canadian in these periodicals, and it does sound many of the basic themes that were to become the hallmarks of the Canadian contingent. Three daughters of a missionary stationed in Labrador gain parental permission to take the family's dog-team and sled out on an early morning ride to say goodbye to friends leaving the camaraderie of the winter settlement for their solitary summer fishing cove. Adventures follow the journey: the dogs fight those of another team; the girls prevent being overturned only by jumping out of the sled prior to the mishap; they must then recapture the dogs. The return journey is also eventful: one adolescent sister dallies in her clam digging, making the sisters' departure close to midday, when the river is in danger of melting from the June sun; the runaway dog-team chases after a deer and is only stopped when the girls run the sleigh into a tree; the ice on the river melts under the sleigh runners; and the father at home encourages the sled dogs to their utmost effort in beating the ice break-up by feeding upwind the dogs who remain at home. Unfortunately the story seems to strain for danger, despite it being always genuinely and amply present, so that the author is immediately under suspicion of writing from someone else's experience. Nevertheless, this little story manages to sound some of the main themes of the nineteenth-century Young Adult Canadian short story. Animals, both tame and wild, are ever-present and interactive with humans; adolescents exist within a social structure stimulated by peers and bounded by the family; adolescent work and play is indistinguishable from adventure; nature must never be assumed to be either benign or savage, for it can be beautiful, entertaining, or perilous by turn.

Interestingly, Canadian treatment of certain themes is very different from those of contemporary American authors in a number of respects. R. Gordon Kelly's analysis of stories in the gentry periodicals, *Mother Was a Lady* (1974), outlines the two basic thematic structures as being that of the Ordeal: a ritual rite of passage that involves physical isolation from society for a time followed by a rescue and subsequent absorption into either the old or a new social structure, and a Change of Heart in which the protagonist undergoes a moral enlightenment or some other dramatic shift in understanding in which there is a conscious decision to make change for the better. Both these formulas are infused with what it is to be a gentleman or lady, a member of the gentry "whose moral authority derives from universal law" (49). The gentry, then, are the culture-bearers of American democratic principles who maintain the social, aesthetic, and intellectual standards of refinement, temperance, justice, and courtesy.

Despite the gentry class orientation of the American periodicals both in authorship and readership, many of the Canadian stories accepted for publication in them feature working-class men and boys whose values and commitments present a stark contrast to the sensibilities of the gentry class. Norman Duncan's stories of sailors and sealing involve body-breaking toil in dangerous circumstances. Frank Lillie Pollock's adolescent heroes are often beekeepers as are many of Arthur E. McFarlane's who also writes about such working-class topics as the dangers of deep-sea diving in "Tales of a Deep-Sea Diver," the brutal employment of an eighteen-year-old pile driver in "Haskery's Gang," and a gang of inner-city ruffians who like to swim illegally in the river in the story "The 'Old Docks' and Policeman Lonigran." In addition to his animal stories, Charles G. D. Roberts wrote a significant number of stories about hard-working men and boys. For example, his lumberjack stories for the year 1890 alone include such titles as "Tales from the Lumber Camps," "The Butt of the Camp," "A Brush with Trespassers," "Treed by a Bull Moose," and "Raft Rivals," all published in *Youth's Companion*, plus "Chopping Him Down" in the September issue of *St. Nicholas*.

On the other hand, many of the American authors had spent their childhood in a countryside civilized by generations of gentleman farmers and they tended to juxtapose rural values of serenity, health, and honour against the evils of city life seen as "a debilitating environment for children, one that stunted moral growth when it did not actually promote viciousness" (Kelly 125). Boy characters from the city tend to live either in cruel poverty or in lavish, undisciplined fashion, and are sent to the country to be civilized. City life is a monstrous, exhausting treadmill. But Canadian authors never write this way; they write from a memory of the countryside as one of unremitting toil and hardship as the forest is cut down to make way for the farms. Farmers and fishermen alike face the savage uncertainties of weather, vicious animals, and unprincipled, uneducated neighbours. When protagonists leave their ordeal, they invariably return to the life-saving town where there is knowledge, skills, goods, comforts, food, and help.

A great deal of the writing for the U.S. periodicals was done by American women, so perhaps it is understandable when Kelly notes that the fathers in the stories tend to exert a weak moral force, to hover on the periphery, to be incapacitated by disease or alcohol, or simply are not there (78). By contrast, the Canadian stories are largely written by men (Mrs. Groser being one of several notable exceptions) and they predominantly depict the struggles of men and boys, often together. Of the nearly one hundred adventure stories by E. W. Thomson, only a few characters are female; virtually all of Frank Lillie Pollock's forty-two stories are peopled by male characters; Charles G. D. Roberts' protagonists are nearly exclusively male, as are J. Macdonald Oxley's, to name a few of the most prolific male contributors.

Curiously, the better-known female Canadian authors usually employ male protagonists. Of the five stories by L. M. Montgomery, all involve boys as protagonists, as do the three by Marjorie Pickthall, and the rather longer story of India by Sara Jeannette Duncan, whose British male hero in "The Story of Sonny Sahib" grows to teenhood in rural villages of India and comes to the aid of his country almost by instinct. Lesser-known female writers such as Annie Howells Frechette, Ella J. Fraser, and Mrs. Groser do include stories of adolescent females as well as boy/girl sibling combinations. Ella J. Fraser's historical sketch of "The Great Miramichi Fire," which occurred in 1825, involves a mother in poor health who is taken on a sea voyage by her husband, the captain of a ship. The author describes her thus: "Lisbeth, woman-like, was fearful and timid, but her husband soon gave her no voice in the matter," and the story continues with further references to the voicelessness of this woman (686). Later issues of these periodicals contain fewer fainting females and most girls who appear as protagonists in the stories are generally required to perform some sort of heroic act parallel to those of the male protagonists.

The cultural expectation is for the girl to succeed, but with one attendant corollary—at the end of the excitement/terror/drama, the female protagonist is always required to "break down" immediately, usually to the consternation of a male onlooker. Edward W. Thomson tells the story in "A Heroine of Norman's Woe" of a young girl determined to rescue a teenage stranger in a canoe, who succeeds through sheer force of will, whereupon her brother observes, "women is [sic] curious creatures. My sister burst out crying and left the wheel to me, and flung down into the cabin and lay there sobbing like her heart would break" (347). In Grace Dean McLeod's historical romance set in a Nova Scotian village in 1744, "A Night in an Indian Canoe," an eighteen-year-old Acadian girl has to choose between the British and her Indian friends. After she has successfully completed the heroic action of warning the Indians of an impending massacre, she is comforted by the women of the tribe and lifted into the canoe by the braves as easily as if she were a child, then taken back home (321). With the completion of her heroic deed she is no longer needed in the adult (male) world, and completely reverts to the childlike and the incompetent. Similarly, in a story by Marshall Saunders, "Drusilla and the Cow," when Aunt Melinda capitulates to all the secret desires her niece had confided to the cow, the girl in gratitude "immediately burst into a flood of tears" and impulsively hugs both old ladies (28).

Madge is one of just a few Charles G. D. Roberts' heroines. In "A City Girl Tested," although admittedly afraid of the dark and of cows, she saves herself and her country cousins from a panther who is stalking them by closely heeding the way in which the boys constructed a torch that she then uses to drive off the big cat. "Then, with fading torch and fast-collapsing heroism she ran back to the house, and tumbled half-fainting over the threshold" (80). More promisingly, Roberts' two female characters in "The Panther at the Parsonage" form a split between competence and futile terror. The large illustration on the first page shows a strong and capable woman facing a panther who is peering in a broken window while a young girl kneels on the floor with her back to the panther, clasping her hands together as if in abject prayer. The caption under the drawing captures the two responses: "Susan sank in a heap, while mother with deadly purpose grasped her curtain-pole, expecting instant attack" (524).

Another gender distinction working within the family is the supremacy of the younger and often less experienced male. W. E. MacLellan writes about the heroism of seventeen-year-old Mary and her eleven-year-old brother in keeping a Prince Edward Island lighthouse lit despite the murderous attempts against them by an embittered sailor in the story "The Defence of Norton Light." When all is over, Bobbie "did his best to comfort Mary, who was leaning against the lower door, trembling violently" (385). A modern reader is left to ponder the age appropriateness of the siblings' behaviours. According to the same author, in his story "Don and Sandy" mothers need to be protected by their adolescent sons from stressful kinds of knowledge. When the two sons of a Scottish widow are caught in a snowstorm, their love and concern for each other help in saving their lives. When it is over, they decide not to tell their mother about the events so as to protect her from future worry. Given the same story with a present father, no doubt the boys would have come home in the full flush of success and the parents would have praised their ingenuity and had increased confidence in their son's self-sufficiency. Curiously, the same ethic does not apply with only the female parent present.

There are a few examples of the dawning of feminist thinking in instances of courageous or selfless behaviour, opportunities for assertive movement within the environment, and the pursuit of education. For example, Edward W. Thomson's "Lena Loveland's Night-Watch" tells of how Tom's sixteen-year-old sister uses an umbrella to scare a very large puma up a tree and then keeps him there by building a campfire until she and a small child are rescued. Her brother and his friends say she has earned the privilege of shooting the cat, which task she dispatches tidily (574). Lena only trembles once, although she does admit to being dreadfully frightened while being stalked. Another example is "Cissy Make-Believe" by Arthur E. McFarlane. Born a Canadian, McFarlane moved to the U. S. and never returned, so it is difficult to assess where he acquired his attitudes, but at any rate he gives a scathing opinion of girls' books as that of an adolescent female protagonist:

> For girls' books she had the most burning contempt. They were all alike. No matter how well they began, they all came to the same maddening conclusion. Even if their heroines went out as nurses to the army, it was no time whatsoever before they showed of what miserable stuff they were really made; they fell in love in the very best part of the fighting, and the rest of the book was a dreary waste. (233)

A pre-*Anne of Green Gables* story, Cissy lives in a world of imagination "for in bookland she was no longer a girl; she was a viking discovering Greenland, or a crusading duke, or a captain in the Revolution, or the commander of a monitor in the war." Note that all the options listed are male roles. Cissy succeeds in an act of heroism and is rewarded with a college education and a change of heart about her gender. "Her old secret lamentations over being a girl were giving place to a very outspoken thankfulness for being a woman, for whole new fields for teaching and working and doing good seemed to open before her which could never open to any man" (234). The tendency seems to be for girls' actions in fiction to mirror the responsibilities they must endure in real life. This gender stereotyping includes a veneer of faintness, trembling, or tears as tokens of both gentility and otherness combined with a kind of pioneer grit and fortitude.

The periodicals dictated narrative length to their contributors, and authors responded with almost formulaic action plots in which the Young Adult protagonists overcome various challenges, usually in nature and only occasionally in relationship to other people. Characterizations routinely employ racial stereotypes, so grating to contemporary ears. For example, the light-hearted but improvident French Canadian and the alternately noble or ignoble savage are proscriptive patterns, generally modified in the stories for children, as if subsumed under the greater need for community order that can only arise from teaching young people the gentlemanly discipline of courtesy.

While the U.S. stories seem to repose virtue more directly onto the culture-bearers, the gentry class, as agents of moral arbitration, in Canadian stories, courtesy is still connected with respect for God and His commandments for living by moral precept. Sometimes this religiosity is sweet and simple as in E. W. Thomson's "Little Baptiste; A Story of the Ottawa River" in which the French-Canadian family has run out of food and credit, and even the possibility for honest labour seems unlikely. The fourteen-year-old son prays to *le bon Dieu* to send breakfast, and in the course of the day, after exhaustive efforts of his own, the family does receive both food and work. The young adult concludes, "We may take as much trouble as we like, but it's no use unless *le bon Dieu* helps us" (522). But sometimes religiosity is mere superstition, as in the lumberjacks in Charles G. D. Roberts's story "In the Rapids of the Ashberish," who carry the belief that their camp is unlucky. Two feuding men, a Métis and a New Englander, apparently willing to fight to the death, make this a tale of revenge and violence. Yet, the ending contains a full-scale resolution in which redemption for both sides is possible. After nearly losing their lives in the rapids, the New Englander explains their truce, "I reckon we got the old scores all washed out, there in the rapids, and kind of come out with a clean slate!" (401). J. Macdonald Oxley's story "Forty Miles of Maelstrom" is a high-adventure canoeing story told in a breathless pace, but the characters are the expert, stolid Indian and the fearful, praying half-breed, both more caricature than flesh and blood (29–30).

In some stories the racial stereotypes are more blatant than in others. Frank Lillie Pollock's tale "My Indian Guest" contains a romantic vision of the life-nurturing Canadian wilderness immediately followed by this description of an Indian, which backwoods survival ethics requires the narrator to feed and house for the night: "His face wore the average Indian's impenetrable look of stupidity, but it seemed to me that there was a more-than average amount of viciousness and brutality in his countenance" (424). D. Ker, an Englishman writing about Canada, offers this description of his Indian guide in "Through the Rapids with Indians": "If you want to know what Indians are like, just fancy two overfried sausages wrapped in dirty brown paper, and you'll have a perfect picture of my 'noble red men,' whose names sounded to *me* exactly like 'Cock-a-doodle-doo' and 'Very-like-a-whale'" (8). A writer by the name of S. E. McDonald contributed one story only, "An Adventure," which reads like a recording of the oral tradition among backwoods yarn-spinners in British Columbia, and it is truly an ignoble savage story. Indians are shot at and left for dead with no mention of body count, self-defence issues, or a subsequent law trial—really a violent little tale. The author is able to deflect the blame south across the border and dismiss the morality of the issues by saying that since they carried "American repeating carbines and cartridges... these redskins were renegade Sioux from across the border" who had come north during the Riel Rebellion, lured by "the hope of scalping and plundering with impunity" (525).

The greatest condemnation in these stories arises from the pattern these "lower orders" exhibit of being less than steady in their adherence to Protestant religious values. In Norman Duncan's "A Point of Honor" the Factor of a Hudson Bay Co. Fort in 1829 allows refuge in the fort to a white man of the lowest principles, and describes his Indian pursuers:

> Even then the Indians were degenerate, given over to idleness and debauchery; but they were not so far sunk in these habits as are the dull, lazy fellows who sell you the baskets and beaded moccasins that the squaws make today. They were superstitious, malicious, revengeful, and they were almost in a condition of savagery, for the only law they knew was the law our guns enforced. (489)

Next in importance to swiftly moving action, humour is the second cardinal rule for writers of Young Adult literature. Here again, the nineteenth-century Canadian Young Adult short story writers excelled, developing the kind of humour that depends on a droll juxtaposition of the expected with the actual, the necessary with the given. Charles G. D. Roberts opens one of his Bay of Fundy stories, "Saved by a Tower of Babel," with this line: "This ledge is known as 'Gannet Ledge', perhaps from the fact that the gannet is one of the few birds never to be found there" (721). In his "Tracked by a Panther" he writes, "It was a very unusual proceeding on the part of an Indian Devil [northern panther], displaying a most imperfect conception of the fitness of things. That I should hunt him was proper and customary; but that he should think of hunting me was presumptuous and most unpleasant" (214). J. Macdonald Oxley, in "Face to Face with an 'Indian Devil': A True Story Retold," develops another form of situational humour in the following droll description of intrepid teenage hunters. "Charlie Peters bore an ancient Dutch musket, warranted when properly loaded to kill at both ends; Johnston had a keen tomahawk, which the Indians had taught him to use like one of themselves; and I carried an old-fashioned smooth-bore shot-gun, dangerous only to small game" (82). Situational irony tends to be the humour of choice to leaven the dangers of life and soften the prescriptive force of the tales as behavioural models.

The most engaging of the six stories by Marshall Saunders, "Drusilla and the Cow," involves a rebellious eighteen-year-old girl who confides her grievances against her two reclusive old aunts to the family cow in the barn. The amusing dialogue she invents for the cow is designed to answer her own real question of what she would do if she had liberty to choose her life for herself: "Oh,... I'd throw open the doors and windows, and say to every fly in Grovetown, 'Come in, inoculate us with some of the spirit of the outside world, soar into these old-fashioned corners, and bring some life into our lives!'" (29). This intertextual resonance might recall Emily Dickinson in "I heard a fly buzz when I died" or it may be an oblique reference to the delayed effects of a malarial mosquito in "Infection in the sentence breeds." Unfortunately Saunders is never subtle, and she expands on the insect imagery by next characterizing Aunt Melinda as "pressing down at her like some gigantic, unfriendly spider calling a halt to a timid fly below." The mythic element is not out of place here, just overplayed; as always, Saunders prefers to rack up her list of didactic points undiluted by art. J. Macdonald Oxley, a prolific contributor, was equally as determined and as lacking in subtlety. In "Mrs. Grundy's Gobblers" a gang of boys vow revenge on Mrs. Grundy and Squire Hardgrit for their stinginess. They manage to put Mrs. Grundy's prize turkeys in the Squire's office building with a very funny climax in which the turkeys are gobbling and the adults are baffled and flustered, and the boys are overwhelmed with glee (217–218).

Much is left to be done in analyzing the artistic qualities of this literature, in investigating the form and structure of these adventure tales, and in understanding the significance of family, education, and religion in the values of the Young Adult reader. But this investigation demonstrates that there was in fact a healthy legacy of Young Adult literature produced by the same forces that generated the adult short story market in the late nineteenth century. With their more inclusive social spectrum and attendant stereotypes unfolding along gender and racial lines, these stories illustrate a genuine balancing of didactic and artistic intentions along with market expectation.

WORKS CITED

Duncan, Norman. "A Point of Honor." *Youth's Companion* 77 (October 22, 1903): 489–490.

Duncan, Sara Jeannette. "The Story of Sonny Sahib." *Youth's Companion* 68 (July to August 1894): 317ff.

Fraser, Ella J. "The Great Miramichi Fire." *Golden Days for Boys and Girls* 28 (September 1, 1906): 686–687.

Groser, Mrs. C. E. "A Summer Ride in Labrador." *St. Nicholas* 4 (1876–77): 689–695.

Hunt, Caroline. "Young Adult Literature Evades the Theorists." *Children's Literature Association Quarterly* 21:1 (Spring 1996): 4–11.

Kelly, R. Gordon. *Mother Was a Lady: Self and Society in Selected American Children's Periodicals, 1865–1890*. Westport, Conn.: Greenwood P, 1974.

Ker, D. "Through the Rapids with Indians." *Harper's Young People* 2 (November 2, 1880): 8–10.

McDonald, S. E. "An Adventure." *Youth's Companion* 60 (November 24, 1887): 524–525.

McFarlane, Arthur E. "Cissy Make-Believe." *Youth's Companion* 76 (May 8, 1902): 233–334.

———. "Haskery's Gang" *Youth's Companion* 78 (November 3, 1904): 552–553; (November 10): 565–566.

———. "The 'Old Docks' and Policeman Lonigran." *Youth's Companion* 77 (July 23, 1903): 349–350.

———. "Tales of a Deep-Sea Diver." *Youth's Companion* 76 (January 30, 1902): 49–50; (February 13): 77; (March 13): 125–126; (March 20): 155.

MacLellan, W. E. "The Defence of Norton Light." *Youth's Companion* 71 (August 19, 1897): 384–385.

———. "Don and Sandy." *Youth's Companion* 70 (December 31, 1896): 699–700.

McLeod, Grace Dean. "A Night in an Indian Canoe." *Youth's Companion* 59 (August 26, 1886): 321–322.

Moyles, R. Gordon. "Young Canada: An Index to Canadian Materials in Major British and American Juvenile Periodicals, 1879–1950." *Canadian Children's Literature* 78 (Summer 1995): 6–64.

Oxley, J. Macdonald. "Forty Miles of Maelstrom." *Youth's Companion* 64 (January 8, 1891): 29–30.

———. "Mrs. Grundy's Gobblers." *Golden Days for Boys and Girls* 9 (February 25, 1888): 217–218.

———. "Face to Face with an 'Indian Devil': A True Story Retold." *Harper's Young People* (November 29, 1892): 81–82.

Pollock, Frank Lillie. "My Indian Guest." *Youth's Companion* 72 (October 15, 1898): 424.

Roberts, Charles G. D. "Chopping Him Down." *St. Nicholas* 17 (September 1889–90): 928-931.

———. "A City Girl Tested." *Youth's Companion* 70 (February 13, 1896): 80.

———. "The Panther at the Parsonage." *Golden Days for Boys and Girls* 10 (July 13, 1889): 524–525.

———. "The Raft Rivals." *Youth's Companion* 63 (May 15, 1890): 262–263.

———. "In the Rapids of the Ashberish." *St. Nicholas* 27 (March 1899–1900): 397–401.

———. "Saved By a Tower of Babel." *Golden Days for Boys and Girls* 13 (October 8, 1892): 721–722.

———. "Tales From the Lumber Camp." *Youth's Companion* 63 (1890)
- 2. "The Butt of the Camp." (January 16): 35.
- 3. "A Brush with Trespassers." (January 23): 47.
- 4. "Treed by a Bull Moose." (February 20): 95.

———. "Tracked by a Panther." *St. Nicholas* 17 (1889–90): 213–216.

Saunders, Marshall. "Drusilla and the Cow." *Youth's Companion* 77 (January 15, 1903): 28- 29.

Thomson, Edward W. "A Heroine of Norman's Woe." *Youth's Companion* 68 (August 2, 1894): 346–347.

———. "Lena Loveland's Night-Watch." *Golden Days* 14 (July 29, 1893): 573–574.

———. "Little Baptiste: A Story of the Ottawa River." *Youth's Companion* 60 (November 24, 1887): 521–522.

"Just Above the Breadline": Social(ist) Realism in Canadian Short Stories of the 1930s

JAMES DOYLE

DOROTHY LIVESAY'S 1936 SHORT STORY "Case Supervisor" opens with a senior social worker trying to escape the real world of the Depression by going to the cinema. But there is no escape: the newsreels flash images of "war, breadlines, crisis, drought," and even the feature film begins by evoking what looks like the milieu that social workers deal with every day. A young woman on the screen climbs "rickety stairs" to a "threadbare room," "hot and angry after standing all day long behind a counter." The film turns out to be an escapist Hollywood fantasy, a romantic comedy of "department store love." But it begins with images that locate this comedy in relation to the real world outside the cinema, "just above the landlord's dispossess [sic], just above the breadline" (Livesay 103).

This cinematic prelude to Livesay's story suggests something of the nature and function of the prose fiction in which it is contained. Livesay's characters might be seen as imaginative constructs like the people on a movie screen, existing "above" the disastrous economic and political actualities of North America in the 1930s. Like the Hollywood fantasy, furthermore, Livesay's literary fiction has the potential to serve as a means of escape or revelation, by producing either romantic improbabilities or reflections of social, economic, and political problems in the real world.

The implications about the nature and purpose of art that Livesay briefly invokes in her cinematic metaphor were the focus of a great deal of critical attention throughout the 1930s, most of it emanating originally from the Soviet Union. As James F. Murphy and Barbara Foley have recently demonstrated, contrary to popular anti-Communist belief, the form and subject matter of art in the new historical era were not dictated by Communist Party bureaucrats, but were debated vigorously by practising artists within and outside the Party. In 1931, articles deriving from this debate began to appear in *Literature of World Revolution* (renamed the following year *International Literature*), the first Soviet literary periodical widely available in an English edition (Murphy 88).

One of the first of such articles, a report of a conference of the Union of Soviet Writers, offered a definition of the currently popular term "socialist realism":

> By socialist realism we mean the reflection in art of the external world... in all its essential circumstances and with the aid of essential and typical characterization. We mean the faithful description of life in all its aspects, with the victorious principle of the forces of the socialist revolution. ... We set socialist realism against idealism, subjectivism, the literature of illusion in any form whatsoever, as an untrue and distorted reflection of reality. (Qtd. in Murphy 100; Murphy's ellipses)

A Canadian debate about the interaction of art and revolutionary politics appeared around the same time as the *International Literature* discussion of socialist realism, in a series of articles published between 1932 and 1934 in the Toronto magazine *Masses*. An attempt to produce in Canada a periodical like the American *New Masses*, the Toronto *Masses* was published by the Progressive Arts Club, a group of writers and graphic artists, most of whom were members of the Communist Party. Livesay was a member of both the club and the Party, as well as an occasional contributor to *Masses*, and although she took no part in this specific controversy, she must have read the series with attention.

The *Masses* debate was a discussion of a common question in American and European Marxist literary circles throughout the 1920s and '30s: whether a politically correct artist should express only socialist ideas or is free to create in any way that seems appropriate. In reply to a correspondent who defended modernist experimentalism and the ideal of "pure art," the *Masses'* editorial collective came down emphatically in favour of socialist commitment as the only true artistic purpose, and of socialist realism as the only valid approach to technique and form. In "Propaganda and Art" (*Masses,* January 1934), Edward Cecil-Smith invoked the authority of such Soviet intellectuals as N. Bukharin and A. V. Lunacharsky to denounce "bourgeois realism" as "static" and "negative," and tinged with "a hidden admixture of romanticism" (10–11). According to Cecil-Smith, the "bourgeois realist" is content with reflecting observed reality, making negative criticisms of it or (like the Hollywood myth-makers who deal in the fantasies of "department-store love") sometimes subordinating it to an ultimately romantic purpose. But the socialist realist interprets the world to show how it can and must be changed.

Cecil-Smith's label "bourgeois realism" is a pejorative variant of what the Hungarian Marxist critic Georg Lukács more neutrally designated "critical realism," and what many non-Marxist literary critics by the 1930s were calling "social realism." Like its socialist counterpart, social realist fiction often reveals the evils of industrial capitalism; but it does not necessarily attempt to analyze the causes of these evils or offer any explicit solutions to them except, occasionally, improbable romantic ones. Socialist realism, on the other hand, conveys lessons about such concepts as the class struggle, the processes of dehumanization ("commodification," or "reification" in Marxist terminology) created by capitalism, the inevitability of proletarian revolution, and the ultimate reconstitution of society.

But contrary to the impression created by the *Masses* debate, Canadian writers in the 1930s were not producing a great deal of either social or socialist realism. As Daniel Aaron, James F. Murphy, Barbara Foley, and other American literary historians have shown, dozens of so-called "proletarian" novels were published in the United States in the decade following the Wall Street crash of 1929. Canadian literary scholars, by contrast, could probably name only a few comparable works published in this country, perhaps including Morley Callaghan's *They Shall Inherit the Earth* (1934) and Irene Baird's *Waste Heritage* (1939), and only one that is explicitly Marxist, Ted Allen's *This Time a Better Earth* (1939). In the same year that her "Case Supervisor" was published, Livesay could write categorically that "there is no proletarian literature in Canada" (230).

There are several reasons for the Canadian neglect of the social and socialist realist novel in the 1930s, including the familiar economic factors that perennially plague Canadian authors and publishers and which were especially severe during the Depression. But as Livesay's own ventures into fiction suggest, if novels were an economic uncertainty in Canada, the situation was a bit better with regard to short stories, for which there was at least a small if unremunerative market. Canadian outlets for stories with reformist or revolutionary political themes included, besides the short-lived *Masses*, the two newspapers published by the Communist Party of Canada, the weekly *Worker* (1922–36) and the *Daily Clarion* (1936–39). A "united front" coalition of Communists, democratic socialists and non-partisan liberals brought out an independent arts magazine, *New Frontier* (1936–37), which attracted short stories by writers such as Ted Allen, Thomas Murtha, Mary Quayle Innis, A. M. Klein, and Livesay. Writers of leftist political inclinations also looked to the *Canadian Forum*, which published many short stories in the 1930s.

Although Livesay and her contemporaries wrote short stories primarily for the practical reason that stories were easier to get published than novels, they chose a genre that turned out to be appropriate to their purposes. A short story is usually better suited to political didacticism than a novel, for at least one obvious reason. When a novel has a narrow ideological focus it is liable to lapse into repetition. In Baird's *Waste Heritage*, for instance, the main character's anger and frustration and the hopeless efforts of the unemployed men to influence official attitudes are established early in the novel, then repeated through a series of parallel incidents. A novelist might avoid repetition by subtleties of plot and characterization, but such subtleties are also liable to draw attention away from the social message. The short story writer, on the other hand, can limit plot and characterization in order to bear down harder on the message, making up in clarity and emphasis for the story's lack of subtlety. As many politically militant writers were discovering in the 1930s, a work of fiction with a didactic purpose, like a sermon, can be more efficiently presented to its audience and is likely to have a more striking effect if it is kept brief.

By the same token, the effective socialist realist story is concisely focussed on the illustration of one doctrinal principle or ideological dialectic. In "The Way to Life" (*Daily Clarion*, June 24, 1938) by "France [Frances?] Hale," the Jewish wife of a German scientist exiled by the Nazis comes to realize the necessity of suppressing her "middle-class pattern of thought and action," and committing herself to the ideal of solidarity between intellectuals and workers in the struggle to overthrow "the brute that was crushing us all." John Weir's "The Grouser" (*Daily Clarion*, February 25, 1939) demonstrates the effectiveness of the united front against fascism through the story of a volunteer in the Spanish Civil War who contemptuously denies being "one of those political comrades," yet who sacrifices his life for what he recognizes as a "good cause." Len Zinberg's "Across the Line" (*Daily Clarion*, May 2, 1939) dramatizes the primacy of the class struggle in the story of an Afro-American woman who passes for white in order to get a job, but finds herself as degraded by wage slavery as she had been by racism: "I guess," she recognizes, "that what makes the difference is not black or white, but rich or poor. And you can't pass for rich."

In the best examples of socialist realism, the political message emerges not simply as an articulated moral, but as a theme that suffuses the whole narrative. This is the process that Georg Lukács described as "writing from the inside"—that is, assuming Marxist ideology as the social and political norm and allowing the ideology to emerge naturally through the interaction of sympathetic characters (93). Dyson Carter's "East Nine" (*New Frontier*, June 1936; reprinted in Phillips) involves a factory repairman who is fatally injured when his boss ignores safety rules to speed up production and fill a much-needed contract. The capitalist in this story is not an ogre, but a sympathetic employer with a genuine concern for his workers. A factory shutdown, however, would bring disaster not only to himself through lost profits, but to his workers through lost wages. The great evil is identified not as a person, but as the dehumanizing processes of industrial capitalism that engulf worker and employer alike. Carter, unfortunately, was unable to let his narrative speak for itself. At the end of the story a choric voice representing the other patients of "East Nine," the industrial accident ward, expresses pity and anger over the victim's death, as well as a revolutionary prophecy: "Fellow man, worker, comrade, farewell. ... We of East Nine who struggle and have yet to die, salute you. No volley will be fired. Some other dawn-time guns will greet your memory" (Phillips 86).

Norman Bethune's only published short story, "The Dud" (originally in the *Clarion* 1939, and frequently reprinted), is more subtly done. Another great modern evil, imperialist warfare, is dramatized in the narrative of an old peasant who finds an unexploded artillery shell in his field in Japanese-occupied China. The evils of imperialism are epitomized by the weeds in his scant field. "His life seemed to him to be just one great neverending struggle with his enemy—weeds," and China itself is "one big fertile acre of earth" overrun with weeds. In an attempt to connect his struggle to the larger political and military conflict, the old peasant sets out to carry the shell back to the Chinese partisans who fired it so that it will not be wasted. Wandering through a land in the grip of a murderous enemy, the old man fulfills his self-imposed mission through an innocent belief in the cause to which he has committed himself. Although the partisans at first laugh at the old man, they recognize how important his mission is to him, and restore his dignity by praising him. Through his quixotic gesture, the old man reveals a vital force opposing the weed-like processes of war. The shell he has carried so far and so faithfully is a useless dud, and the whole journey, to a cynical mind, is meaningless. But the old man is allowed to believe that he has "done something to clear the field of China" (121). In Marxist-Leninist theory, each worker and peasant has a role to play, no matter how small or apparently insignificant, in the revolutionary drama. Bethune suggests that in this drama the ability to believe in the relevance of one's actions to the cause is more important than the relative significance of the actions themselves.

While stories of socialist realism dramatize and express confidence in Marxist doctrine, social realism is either non-committal or pessimistic. Presenting a photographic representation of human suffering, such stories leave to the reader's judgment any inferences about the causes and possible remedies of that suffering, or they imply that the causes are obscure and the remedies elusive. Many stories of this sort appeared in the *Canadian*

Forum in the 1930s, although they occasionally appeared in Communist publications as well. "The Death of a Derelict," by "R. M.," in the *Clarion* of June 24, 1938, is a brief and gruesome account of a homeless man killed by a streetcar. The bystanders express self-centred or indifferent reactions, and in the end "the ambulance [drives] away with its bell ringing," while the police set to work clearing up the traffic jam. Such relentlessly described revelations of the realities of modern life are sometimes reinforced by irony, as in Maurice Lesser's "Bread Line" (*Forum*, September 1933; reprinted in Phillips), where a derelict man hopes to recover a lost one hundred dollar bill but finds only a charity meal ticket.

Realism and irony are likewise combined in Mary Quayle Innis's "The Party" (*Forum*, June 1931; reprinted in Phillips), where a socially competitive woman learns at the end of her pretentious social gathering that her husband has lost his job. But Innis's story has more to do with the psychology of gender relations, the breakdown of communication between a man and a woman, than with the socio-economic situation. The point of the story is the woman's foolish pride and insensitivity to her husband's emotional crisis. In Marxist terms, the wife with her determination to show her neighbours how well-off she is lacks a sense of class solidarity; but Innis is more concerned with her denial of reality, her desire to "have the kind of [household furnishings] you saw in the movies," than with the implied political lesson. Like Livesay in "Case Supervisor," Innis uses the cinema to represent bourgeois escapist mentality; Innis does not, however, go on to suggest how this mentality can be overcome by political enlightenment.

Political enlightenment is always the climactic focus of Livesay's socialist realist stories. Her "Out West" (written c. 1936 and printed in *Right Hand*) focusses on the aimless journeys of unemployed young men, counterpointed by the confinement of the jail cell in which the framing circumstances of the story take place. The young working-class protagonist, Sean, is characterized by his eagerness and ability to learn, dramatized early in the story by his quick mastery of the Morse-like code the inmates have contrived to communicate with each other. From his more politically knowledgeable fellow prisoners he learns the necessity of revolutionary struggle: "We will be castaways all our life unless we fight for our future" (188). The new "fight for the future" reminds Sean of his own father's commitment to the old western ideal of subjugating the frontier; but Sean's father was a dreamer whose ideal became reduced to the phrase "mebbe someday" (190). Similarly, his mother dreamed materialistic dreams of money, electric appliances, automobiles—all resolving into the words "some day" (190). The parents' words are echoed in the refrain Sean hears from prospective employers when he looks for a job: "maybe next year things will pick up" (191).

Sean has the advantage over his parents, however, in his intellectual vitality. He "devours history books," and his academic interest in the past not only contrasts with his father's vague frontier dreams, but also underscores his openness to systematic historical knowledge, a prerequisite to Marxist enlightenment. While Sean's mother blames her son for his own failure, Sean has made a beginning toward understanding the real causes of the crisis that has engulfed his generation. He cannot have the bourgeois respectability of a "real job," but through camaraderie with his fellow victims he is discovering working-class solidarity, one of the first steps toward proletarian revolution. The story ends, however, not with a melodramatic gesture of rebellion, but with a tentative question, a hint of defiance, and a reminder of Sean's eagerness to learn: "his generation—the crowd around him... would they go on taking it? He wanted to know" (195).

Livesay's "Six Years" (*New Frontier*, April 1936; *Right Hand*) also upholds the principle of class solidarity and collective action, and reveals the folly of bourgeois notions of individualism. Mrs. Dakin's attempt to support her husband's ambitions by denying her class consciousness and by remaining aloof from her neighbours eventually breaks down under the weight of economic circumstances. Her illumination comes, ironically, when the electric company cuts the power off to her house, and she is forced to admit to her neighbour that her husband has lost his job. The neighbour, the wife of another unemployed worker, serves as the narrator of the story and spokesperson for the point of doctrine being illustrated. The story exposes the fallacy of bourgeois individualism in terms that recall Lenin's denunciation of ideological error as "immature" or "infantile." "She was so young," says the narrator about Mrs. Dakin, "and she thought she could do everything by herself" (172).

At the end of the story the young wife has recognized her error and is resolved to convert her husband. "I'll tell Everett," she promises her neighbour. In this story, unlike "Out West," Livesay combines socialist realism with feminism; but the feminism relates to solidarity in the class struggle rather than to antagonism between the sexes. Unlike Innis, who sees the social problems of poverty and unemployment as aggravating the gender conflict, Livesay suggests that when working-class men are defeated by circumstances or their own weakness, the women must take action, not as a gesture of anti-male reproof or as an assertion of feminist power, but as a necessary act of intervention in maintaining working-class control over the inevitable processes of revolution.

In other stories, Livesay does associate power and aggression with men and victimization with women, but she makes it clear that this gendered power structure is a consequence of the corruption of capitalism. In

"Case Supervisor" women are oppressed by this power structure both directly through their economic inferiority, and indirectly by being deluded into serving the capitalist system. In contrast to the sympathetic and politically knowledgeable narrative voice of "Six Years," the point of view of "Case Supervisor" is the deluded consciousness of the title character, Miss Chilton, who tries to evade her complicity in the failure of social institutions to relieve human misery. She takes refuge in the manufactured illusion of the cinema, and when that recourse fails she hides behind bureaucratic impersonality. In the latter strategy she follows the example of her superior, a woman who sees the agency's work in terms of budget priorities and procedural efficiency, and who invokes as her authority the "businessmen" on the governing board who complain about the inefficient management of the agency. Chilton, like her superiors, tries to keep the people on relief at a distance, to commodify them as "cases," or to perceive them as icons of bourgeois romanticism, like characters on a movie screen. But while she and her superiors retreat into one form or another of evasion, one of the younger social workers on Chilton's staff replaces the bureaucratic procedures with human generosity, by paying for the fuel of a poverty-stricken family out of her own meagre earnings.

When the young woman tells Chilton what she has done, Chilton expresses shock and feeble protest, and takes refuge, as always, in evasion. The case supervisor addresses the young woman ironically as "child," but it is Chilton and the bureaucracy behind her who are the symbols of historical immaturity. Like the old man in Bethune's "The Dud," the young woman, by her act of personal commitment, brings the new era based on social justice one step closer to realization.

Livesay's stories demonstrate the dramatic flexibility inherent in the narrow ideological scope of the socialist realist short story. But Livesay devoted her main literary energies to poetry after she left the Communist Party in the early 1940s. The entire literary tradition of Canadian socialist realism, never substantial at any time, was virtually annihilated by the suppression of the Communist Party and its publications in 1939–40. After the war there were some attempts to revive Communist-sponsored literary activity in Canada, and short stories appeared occasionally in the Party's weekly newspaper and a short-lived successor to *New Frontier*. But the limitations of the form became especially evident in these derivative and somewhat old-fashioned stories. Socialist realism flourished in eastern Europe until quite recently, and continues to be the object of critical and historical interest, as illustrated for instance by the volume of conference proceedings from McMaster University, *Socialist Realism Revisited* (1994). As that volume demonstrated, however, in eastern Europe socialist realism evolved from a relatively flexible revolutionary voice to a government-approved ideology concerned with defending established political regimes.

Social realism, untainted by association with partisan Communism, has been a little more durable, and the label could be applied to some stories being published today. But postmodern critical attacks on older literary forms and changing fashions among creative artists have discouraged the practice of traditional literary realisms. As Barbara Foley has pointed out, the post-structuralist tendency to identify reality with textuality has led to a scepticism toward any text that purports to base its "truth-value" on assertions about a world external to itself (253–254). In the 1930s, however, it was difficult even for the most sceptical of readers or writers to deny the truth of unemployment, poverty, and starvation. It was difficult, too, for writers to refrain from portraying and evaluating these problems, even if their portrayals might never be able to reach and influence the real human misery. Even though the writers were confined to their position "just above the breadline," they searched for a language and literary form that might contribute to the elimination of the breadline and the transformation of society.

WORKS CITED

Aaron, Daniel. *Writers on the Left: Episodes in American Literary Communism.* 1961. New York: Columbia UP, 1992.
Bethune, Norman. "The Dud." *The Mind of Norman Bethune.* Ed. Roderick Stewart. Toronto: Fitzhenry & Whiteside, 1977.
Cecil-Smith, E. "Propaganda and Art." *Masses* 2 (January 1934): 10–11.
Foley, Barbara. *Radical Representations: Politics and Form in U.S. Proletarian Fiction, 1929–1941.* Durham: Duke UP, 1993.
Hale, France. "The Way to Life." *Daily Clarion* (24 June 1938):2.
Kolesnikoff, Nina, and Walter Smyrniw, eds. *Socialist Realism Revisited: Selected Papers from the McMaster Conference.* Hamilton: McMaster UP, 1994.
Livesay, Dorothy. *Right Hand, Left Hand.* Erin: Press Porcepic, 1977.
Lukács, Georg. *The Meaning of Contemporary Realism.* London: Merlin, 1963.
Murphy, James F. *The Proletarian Moment: The Controversy over Leftism in Literature.* Urbana: U of Illinois P, 1992.
Phillips, Donna, ed. *Voices of Discord: Canadian Short Stories from the 1930s.* Toronto: New Hogtown, 1979.
"R. M." "The Death of a Derelict." *Daily Clarion* (June 24, 1938): 4.
Weir, John. "The Grouser." *Daily Clarion* (February 25, 1939): 4.
Zinberg, Len. "Across the Line." *Daily Clarion* (May 2, 1939): 6.

The Language of the Law: The Cases of Morley Callaghan

GARY BOIRE

THIS DISCUSSION HAS TWO DISCRETE, yet intersecting, points of departure. I want to consider, first, Morley Callaghan as an experimental short story writer—more specifically, a postcolonial writer intensely aware of his own resistant activity within a well-established colonialist genre. I want to consider, in other words, Callaghan's radical experimentations with both the language and genre of the short story form. Second, I want to consider how this experimentation intersects with what proved to be Callaghan's lifelong boredom and fascination—his fear and temptation, if you will—with the language of law. In the interests of clarity, I want to concentrate here, furthermore, on the cluster of stories published between 1925 and 1928—the years during which Callaghan attended Osgoode Law School, corresponded with Ernest Hemingway in Paris, and began drafting the first of his many short "legal fictions."

My argument, in a nutshell, is that figures of law permeate many of the works of Morley Callaghan, and that these figures function not simply as an image of authority or as an emblem of socially sanctioned force. Rather, law (its imagery, vocabulary, rituals, and institutions) functions in Callaghan as a type of social "genre," one made up of multivalent foundational "languages," which, in turn, are sedimented throughout his *oeuvre*. These legal languages come to represent a variety of delimitations, for in Callaghan the law is not only always and already an ass, but usually a protean site of authoritarian desire.

By continually invoking this site in a variety of his short stories Callaghan uses the story genre to construct a meticulous, ongoing counter-discourse, a deliberate demystification of authority's chameleon-like forms and strategies. As literary "case histories," the stories come to be, not simply poignant vignettes or tales, but powerful—anarchic—interrogations of both inherited "genres" and imposed "languages." To adapt a comment made in a different context by W. H. New, Callaghan's "open, broken forms of the short story... constitute a generic opportunity for authentic speech"(x).

That Callaghan was aware of himself as an anticolonial writer is evident from a number of sources. Most obvious, of course, is the highly stylized self-portrait in *That Summer in Paris* (1963), where he continually declares his literary independence from everything and everyone with the exception of Sherwood Anderson. This kind of aggressive constructed independence, a public persona of anarchic freedom, gains an interesting twist when we consider three additional statements made, respectively, in 1928, 1938, and 1964. Each corroborates Callaghan's stated need to achieve artistic independence; but each also discloses his evident sympathy with writing that self-consciously breaks away from colonial traditions.

The first is from Callaghan's 1928 letter to Raymond Knister on the publication of the latter's *Canadian Short Stories* (1928). The anthology enraged Callaghan because, along with his own story "Last Spring They Came Over" (which I will discuss later), it also included works by Scott, Roberts, and Parker. In a fit of pique, Callaghan rebuked Knister for his colonialist conservatism:

> Today I got a copy of the Canadian stories. I read the Introduction and then I read D. C. Scott's story in the book. What is the matter with you? Though it will come as a relief to many schoolmarms throughout the country to learn that the venerable Duncan is a great writer, since they have always suspected it, you know better. Then why do you do it? Are you thinking of retiring definitely? You had a chance to point the way in that introduction, and you merely arrived at the old values that have been accepted here for the past fifty years; id est, Duncan C. Scott, G. D. Roberts and Gilbert Parker are great prose writers. (Letter to Raymond Knister, August 15, 1928)

Callaghan's passionate interest in breaking away from what he saw as outworn colonial styles—the sketch, folktale, humorous anecdote, exemplum, or animal fable—reappears ten years later in an obscure *Saturday Night* review (interestingly entitled "Honesty of Purpose"). Commenting on C. R. Allen's *Tales of New Zealanders*, Callaghan remarked,

> from a Canadian point of view this collection of New Zealand stories has a special interest... are [New Zealanders] still writing colonial literature, or have they got something of their own? The fine thing to be said about most

> of these stories is that the authors of them are obviously seeing the people against the background of their own country. But once that has been said the other questions arise: what are they doing with the language? Does there seem to be any kind of native sensibility of imagination? ("Honesty" 6)

Intriguingly, Callaghan would continue to apply these very questions to himself, offering along the way a number of tentative answers.

By 1964, for example, he was able to offer the following, sepia-tinted retrospective, one that champions his own anticolonial achievements:

> I had become aware that the language in which I wanted to write, a North American language I lived by, had rhythms and nuances and twists and turns quite alien to English speech. When I showed some of my first stories to academic men highly trained in English literature, I could see them turning up their noses. "A failure of language," one said to me; and feeling encouraged I said, "No, a failure on your part to understand the language." ("Ocean" 17)

It is a tribute to Callaghan's sensitivity and self-awareness that his staunch defence of a "North American" standard of taste shares the profound insights of theorists like Frank Davey and W. H. New—both of whom have argued critically along the same lines.

Davey, for example, rightly argues that "the development of the Canadian short story... occurred almost entirely outside [the] twentieth-century Anglo-American theory of the unified and autotelic story"; he continues that any examination of the *Canadian* short story necessarily "requires a much more pluralistic and eclectic view of the story and a more 'generous' sense of its generic language" (142–143). W. H. New takes a postcolonial approach to the genre and argues similarly that,

> one should not expect American or English rhetorical patterns to be universal ones... to presume that Canadian or Australian or New Zealand patterns would not be different is to fail to conceive of the possibility of working alternatives, alternatives of working cultural pattern and of functionally different narrative modes to those in currency in, say, England or America. (16)

Pace Jacques Derrida and "the law of genre," Callaghan, by 1964, had quite joyfully mixed genres, bastardized forms, and defiled the supposed purity of inherited literary shapes. On one hand, the clipped, pared-down journalistic prose, combined with urban landscapes and impoverished "little people," seemed to subvert the imposed laws of "proper" literary language and thereby place Callaghan firmly within the canon of modernist realism. Yet his well-known transgressive hybridizations of tale, vignette, romance, journalistic profile, Christian parable, and realistic sketch deliberately questioned even the possibility of a "law of genre," and formally re-enacted his thematic concerns with the breakage of law. As Davey reluctantly admits, "it is possible to find in Callaghan's stories a mixture of codes" (145). And it was precisely this mixture, this "illegality" of multiple forms that Callaghan would re-create analogically within the thematics and language of his many stories.

In this same essay in 1964, moreover, Callaghan expresses his sympathy for the devil as it were, for the kind of writing that aligns itself not only with generic oddity, but (interestingly enough for my purposes) criminal transgression, outlawed passion, and the breakage of both literary form and social law. In addition to Sterne's *Tristram Shandy* and Bronte's *Wuthering Heights*, Callaghan praises both a famous novelistic magistrate (Henry Fielding) as well as a famous novelistic outlaw (Daniel Defoe, particularly his *Moll Flanders*). This intriguing blend of sympathies—for the anticolonial reappropriation of language and form, and for the transgressive resistance toward authoritarian law—flourishes in Callaghan's own legal and literary experiences of 1925–28.

That Callaghan had an ambivalent relationship with the law is evident from both his earliest letters to Hemingway and his later memoirs and interviews. Writing to Hemingway on October 11, 1925, Callaghan quipped, "I'm now a law student. Have a lot of time and could do a good deal of writing." Similarly, the references in *That Summer in Paris* stress his lackadaisical approach to legal studies: "I used to go to morning law classes and often doze in my chair.... If Joe Sedgewick [with whom Callaghan articled] wanted a title searched I did it for him. Otherwise, with him out on business, I would sit in his office at my typewriter working on a short novel" (47). In the end, Callaghan's decision to complete his degree owed more to filial duty than to any real commitment to a legal career. (Callaghan seems, in fact, to have received more satisfaction at the *Toronto Star*—where he worked the crime desk, the police reports, and the courts!)

Notwithstanding this kind of comic portrayal, Callaghan's experiences at Osgoode left their mark in more than pragmatic ways. In one sense Osgoode simply consolidated what had been, and what would remain, one of Callaghan's most fertile and challenging areas of literary exploration: throughout his career Callaghan would conduct a lifelong literary and moral struggle with the concepts of natural justice, transgression, and legality. Law and its mechanisms; the themes of retribution, discipline, penitence, and punishment; an implacable unjust justice system—all of these would appear throughout his entire *oeuvre*.

At the simplest level, cops and robbers, lawyers and pimps, murderers and judges, prostitutes and thieves form something of a retinue or relentless metaphor in Callaghan—a thematic repertoire that he often deploys to represent repression, social violence, puritanical oppression, censorship or whatever. Consider, for example, the gangster mayhem of *Strange Fugitive* (1928); the prisons of *It's Never Over* (1930) and *More Joy in Heaven* (1937); the trial scenes of *Such Is My Beloved* (1934) and *The Many Colored Coat* (1960), not to mention the murders of *They Shall Inherit the Earth* (1935), *The Loved and the Lost* (1951), *A Fine and Private Place* (1975), and *Close to the Sun Again* (1977); as well as the all-pervasive illegality of *The Enchanted Pimp* (1978), *A Time for Judas* (1983), *Our Lady of the Snows* (1985) and *A Wild Old Man on the Road* (1988). Emblems of law and authority, in other words, permeate Callaghan's fiction from his earliest known published article onward. (Even "A Windy Corner at Yonge-Albert," Callaghan's first publication written in 1921, has a policeman who breaks up a public political debate.) In the simplest of senses, this retinue lends itself to Callaghan's interests in justice and transgression, to his desire to explore such themes as crime and punishment.

But the law forms more than just an imagistic resource for Callaghan's thematic polemics. Law forms part of a political unconscious in Callaghan, a sedimented archeology or "genre" of thought always associated ultimately with some corrupt component of authoritarian desire. At this point it is helpful to recall a comment made in Fredric Jameson's masterful work, *The Political Unconscious*, where he argues that,

> In its emergent strong form a genre is essentially a socio-symbolic message, or, in other terms, that form is immanently and intrinsically an ideology in its own right. When such forms are reappropriated and refashioned in quite different social and cultural contexts, this message persists and must be functionally reckoned into the new form... the ideology of the form itself, thus sedimented, persists into the latter, more complex structure, as a generic message which coexists—either as a contradiction or, on the other hand, as a mediatory or harmonizing mechanism—with elements from later stages. (140-141)

Jameson's complex remark here cuts (at least) two ways. In one sense we can apply it to ourselves reading Callaghan—we read his texts through the sedimented layers of the interpretive industry surrounding his canonized status: that is, Callaghan the humanist, the Christian personalist, the individualist, the anarchist, and so on. But on the other (more interesting) hand, Jameson's remark helps us to detect a peculiar kind of "sedimentation" at work in Callaghan's writing when it comes to the sedimented presence of law. For the very prevalence of legal imagery suggests that when

Callaghan "reads" the world (and therefore its language) in his writing, he simultaneously "reads" and interrogates their organization by means of power relations, by means of legal formulae. If every one of Callaghan's texts constitutes a reading of the social text that identifies its various sedimented layers of control, then every one of these readings performs a quiet but resistant act of demystification. Particularly as each of these short stories under examination leads to a readerly epiphany: a moment of sudden multivalent illumination.

Now if law, as Pierre Bourdieu argues, is more than just socially sanctioned force, what we have in Callaghan's legal fictions is a much more complex issue than mere thematics. For Bourdieu, as for Callaghan, law is first and foremost a genre constituted by a grammar of control, a type of language that "consecrates the established order by consecrating the vision of that order which is held by the State" (838). In an eerie echo of Callaghan's own sentiments in *A Fine and Private Place* (where Eugene Shore complains that most people "register" their words with the police), Bourdieu argues that "the law is the quintessential form of 'active' discourse, able by its own operation to produce its effects. It would not be excessive to say that it creates the social world, but only if we remember that it is this world which first creates the law" (839). As this kind of language, complete with its own deep structures and hegemonic apparatuses, law becomes, as it were, every State's mother tongue, every citizen's first "sentence." Uncritically internalized, the law functions, as Callaghan (and Bourdieu and Foucault and de Certeau and Althusser) reminds us, essentially as an unconscious interpellative force—a language, a sedimented story within each citizen's imaginative repertoire. As Bourdieu quips with uncharacteristic clarity, "the specific property of symbolic power is that it can be exercised only through the complicity of those who are dominated by it. This complicity is all the more certain because it is unconscious on the part of those who undergo its effects—or perhaps we should say it is more subtly extorted from them" (844). Like Frankenstein's monster (or society's corrupt policeman, Jason Dunsford, in *A Fine and Private Place*), the law is a created thing, an energy that turns back upon its creators, itself creating within them an alienated acceptance of self-imposed restriction.

It is precisely this kind of all-pervasive, virtually panoptic power that characterizes Callaghan's presentation of the law (and its mechanisms) throughout his entire career. As mentioned earlier, many of the novels are explicitly grounded in legal rituals: either criminal activity, police investigations, trials, prisons, or murders. Law, in these works, is everywhere. And so it is not surprising that in seven of the ten stories (not to mention the one novel) published between 1925 and 1928 we have an incredible "word-hoard" of crime and punishment, a virtual storage house of transgression and imposed discipline.

In "A Girl with Ambition" (1925–26), for example, the nerdish Harry Brown stands as a symbol of propriety and good-breeding for the working-class Mary Ross—and paramount in his symbolic capital is the fact that "he was going to be a lawyer" (239). "Amuck in the Bush" (1927) and "A Country Passion" (1928) are both examples of Callaghan's much-touted interest in what early critics called the "sub-normal personality." Both involve grotesque sexual assaults where the perpetrators, Gus Rapp and Jim Cline respectively, are arrested and imprisoned. In both stories Callaghan carefully constructs the personality of the protagonist—the case history—first, and then concludes both stories with the crime and then with the inexorable arrival of law: police cars, constables, handcuffs, jail cells and so on. More complex is the rudely named Joe Harding who seduces his sixteen-year-old niece in "An Autumn Penitent" (1928). In this long short story of sexual transgression, suicide, and public confession, Callaghan slyly insinuates Joe's various "trials" and tribulations by having him read the "police-court news" and reports of a "murder trial" (2). Even so innocuous a story as Callaghan's famous "A Predicament" (1928) involves a young priest, Father Francis, who feels he must learn to exercise his officially sanctioned "judgement" (19) instead of a pragmatic (but very effective) hypocrisy.

What makes these short stories so intriguing is that here Callaghan deploys a more elusive technique, almost the diametric opposite of explicit foregrounding. To borrow an insight of W. H. New's, Callaghan's "legal" short stories operate through a strategy of indirect form and oblique commentary (x). The stories, in fact, are marked by a broken scattering of references, a series of fleeting, off-handed, almost buried legal "punctuation marks." Only one of the stories has any prolonged representation of legal ritual; but the vast majority of them are dotted throughout with a vocabulary taken from the law; legal diction—or at least a diction resonant with law's power—is omnipresent. The result is that law haunts these imaginative worlds like an ever-present but invisible force, remaining always the emblem of enforced norms, yet constantly changing its specific significations.

This is especially true of two stories written and published by Callaghan during his Osgoode years, "Last Spring They Came Over" (1927) and "A Wedding Dress" (1927) (both of which Callaghan sent to Hemingway in Paris in 1925–26.) The former tells the story of two aptly named British brothers, Alfred and Harry Bowles, who emigrate to Toronto to work at a local newspaper. Alfred writes numerous comic letters home about the locals; Harry, however, withers soon after arrival and dies; Alfred then disappears at the end of the story never to be seen again.

Initially, the story is Callaghan's tongue-in-cheek satiric response to British pomposity. This tale about a mediocre British journalist is written in a crisp mediocre journalistic style; both brothers, moreover, are pretentious colonial bores, and so appropriately appear in a story that mockingly hybridizes such imperial genres as the allegory, anecdote, biography, fabliau, initiation story, mystery story, parable, sketch, and vignette. Callaghan's narrator slyly mocks the brothers' colonialist attitudes and pointedly mimics their British slang:

> They talked of the Englishman in Canada, comparing his lot with that of the Englishman in South Africa and India. They had never travelled but to ask what they knew of strange lands would have made one feel uncomfortable. ... Once in a while, after walking a block or two, one of the brothers would say he would damn well like to see India and the other would say it would be simply topping.[1] (40)

This whimsical mimicry gains particular force when we notice Callaghan's ever-so-subtle manipulation of the legal metaphor. Alfred's first assignment is "doing night police," which makes him feel "important" (39); but being inept, he soon bungles his assignment and instead has to help "a man do courts at the City Hall" (41). Alfred's double failure as a legal reporter is not insignificant.

Convinced as he is of his own superior status, Alfred sees the law as a desirable type of social capital; this is especially evident when we realize the importance he attributes to legal power and how he affiliates it with the hegemony of Empire itself:

> The night editor took a fancy to him because of the astounding puerility of his political opinions. Alfred was always willing to talk pompously of the British Empire *policing* the world and about all Catholics being aliens, and the future of Ireland and Canada resting with the Orangemen. ... The night editor liked him because he was such a nice boy. (39; my emphasis)

Here the Irish-Catholic-Canadian-law-student-part time-journalist Callaghan is at his best. The alignment of "policing" with British imperialism not only works hard to deliver a satiric thrust at a satirized character, but in the characterization itself, Callaghan implicitly deploys the figures of law to interrogate imperial attempts to contain both Irish independence and Canadian nationalism. This moment of ironic diction—"policing"—constitutes, in effect, a miniature resistant event, a small one-word "short story" about the language of power.

Callaghan's portrayal of the law as a restrictive discourse, an official state signature that seeks to right and rewrite the minds and souls of its citizenry is most evident in his well-known story "A Wedding Dress." The narrative is again a generic experimentation: a case history or an example of "police court news" that ironizes the sentimental tale, vignette, and sketch. The character is introduced, her personality is developed through vague hints, the criminal event is described, and legal retribution follows soon after.

The story, however, is also an exercise in sexist pathos: Lena Schwartz is an "old maid" whose wedding day finally arrives. Callaghan's narrator emphasizes her idealistic anticipations and her wish to appear desirable to her fiancé, Sam Hilton. She goes shopping for a wedding dress but, according to her lawyer, "become[s] temporarily a kleptomaniac" (61), and steals an expensive gown from a department store. In short order, she is arrested and spends the night in a police cell. The next morning Sam arrives from Windsor, and watches Lena's trial, which Callaghan presents in sparse detail. After Sam's character testimonial, Lena is put on remand and ordered by the magistrate to "go out and have a quiet wedding" (61). The story ends with Lena blinking confusedly, being led out of the court and out of the story by Sam to get married.

Throughout, Callaghan's narrator carefully establishes Lena's sexuality as a potentially unruly force—a force that she herself finds alienating. The narrator continually draws attention to her untouched, virginal body through both direct description and indirect (leering) commentary: "her hair was straight, her nose turned up a little and she was thin" (56); the male members of her rooming house nudge one another and chuckle that "it will really happen to her all right. ... The Lord knows she waited long enough" (56). As Lena goes shopping for her wedding dress, Callaghan places his narratorial emphasis almost exclusively on her suppressed sensuality and desires, on her desire for attention and seduction. The narrator remarks that "she had a funny aching feeling inside" and that "her arms and legs seemed almost strange to her" (57).

This state of sensual discombobulation continues when Lena decides she wants a "special [dress] to keep alive the tempestuous feeling in her body, something to startle Sam" (58). When she finally finds the dress of her dreams—what is really a displaced version of herself as she wishes to be: a desired love-object—Lena "liked the feeling it left in the tips of her fingers" (58). The narrator emphasizes that Lena's mind "play[s] with thoughts she guiltily enjoyed" and that she "imagines herself wantonly attractive in the dress, slyly watched by men with bold thoughts as she walked down the street with Sam" (58). Driven by these desires Lena steals the dress, returns home and wears it alone in her room.

The rest, as they say, is history: when the detective arrives Lena feels "that she might just as well be walking downstairs in her underclothes; the dress was like something wicked clinging to her legs and body" (59). At her trial next day, "everybody looked at her, the dress too short and hanging loosely on her thin body, the burnt orange petals creased and twisted. The magistrate said to himself: 'She's an old maid and it doesn't even look nice on her'" (61).

What makes Lena Schwartz's trial so interesting is that it functions within the story, not simply as a tragi-comic resolution, but as a male-centred normalizing ritual. Not for a moment am I claiming that Callaghan is a feminist author, but I am arguing that in this story—and in this conclusion—he shares the insights of a legal theorist like Bourdieu. For Callaghan, only a simpleton (like Alfred Bowles or Joe Harding) believes that state trials provide just decisions; what they do provide is a legitimized version of what most ruling interests agree is the truth. Bourdieu agrees when he remarks that,

> the judgement of a court, which decides conflicts or negotiations concerning persons or things by publicly proclaiming the truth about them, belongs in the final analysis to the class of acts of naming or of instituting. The judgement represents the quintessential form of authorized, public, official speech which is spoken in the name of and to everyone. These performative utterances, substantive... decisions publicly formulated by authorized agents acting on behalf of the collectivity, are magical acts which succeed because they have the power to make themselves universally recognized. (838)

Like the British Empire "policing" the world, Lena Schwartz's trial is a process of definition, inscription, and therefore delimitation. Whereas up to this point Lena has been portrayed as a sexualized body whose energy is potentially transgressive (indeed wanton!), here in the legal rituals of normalization her desires are placed squarely back within the confines of a mandated heterosexual marriage. The magistrate speaks in the name of and to everyone, and, on behalf of the collectivity, quietly silences all that potential sexual noise. In this poignant moment, law (and not love) triumphs; individual desire is subjected and made abject.

Morley Callaghan's deployment of law in the 1925–28 cluster of stories is important for a variety of reasons. The ever-presence of legal diction and legal metaphor attests, on one hand, simply to the fact that a young writer was simultaneously attending law school and writing his first stories.

I have tried to argue, however, that in a more complex sense, this ever-presence of law constitutes a sedimented genre, an interwoven filament of authoritarian thought that Callaghan continually explores, sometimes comically, sometimes ironically, sometimes approvingly.

This cluster of stories, moreover, forms the nucleus of Callaghan's entire life work, a vast body of experimental stories and novels that would continually return to themes of justice and control, crime and punishment, stories that would continually deploy legal language as part of Callaghan's own appropriation of the short story genre. The cluster, finally, in all of its fragmented usage of legal language, also points to a different deployment: the fragmented legal references, scattered as either words or metaphors across hundreds of later stories, constitute a metanarrative, a series of broken short stories, about the omnipresence of law in our imaginations, an interpellative force that necessitates continual resistance. It is in this continual resistant stance that Morley Callaghan emerges in his short stories as one of Canada's finest gadflies, one of the Canadian state's necessary anarchists.

NOTE

1. I am indebted here to Louis MacKendrick, who in private conversation at The Elephant and Castle pub (Rideau Centre, Ottawa) pointed out Callaghan's punning reference here to both the British game of "bowls," as well as the less salubrious implication of "bowels." MacKendrick also drew my attention to Callaghan's lurid suggestion that the brothers engage in an incestuous relationship: they sleep together, prefer boys to girls, and live on "Mutual" street. It goes without saying that Callaghan also playfully invokes the names of two British kings: Alfred and Harry.

WORKS CITED

Bourdieu, Pierre. "The Force of Law: Toward a Sociology of the Juridical Field." Trans. Richard Terdiman. *The Hastings Law Journal* 38 (July 1987): 805–853.

Callaghan, Morley. "Amuck in the Bush." (1927) *Morley Callaghan's Stories*. Toronto: MacMillan, 1959.

———. *An Autumn Penitent* (1928).Toronto: MacMillan, 1973.

———. "A Country Passion" (1928). *Morley Callaghan's Stories*. Toronto: MacMillan, 1959.

———. "A Girl with Ambition" (1925–26). *Morley Callaghan's Stories*. Toronto: MacMillan, 959.

———. "Honesty of Purpose." Rev. of *Tales of New Zealanders*. Ed. C. R. Allen. *Saturday Night* (July 23, 1938): 6.

———. "Last Spring They Came Over" (1927). *Morley Callaghan's Stories*. Toronto: MacMillan, 1959.

———. Letter to Ernest Hemingway. October 11 [1925]. Ernest Hemingway Papers. John Fitzgerald Kennedy Library, Boston.

———. Letter to Raymond Knister. August 15, 1928. Raymond Knister Papers. William Ready Division of Archives and Research Collections. McMaster University, Hamilton, Ontario.

———. "An Ocean Away" (1964). *Morley Callaghan*. Ed. Brandon Conron. Critical Views on Canadian Writers. Toronto: McGraw-Hill Ryerson, 1975.

———. "A Predicament" (1928). *Morley Callaghan's Stories*. Toronto: MacMillan, 1959.

———. *That Summer in Paris: Memories of Tangled Friendships with Hemingway, Fitzgerald, and Some Others*. Toronto: MacMillan, 1963.

———. "A Wedding Dress" (1927). *Morley Callaghan's Stories*. Toronto: MacMillan, 1959.

Davey, Frank. *Reading Canadian Reading*. Winnipeg: Turnstone Press, 1988.

Jameson, Fredric. *The Political Unconscious: Narrative as a Socially Symbolic Act*. Ithaca: Cornell UP, 1981.

New, W. H. *Dreams of Speech and Violence: The Art of the Short Story in Canada and New Zealand*. Toronto: U of Toronto P, 1987.

Rediscovering the Popular Canadian Short Story

ALLAN WEISS

HISTORIES OF THE CANADIAN SHORT STORY before 1970 generally focus on a limited and well-accepted group of writers, from Charles G. D. Roberts to Stephen Leacock to Morley Callaghan and on to the writers who emerged during the flowering of Canadian literature in the 1960s. The impression one gets is that during this period, especially during the middle decades of the twentieth century, only a few writers were working in the field—those writing fairly serious work. A major reason for this misapprehension is the inaccessibility of many of the works that in fact formed the bulk of Canada's short fiction for much of the century: popular short stories.

The term "popular short story" refers to works published in general-interest magazines and designed to appeal to as broad an audience as possible. It also encompasses certain genres like romance, detective, and science-fiction stories that have been traditionally distinguished from "mainstream" and "literary" fiction.[1] While recent scholars have taken popular fiction more seriously as a cultural expression—if not on aesthetic grounds—the popular short story remains a largely unexplored field, especially in Canada.[2] Yet even the widely anthologized writers of the pre-1970 period wrote for large-circulation magazines; Callaghan, Hugh Garner, and W. O. Mitchell published in *Maclean's* magazine, the Canadian *Liberty*, and so on, and Alice Munro's earliest professional publication was in *Mayfair*. Many writers worked exclusively in popular fiction, but their names have been forgotten and so have the works they produced in surprisingly large numbers. Indeed, the most widely read and well-liked of these writers are unknown to most scholars today.

One reason for their obscurity is that their works were designed to be disposable. The stories were formulaic, providing the kind of instant gratification that television shows do today, and they appeared in monthly or biweekly magazines that were simply discarded after reading. More importantly, such stories were seldom collected, either by the authors themselves or by anthology editors who paid scant attention to such ephemera on aesthetic or practical grounds. Certainly the stories seldom reached levels of quality that would make them memorable. Unless a story appears in book form, it is unlikely to become part of a country's fictional canon, but will moulder in justified or unjustified obscurity in a library's stacks—if the magazine in which it appeared exists at all.[3]

Among these lesser-known but prolific writers were R. Ross Annett (1895–?), Leslie Gordon Barnard (1890–1961) and his wife Margaret, Louis Arthur Cunningham (1900–1954), David K. Findlay (1901–   ), John Patrick Gillese (1920–   ), H. Gordon Green (1912–1991), Rhoda Elizabeth Playfair, and Kerry Wood (1907–   ). Their stories appeared in both Canadian and foreign general-interest and women's magazines; among the Canadian periodicals were *Canadian Magazine*, *Maclean's*, the Toronto *Star Weekly*, the *Family Herald and Weekly Star*, *Saturday Night*, the *Canadian Home Journal*, and *National Home Monthly*. Some achieved success and even fame in the American general-interest magazines, notably R. Ross Annett, whose "Babe" stories appeared regularly in *The Saturday Evening Post*—a number of these stories were collected in *Especially Babe* in 1942 and reissued by Tree Frog Press in 1977 with an introduction by Rudy Wiebe.

The popular short story in Canada reached its height during the period from about 1920 to the mid-1950s, quite naturally following the changing fortunes of the magazines themselves. What is truly remarkable about this period is the extent to which editors had a nationalist purpose or consciousness. We think of the small presses and little magazines as the nationalist voices, and the 1960s as the period when book and magazine editors, caught up in the nationalist fervour that attended the Centennial celebrations, provided the outlets for an unprecedented burst of Canadian literary activity. Yet the editors of some general-interest magazines between the wars also sought to promote Canadian writing, or at least made a point of noting when they published a Canadian writer. It is true that periodicals like the *Star Weekly* and the *Canadian Home Journal* published primarily foreign writers, buying stories from syndicates without regard to national origin, but the editors of the *Family Herald* and *Canadian Magazine*, and to some extent *Maclean's*, resolved to support local talent. Indeed, for quite some time until the early 1930s, *Canadian Magazine* published *only* Canadian writers, and its editors believed that the magazine could not merely survive but thrive by appealing to its readers' nationalist sentiments. For example, editor Joseph Lister Rutledge said in an editorial in 1929:

> It has been rather a favorite idea of ours, this producing a magazine that, whatever its faults might be, was at least exclusively Canadian. We believed that it was not only a good idea from a patriotic standpoint, but from a business standpoint as well; and naturally, being human, we are not quite blind to the bread and butter end. (Rutledge 1)

R. S. Kennedy and (as of 1948) H. Gordon Green had similar nationalist aims as editors of the *Family Herald* (Green, "Happy" J2).

A sampling of the stories published during the period from 1929 to the late 1950s—when the magazines began to cease publishing fiction or suspended publication altogether—reveals a broad range of styles and genres. Some of these differences reflect the authors' individual proclivities; for example, Frederick B. Watt focussed on the sea, while David Kirkpatrick Findlay wrote about bush and military airmen. Phyllis Lee Peterson's stories, like Annett's, feature child characters or even protagonists. But most writers worked within a variety of fictional genres, primarily romance, war, western, and detective fiction.

What the stories have in common, regardless of author and genre, is that they almost all end happily. In my 1988 study comparing popular and "literary" fiction during the 1950s and 1960s, I noted that popular fiction features a largely comic structure while literary fiction uses a largely tragic one (see Weiss 227).[4] In other words, in the popular short story events turn out well for the hero and/or heroine no matter how many complications arise during the course of the story. At the very least, justice prevails. The plot twists may involve mistaken identities and other misunderstandings; for example, in Leslie Gordon Barnard's "Crime Comes to South Street," all the evidence suggests that Henry and Ellen Abercorn's son George has become a criminal. But we learn at the end that he has been forced into helping two fugitives escape and then being in their car when they shoot his friend, who has threatened to go to the police. In Barnard's "A Friend of Beau's," Joe Morton seems to be the villain of the piece, but turns out to be a police officer trying to warn Sadie Smith against pursuing a relationship with Beau, a criminal. Predictably, Sadie and Joe end up marrying after she discovers Joe's identity. In Louis Arthur Cunningham's "Spring and Miss Heather," bachelor Roger Gilman is fooled into thinking that Heather, with whom he works and is enamoured, is engaged, and he fools her into thinking he is also engaged so that he can buy her an expensive trousseau (with her unwitting assistance). Their confusion is cleared up, and their marriage is inevitable.

The characterization in the stories depends heavily on stereotypes, as one might expect, including racial ones. Indeed, a number of stories in *Canadian Magazine* concern French Canadians who fit the standard image of the quaint Habitant. In D. M. Currie's "And Be My Love" the stubborn young people destined to be married at last are stage Irish, capable of saying lines like, " 'Kitty... why do you not listen to me at all, at all?' " (58). By and large, however, protagonists, especially in love stories, are middle-class WASPs. Heroes are good-looking and conventionally virtuous (except for the somewhat Byronic protagonist of Mary Shannon's "Leader of the Twilight Band," but it is noteworthy that he is Latin American and therefore exotic). Heroines are, of course, almost all young and attractive, except for stories where the theme demands otherwise, as we will see. Villains seldom cause real or lasting damage, and are generally brought to justice, although once more there are exceptions, such as David K. Findlay's "Brief Career of Mr. Stott, Detective," in which an amateur sleuth makes what is apparently a fatal error in identifying Carolyn Heargreaves' killer.

The settings, as critics of the period's fiction have noted, are not reflective of the times. Canada was becoming a primarily urban society—indeed, sixty percent of the population lived in cities by 1951—but the fiction almost invariably concerns characters in small towns, on farms, or in fishing villages. As one might expect, stories published in Canadian magazines are more likely to be set in clearly identified Canadian places, notably works published in the *Family Herald* and those featuring French-Canadian or historical subjects. Otherwise, the settings are fairly generic, or, as in "Crime Comes to South Street," identifiably foreign (in this case, London). Annett's "Babe" stories, it should be noted, despite their foreign publication are unapologetically set in the Saskatchewan prairie. Critics may therefore have exaggerated the tendency of popular short stories to have unspecified settings or be set in the country of publication.

The stories usually have a moral purpose as well as an intent to entertain. In the broadest sense, popular stories seek to portray the transcendent power of love or the benefits, through clear rewards, of virtuous behaviour (Fowler *passim*). Critics have long noted the conservative ideology expressed by popular fiction, which reinforces romantic views of love and the tenets of conventional morality (e.g. Cawelti *passim*; Radway *passim*; although cf. Birch 85; Hilfer *passim*).

The power of love is evident in Leslie Gordon Barnard's stories about old age, like "Gift of the Colver Blood" and "Mudge Lane," published a few months apart in 1929. In both stories, elderly protagonists cling to loves that time has not weakened. In the first, Grandfather Randall dies after being caught in a storm while suffering the delusion that it is fifty years earlier, and that he will stop Jack Colver from stealing his wife. In the second, Mary Gorsby visits her old love Simon despite the scandalized looks of other old women. Both demonstrate the strength not just of love but of the life force itself, in the face of death and time's passage. Similarly, stories often advance sentimental views of the family, as in Rhoda Elizabeth Playfair's "His Wonders to Perform," where a young boy melts his mother's heart by his tender caring for a stray cat, and his offer to help his mother with her chores, causing her to reverse her earlier refusal to let him keep it.

Sometimes the stories have more specific messages that constitute their themes. For example, Rhoda Elizabeth Playfair's "The Girl Who Wasn't Pretty" is designed to teach the reader that looks are not everything; Mark Williams learns by seeing the loving relationship of George and Peggy Preston that he should look beyond Alice Trescott's appearance and stop pursuing the beautiful but unsuitable Sandra Cunningham. Playfair's "The Affair of Able Willie" is an attack on racial prejudice—Mrs. Manders is the only person in town who does not discriminate against Abraham Williams, an Indian boy.

One thing that is notable about the stories is that they are often very closely tied to the circumstances in which they were written and read. Contrary to expectation, they are not mere escapist fare in all cases. Annett's "Babe" stories appeared during the Depression and strongly reflect this context. It should be remembered, however, that their portrait of Depression life is tempered by humour, which, as Wiebe notes in his introduction, serves in part to reduce the potential for sentimentality (Annett 12). Still, writers sought to evoke strong and immediate reactions in their readers, and references to current events such as the Depression and World War II are obvious means of doing so. Sometimes there is a clear degree of wish-fulfillment involved, such as the stories about upper-class characters like those in Margaret E. Barnard's "Second Wedding," published in 1934. On the other hand, her husband's "Nothing to Quarrel About" concerns two now-poor characters—both ruined by "the Finchell crash"—who strive to present a wealthy front at a weekend visit to wealthy Mrs. Pomfret. Here, readers can see the high life in all its splendour, much as in a movie musical of the period, while at the same time being able to identify more closely with the not-so-rich characters. John Patrick Gillese's "The Washing Machine" shows in idealized form how the Depression forced people to make great sacrifices for each other, as the narrator's father sells the pump engine to buy the washing machine his wife has been dreaming of; although written after the fact, the story would certainly evoke strong feelings in those who remembered the hardships of the 1930s. Gillese's message is clear: his narrator says of his parents, "I do know that in the hardest times of our lives they were richer than many people ever are, because they knew how to take richness out of sacrifice for each other" (209).

Of course, during the war years fiction reflected the dominant preoccupation of the day. Stories about soldiers, sailors, and airmen filled magazines. Popular fiction had always had a didactic purpose, but it was at this point that the line between fiction and propaganda blurred almost to nothing. Very characteristic is David Kirkpatrick Findlay's "Bugles, Blow for These," about a downed, injured airman and the air-raid volunteer he meets. Katherine Fitzhugh is a symbol of England herself: "She was the flowering of a thousand years. England had shaped her, colored her and allowed the strange and beautiful accident of her midnight air and exotic winglike brows" (27). Before returning to the war effort, Flight Lieutenant Vincent tells her he is joining a night fighter unit: " 'We've hated war—let's make them feel that hate. Let's sear it into their souls until it becomes a weapon that fights for us. Let's be as tough to protect as they are to kill' " (29). The story celebrates the bravery of the English people during the Blitz, striving to boost morale—and hatred for the Germans.

It would be a mistake to dismiss the stories as entirely lacking in technique or depth. Many, like Theodore Goodridge Roberts's poor imitation of *Huckleberry Finn*, "There's Lots of Time," are indeed superficial and incredible, and merit little attention. But others strive to enrich the plots with character development and symbolism, although often of a fairly crude kind. In Leslie Gordon Barnard's "Gift of the Colver Blood," the life force discussed above is symbolized by an orange scarf passed down from grandmother to granddaughter; Barnard contrasts its vivid colour with the otherwise grey and dour setting. It represents the vitality of youth, as does the blue and white chinaware Mary Gorsby owns in "Mudge Lane." Both stories focus more on character than plot, and their endings are less pat than the norm. We have already noted the Byronic energy of Conquistador, the protagonist of Mary Shannon's "Leader of the Twilight Band"; he is insistently associated with the title character, a wild horse that is just as regal and proud as the man pursuing it. The sorrel saves Conquistador's life, and the latter expresses his gratitude in a gesture that "was not a salute. Rather, was it the homage of conqueror to conqueror" (31).

Overall, the focus on character generally comes with the exploration of one theme that appears most frequently in these stories: the triumph of the human spirit in the face of adversity. Stories concern dangers on the sea, dangers in the air, dangers from wild animals or human enemies, and the ability of characters to display courage and rise above them. In Louis Arthur Cunningham's "The Landsman," for example, Anthony Ruddock cannot bring himself to join the rest of his family out on the sea;

because of an early shipwreck he is traumatized, and stays home while others go out on fishing or rescue boats. After one particularly embarrassing exhibition of cowardice he leaves the village, only to return—in disguise—as a parachutist working with a stunt pilot. He uses his new skill to perform a sea rescue, proving himself before his ex-neighbours (and, incidentally, the girl who loves him). Other characters must conquer their own fears, natural disasters, economic hardships (as in the Depression-era stories), or the Nazis, and usually succeed.

In sum, the stories of the period provide emotionally if not always aesthetically satisfying conclusions. Characters defeat the forces—whether human or natural, whether internal or external—that block their happiness; they end up proving themselves, getting married, or otherwise reintegrating into society in keeping with the stories' comic structure. The endings validate middle-class values of marriage, family life, modest material comfort (as opposed to aristocratic opulence or working-class squalor), and social respectability. We would be mistaken to see the sentimentality as entirely false, however; we have to place ourselves in the position of people enduring the hardships of the Depression, the Second World War, and the struggle to live in harsh environments to appreciate the reality of what the authors often portray.

The large magazines began to perish as long ago as 1939, for one main reason: the loss of advertising revenue to the new media of radio and, later, television. In his last editorial, Rutledge complained about how government policy effectively killed *Canadian Magazine*. By 1938 it had a circulation of over 137,000, but the government's favouring of the Canadian Broadcasting Corporation, high taxes, and foreign competition made it no longer viable to publish "magazines edited exclusively for the benefit of Canadians" (3). In the 1950s, most of the large-circulation magazines succumbed as television drew off their advertisers; the rest published less fiction or none at all.

But this does not mean that the popular Canadian short story disappeared entirely. Romance stories continued to appear in *Chatelaine*, and writers who had found ready markets in mainly American pulp magazines of detective and science fiction continued to publish there. The popular short story thus fragmented, and writers specialized in genre fiction: for example, Ernest Harrison and William Bankier in detective fiction, Phyllis Gotlieb in science fiction. The main outlet for general-interest fiction during the 1960s, ironically, was the Canadian Broadcasting Corporation, although Robert Weaver's "Anthology" favoured literary fiction over the more popular form. The genres maintained some of the features that characterized the popular short story: emphasis on plot and action, often happy endings (in some cases represented by the successful solution of technological or detective problems), and the theme of human triumph over difficulties. During the 1960s, the university-based literary magazine replaced the large-circulation general-interest magazine as the main outlet for fiction, and the nature of what was published changed accordingly—but that is another story.

The popular short story was a major element of our literary history, if for no other reason than that, in its tendency toward conventionality of form and theme, it was what many literary story writers wrote in opposition to. For decades, the vast majority of Canadian short stories sought a wide readership, for good or ill. It is important to recall what was written and who wrote it, to rediscover a part of Canada's short-story history that has been forgotten, and to fill a gap so many scholars do not even realize exists. The fact that the writers discussed achieved so great a reputation among so many people makes it imperative that we take their role in our cultural history seriously.

NOTES

1. For the distinction between "high" and "mass" or "popular" culture, see Lowenthal, Bradbury, Gans, Hall, and Schücking, among many others.
2. For studies of American and British popular short fiction, see Berelson and Salter, Johns-Heine and Gerth, and Fowler; on Canadian popular stories, see Zureik and Frizzell.
3. Ironically, the wider the circulation of a magazine the more likely it is to disappear entirely after a short time. The Canadian *Liberty* was entirely unavailable in Toronto until a donation was made to the Metro Reference Library some ten years ago.
4. Compare Fowler's comments on the British popular short story, especially p. 95.

WORKS CITED

Primary Works
Annett, R. Ross. *Especially Babe*. Introd. Rudy Wiebe. 1942; Edmonton: Tree Frog Press, 1978.
Barnard, Leslie Gordon."Crime Comes to South Street." *National Home Monthly* 40 (April 1939): 12–13, 31, 33, 35, 47.
——— . "Don't Let It Change Us." *Family Herald* (July 17, 1952): 20–21.
——— . "Four Men and a Box." *Cavalcade of the North*. Ed. George E. Nelson. Garden City: Doubleday, 1958. 633–636.

———. "A Friend of Beau's." *Family Herald* (August 31, 1950): 16–17, 22.
———. "Gift of the Colver Blood." *Canadian Magazine* 71 (June 1929): 5–6, 42–43.
———. "The Harpoon." *Star Weekly* (June 23, 1951): Sec. I, 9.
———. "The Little Green Hat." *Family Herald* (September 29, 1960): 24–25, 28.
———. "Mudge Lane." *Canadian Magazine* 71 (March 1929): 11–12, 45–46.
———. "Nothing to Quarrel About." *Canadian Magazine* 82 (September 1934): 3–5, 28.
———. "Short Cut for Mr. Poppin." *Weekend* 1 (November 24, 1951): 18.
———. "The Two Boats." *Family Herald* (April 19, 1950): 28–29.
Barnard, Margaret E. "Second Wedding." *Canadian Magazine* 81 (February 1934): 10–11, 38.
Clare, John. "The Strange Death of Sam Fletcher." *Maclean's* 63 (September 1, 1950): 20, 33, 35–37.
Cunningham, Louis Arthur. "The Landsman." *Canadian Magazine* 71 (February 1929): 16–17, 36.
———. "Sea Fever." *Maclean's* 47 (January 1, 1934): 15, 38.
———. "Spring and Miss Heather." *Canadian Magazine* 73 (April 1930): 9–10, 20.
———. "The Terrible Secret of M. Laroche." *Maclean's* 63 (November 1, 1950): 18–19, 32–33.
Currie, D. M. "And Be My Love." In *Stories to Read Again*. Ed. H. Gordon Green. Fredericton: Brunswick Press, 1965. 55–69.
Findlay, David Kirkpatrick. "Brief Career of Mr. Stott, Detective." *Canadian Magazine* 90 (October 1938): 24–25, 59–62.
———. "Bugles, Blow for These." *Maclean's* 55 (April 1, 1942): 8–9, 26–30.
———. "The Decoy Is for Ducks." *Star Weekly* (November 25, 1950): Sec. I, 8, 12.
———. "Love Comes Home Again." *Star Weekly* (May 19, 1951): Sec. II, 3, 12.
———. "Miss Hubbard Went to the Cupboard." *Star Weekly* (May 24, 1952): Sec. I, 1, 12.
———. "Star Performance." *Star Weekly* (January 7, 1950): Sec. II, 1.
Gillese, John Patrick. "The Washing Machine." In *Stories to Read Again*. Fredericton: Brunswick Press, 1965. 201–209.
Green, H. Gordon. "Cocooney Kelly." *National Home Monthly* 46 (March 1945): 17, 37–40.
———, ed. *Stories to Read Again*. Fredericton: Brunswick Press, 1965.
Mayse, Arthur. "Bush Job." *Maclean's* 53 (February 15, 1940): 5–7, 36.
Peterson, Phyllis Lee. "The Facts of Life." *Weekend* 2 (February 23, 1952): 10–11.
———. "Monsieur Pantoufles." *Weekend* 2 (March 29, 1952): 36.
———. "Pete's Rubbers." *Weekend* 2 (February 9, 1952): 12.
Playfair (Stein), Rhoda Elizabeth. "The Affair of Able Willie." *Family Herald* (May 1, 1958): 6–17.
———. "The Girl Who Wasn't Pretty." *Family Herald* (June 23, 1960): 18–19, 24.
———. "His Wonders to Perform." *Family Herald* (December 21, 1950): 22–23.
Roberts, Theodore Goodridge. "There's Lots of Time." *National Home Monthly* 40 (May 1939): 10–11, 41, 44.
Rutledge, Joseph Lister. Editorial. *Canadian Magazine* 72 (August 1929): 1.
———. Editorial. *Canadian Magazine* 89 (April 1939): 3.

Shannon, Mary. "Leader of the Twilight Band." *Canadian Magazine* 71 (January 1929): 20–21, 31.
Sturdy, John Rhodes. "Oh, Danny Boy." *Weekend* 1 (November 24, 1951): 24–25, 32.
———. "A Question of Time." *Maclean's* 56 (July 15, 1943): 10–11, 35–36, 53.
———. "The Third Bullet." *Weekend* 1 (September 8, 1951): 16, 44–45.
Tench, C. V. "Nine Must Die." *National Home Monthly* 51 (February 1950): 8–9, 20–21.
Watt, Frederick B. "Three Laughing Ghosts." *Canadian Magazine* 74 (September 1930): 6–7, 55–56.

Secondary Works

Bennett, Tony, ed. *Popular Fiction: Technology, Ideology, Production, Reading*. London: Routledge, 1990.
Bensman, Joseph, and Israel Gerver. "Art and the Mass Society." *Social Problems* 6 (1958): 4–10.
Berelson, Bernard. "Who Reads What and Why?" *Saturday Review* (May 12, 1951): 7–8, 30–31.
Berelson, Bernard, and Patricia J. Salter. "Majority and Minority Americans: An Analysis of Magazine Fiction." *Public Opinion Quarterly* 10 (1946): 168–190.
Birch, M. J. "The Popular Fiction Industry: Market, Formula, Ideology." *Journal of Popular Culture* 21:3 (1987): 79–102.
Bradbury, Malcolm. *The Social Context of Modern English Literature*. Oxford: Basil Blackwell, 1971.
Cawelti, John. *Adventure, Mystery, Romance: Formula Stories as Art and Popular Culture*. Chicago: U of Chicago P, 1976.
Fluck, Winfried. "Fiction and Fictionality in Popular Culture: Some Observations on the Aesthetics of Popular Culture." *Journal of Popular Culture* 21:4 (1988): 49–62.
Fowler, Bridget. " 'True to Me Always': An Analysis of Women's Magazine Fiction." *British Journal of Sociology* 30 (1979): 91–119.
Gans, Herbert J. *Popular Culture and High Culture: An Analysis and Evaluation of Taste*. New York: Basic Books, 1974.
Green, H. Gordon. "Happy Ending with a Twist Never Made the Herald." *Toronto Star* (March 16, 1991): J2.
Hall, John. *The Sociology of Literature*. London: Longman, 1979.
Hilfer, Anthony C. "Inversion and Excess: Texts of Bliss in Popular Culture." *Texas Studies in Literature and Language* 22 (1980): 125–137.
Johns-Heine, Patricke, and Hans H. Gerth. "Values in Mass Periodical Fiction, 1921–40." *Public Opinion Quarterly* 13 (1949): 105–113.
Lowenthal, Leo. *Literature, Popular Culture, and Society*. Palo Alto: Pacific Books, 1961.
McCormack, Thelma. "Writers and the Mass Media." *Canadian Literature* 20 (1964): 27–40.
Radway, Janice A. "Phenomenology, Linguistics, and Popular Literature." *Journal of Popular Culture* 12:1 (1978): 88–98.

Sanders, Clinton A. "Structural and Interactional Features of Popular Culture Production: An Introduction to the Production of Culture Perspective." *Journal of Popular Culture* 16:2 (1982): 66–74.

Schücking, Levin L. *The Sociology of Literary Taste.* Chicago: U of Chicago P, 1966.

Weiss, Allan. "Magazines and the English-Canadian Short Story, 1950–1970." *Visions critiques* 5 (1988): 223–230.

Zureik, Eliza T., and Alan Frizzell. "Values in Canadian Magazine Fiction: A Test of the Social Control Thesis." *Journal of Popular Culture* 10 (1976): 359–376.

"Love and Death": Romance and Reality in Margaret Laurence's *A Bird in the House*

NORA FOSTER STOVEL

A BIRD IN THE HOUSE, Margaret Laurence's 1970 collection of short stories set in Manawaka, is a female Canadian *Bildungsroman* chronicling the maturation of protagonist Vanessa MacLeod. *A Bird in the House* is also a metafictional *Künstlerroman* like *The Diviners*, a fiction about fiction narrating the development of an artist, because Vanessa becomes a novelist, like Morag Gunn. Narrated by Vanessa, as an adult remembering her childhood, *A Bird in the House* offers a dual perspective, ironizing the chasm between the child's fantasies and the mature writer's memories. Laurence chronicles the creation of a writer by embedding Vanessa's own stories in the narrative, as her development is measured by the maturation of her fiction. The name "Vanessa," meaning "butterfly," emphasizes the transformational element of the narrative, reinforced by the narrator's retrospections that conclude significant stories—"The Mask of the Bear," the title story "A Bird in the House," "The Loons," and the concluding story, "Jericho's Brick Battlements"—underlining the development from the child's to the adult writer's perception of reality. *A Bird in the House* is not merely metafiction, however; it is "semi-autobiographical fiction" (Laurence, *Dance* 5) in the author's words. Laurence acknowledges, "The character of Vanessa is based on myself as a child, and the MacLeod family is based on my own childhood family" ("Loons" 805).[1]

A Bird in the House is not only autobiographical metafiction; it is also *metabiography,* to coin a term, because stories Vanessa MacLeod writes are the same stories Margaret Laurence wrote. Both actual and fictional authors write a story about pioneers entitled "The Pillars of the Nation," and both write a tale about the fur trade set in nineteenth-century Quebec.

Chronicling Vanessa's development as an artist thus reflects Laurence's own creative growth. Laurence says, "The ways in which memories and 'created' events intertwine in [*A Bird in the House*] probably illustrate a few things about the nature of fiction" ("Loons" 805). This artistic alchemy is illuminated by examining the metabiographical aspect of *A Bird in the House* by tracing Vanessa's own embedded stories.

The story is an ideal genre for conveying the relation between art and life. For Laurence, the short story, with its lyric form, is the perfect vehicle for the theories of memory that she expounds in *The Diviners*, because Vanessa's vignettes, like Morag Gunn's *Memorybank Movies*, dramatize spots of time that mark turning points in Vanessa's life. Each of the stories in *A Bird in the House* recreates an epiphany, a negative epiphany as in James Joyce's *Dubliners*, as Vanessa becomes disenchanted or disillusioned—disabused of her childish faith in fair play in real life.

The creative development Laurence recreates in *A Bird in the House* reflects real experience. Laurence's mother advised her to *write about what you know* when, as a child, she wrote stories about lords and ladies, castles and moats, and Laurence portrays Vanessa learning the same lesson from life. In "The Sound of the Singing," the first story in *A Bird in the House*, Vanessa, age ten, struggles to create "an old-fashioned lady" out of a clothes-peg, pipe cleaners, and crepe paper—inspired by the dresser doll adorned with a curly yellow coiffure and a hoop skirt of fluted apricot crepe de Chine (26), among the treasures in Aunt Edna's bedroom, the gift of an old admirer—but Vanessa becomes frustrated when the lady's skirt refuses to stick properly on the doll:

> It had become, somehow, overwhelmingly important for me to finish it. I did not even play with dolls very much, but this one was the beginning of a collection I had planned. I could visualise them, each dressed elaborately in the costume of some historical period or some distant country, ladies in hoop skirts, gents in black top hats, Highlanders in kilts, hula girls with necklaces of paper flowers. But this one did not look at all as I had imagined she would. Her wooden face, on which I had already pencilled eyes and mouth, grinned stupidly at me, and I leered viciously back. *You'll be beautiful whether you like it or not*, I told her. (22)

Laurence observed, "There is a lot of history in my fiction" (Fabre 208), and she portrays Vanessa here as a would-be historian, marshalling her marionettes to reflect myriad cultures in a manner that allows her to play God, to control the chaos of the past, rather than confront her own present.

Vanessa's Grandmother MacLeod aspires to be an old-fashioned lady, with her Irish linen and Birks silver, in the next story, "To Set Our

House in Order." Vanessa's father explains, just "like Grandfather MacLeod being interested in Greek plays," so "your grandmother was interested in being a lady" (55). Vanessa discovers in her father's own books—"*Seven-League Boots. Arabia Deserta. The Seven Pillars of Wisdom. Travels in Tibet. Count Lucknor the Sea Devil*" (56)—that he aspired to be an explorer, not a doctor. Vanessa becomes an explorer of the heart, realizing everyone cherishes a dream; but the challenge is bridging the chasm between dream and truth.

Both authors, actual and fictional, possess private places to dream, to let the theatre of the mind run rampant and to let their unruly feelings spill over onto the orderly lines of a scribbler. Robert Wemyss built a life-size playhouse for his daughter Peggy, and Laurence gives Vanessa a similar playhouse in *A Bird in the House*. In *Dance on the Earth: A Memoir*, Laurence recalls:

> At the Big House, my play-house changed its function. It became my study, my refuge, my own private place. Even in winter, although the little shack wasn't heated, I used to go there to brood upon life's injustices, to work off anger, or simply to think and dream. In summer, I would climb up to the roof and lie there, hidden from view by the big branches of the huge spruce trees that bent over the gently sloping roof, and read for hours. (64)

Later, Laurence found the loft over the garage for her Grandfather Simpson's McLaughlin-Buick provided privacy for writing: "I used to cheat on my violin practice and whip up to the loft, where I kept my five-cent scribblers in which I was writing a novel entitled 'The Pillars of the Nation'" (67). Vanessa also escapes to the loft to write, hiding her scribblers in Grandfather Connor's old McLaughlin-Buick: she says, "I began to size up the inner situation, which was a relief from the outer. I already had half a five-cent scribbler full of the story I was writing" (164–165).

In *Dance on the Earth*, Margaret Laurence recalls the moment of revelation when she realized her life's vocation: "I have to be a writer" (74). As a novelist, Laurence is a realist *par excellence*, employing verisimilitude as the vehicle for her vision. But youth is romantic, and the progression from romance to realism chronicles the maturation process, as M. H. Abrams defines the terms: "Realistic fiction is often opposed to romantic fiction. The *romance* is said to present life as we would have it be—more picturesque, fantastic, adventurous, or heroic than actuality; realism, on the other hand, is said to represent life as it really is" (174). Giovanna Capone explains this development:

> In Margaret Laurence's *A Bird in the House* the distance between the real and the imaginary is the ordering theme of the cycle of stories, built as they are on the spaces between experience and its imaginative reconstruction.

> As the stories follow one another the confrontation of the narrator's reconstructions with her childhood vision of the world gradually becomes more explicit. (161)

In *A Bird in the House,* Laurence chronicles a progression from romanticism to realism in Vanessa that reflects her own maturation process, as she explains it in her memoir.

As a child Laurence preferred reading romantic tales, as she asserts in *Dance on the Earth*:

> My favourites were adventure stories. I don't think it ever occurred to me that such adventures could never happen to me, a girl. I never pretended, even in fantasy, to be a boy. I saw myself as myself, doing deeds of high bravery on the high seas and the low moors. I was the female version of Alan Breck. Yet what a pity that the girls of my generation had so few women role models in fiction who were bold and daring in life and work. (64–65)

Margaret Laurence and Vanessa MacLeod share a love for Sir Arthur Conan Doyle's historical romance *The White Company* (*Bird* 102; *Dance* 64). In "Books that Mattered to Me," Laurence confesses that she admired both Stevenson's Alan Breck—"my ideal of bravery and adventure"—and Arthur Conan Doyle's boy hero, "the lad Alain, with whom I identified totally" (240).

Peggy Wemyss's writing was equally heroic: in *Dance on the Earth*, Laurence recalls writing "a highly uninformed but jubilantly imaginative journal of Captain John Ball and his voyages to exotic lands, complete with maps made by me of strange, mythical places" (61). Vanessa prefers "stories of spectacular heroism in which I figured as central character" (14). Peter Easingwood is thus correct when he asserts, "The autobiographical impulse is there not only in the incidental detail of realistic presentation but even more decisively in the... element of romance" (24).

In *A Bird in the House* Laurence recreates *a realist's progress*: in "The Sound of the Singing," the opening story, Vanessa, age ten, is beginning to worry about reconciling romance with reality:

> I was planning in my head a story in which an infant was baptised by Total Immersion and swept away by the river which happened to be flooding. (Why would it be flooding? Well, probably the spring ice was just melting. Would they do baptisms at that time of year? The water would be awfully cold. Obviously, some details needed to be worked out here.) The child was dressed in a christening robe of white lace, and the last the mother saw of her was a scrap of white being swirled away towards the Deep Hole near the Wachakwa bend, where there were bloodsuckers. (24–25)

No doubt Vanessa visualizes herself heroically saving the infant from a fate worse than death.

The problem is that Vanessa draws her material from literature, not life, finding her inspiration in the Bible. In "The Sound of the Singing" she explains how she prepares for the catechism of her beloved, devout Grandmother Connor at Sunday dinner at the Brick House:

> I rarely listened in Sunday school, finding it more entertaining to compose in my head stories of spectacular heroism in which I figured as central character, so I never knew what the text had been. But I had read large portions of the Bible by myself, for I was constantly hard-up for reading material, so I had no trouble in providing myself with a verse each week before setting out for the Brick House. My lines were generally of a warlike nature, for I did not favour the meek stories and I had no use at all for the begats.
> "*How are the mighty fallen in the midst of the battle,*" I replied instantly. (14–15)

Vanessa's biblical text refers to her battle with "The Great Bear" (63) himself, Grandfather Connor, reflecting Laurence's conflict with her autocratic Grandfather Simpson. When Timothy Connor criticizes Vanessa's father, Ewen MacLeod, the town doctor, for missing Sunday dinner at the Brick House because he is attending Henry Pearl, Vanessa leaps to his defense: "'It's not his fault,' I replied hotly. 'It's Mr. Pearl. He's dying with pneumonia. I'll bet you he's spitting up blood this very second'" (23). Vanessa's imagination goes to work immediately, turning fact into fiction: "Did people spit blood with pneumonia? All at once, I could not swallow, feeling as though that gushing crimson were constricting my own throat. Something like that would go well in the story I was currently making up. *Sick to death in the freezing log cabin, with only the beautiful half-breed lady* (no, *woman) to look after him, Old Jebb suddenly clutched his throat*—and so on" (23). As Capone observes, "Vanessa is a juvenile storyteller by vocation; and side by side with the life she is living, she lives the story she is currently making up, so that at times a word from reality evokes a literary atmosphere, a sentence, or a paragraph from a would-be story" (165).

Old Jebb may be a figure from Vanessa's novel: in "The Sound of the Singing" she announces proudly, "'I'm writing a story... *The Pillars of the Nation*... It's about pioneers'" (29). When Aunt Edna replies, "'You mean—people like Grandfather?'" Vanessa reacts, "'My gosh'... Was he a pioneer?'" Aunt Edna responds, "'I'll tell the cockeyed world'" (29). The mature narrator explains:

> That had been my epic on pioneer life. I had proceeded to the point in the story where the husband, coming back to the cabin one evening, discovered to his surprise that he was going to become a father. The way he ascertained

> this interesting fact was that he found his wife constructing a birch-bark cradle. Then came the discovery that Grandfather Connor had been a pioneer, and the story had lost its interest for me. If pioneers were like *that*, I had thought, my pen would be better employed elsewhere. (68)

Reality deflates romance. Vanessa is not really interested in writing about actual pioneers, but only in fabricating a glamorous fantasy. As Easingwood explains, "When reminded that her Grandfather Connor was a pioneer, Vanessa at once abandons her juvenile attempt at writing a romance of pioneer life: the prospect of romance is spoiled by this confrontation with the known reality" (22).

In *Dance on the Earth* (73) Laurence gives a strikingly similar account of her own pioneer epic:

> I had just completed my masterpiece, "The Pillars of the Nation," which filled two or three scribblers and was the story of pioneers. I believe it was in that story that the invented name Manawaka first appeared. The only part of the story I recall was a sensational scene in which the young pioneer wife delicately communicates to her husband that she is pregnant by the tactful device of allowing him to arrive home and witness her making a birch-bark cradle. (73)

"I guess if I'd stuck to birch-bark cradles in my fiction, the book-banning elements loose in Canada wouldn't have hit on me as a target" (73), Laurence remarks wryly. She recalls proudly:

> "The Pillars of the Nation" got an honourable mention and I was ecstatic. A few months later, a story of mine called "The Case of the Blond Butcher" was actually printed in the young people's section of the Saturday *Free Press*. It was a murder story in which it turned out that no murder had been committed after all. (In those days I favoured happy endings. I still do—who wouldn't? But nowadays they're not always possible.) (73)

This is the lesson Vanessa has yet to learn, but she still likes love stories to have happy endings:

> I was much occupied by the themes of love and death, although my experience of both had so far been gained principally from the Bible, which I read in the same way as I read Eaton's Catalogue or the collected works of Rudyard Kipling—because I had to read something, and the family's finances in the thirties did not permit the purchase of enough volumes of *Doctor Doolittle* or the *Oz* books to keep me going. (65)

Later, in "The Mask of the Bear," when Aunt Edna asks, "'How's *The Pillars of the Nation* coming along?'" Vanessa's response is terse: "'I quit that one,' I replied laconically. 'I'm making up another—it's miles better. It's called *The Silver Sphinx.* I'll bet you can't guess what it's about.'" Aunt Edna's reaction is gratifyingly obtuse: "'The desert? Buried treasure? Murder mystery?'" Vanessa shakes her head and pronounces only one word: "'Love.'" Edna responds with straight-faced surprise: "'Good Glory. ... That sounds fascinating. Where do you get your ideas, Vanessa?'" Vanessa responds mysteriously, "'Oh, here and there. ... You know'" (69). With no real knowledge of love Vanessa turns to the next best thing to Eaton's Catalogue, the Bible, storehouse of stories:

> For the love scenes, I gained useful material from The Song of Solomon. *Let him kiss me with the kisses of his mouth, for thy love is better than wine,* or *By night on my bed I sought him whom my soul loveth; I sought him but I found him not.* My interpretation was somewhat vague, and I was not helped to any appreciable extent by the explanatory bits in small print at the beginning of each chapter—*The church's love unto Christ. The church's fight and victory in temptation,* et cetera. These explanations did not puzzle me, though, for I assumed even then that they had simply been put there for the benefit of gentle and unworldly people such as my Grandmother Connor, so that they could read the Holy Writ without becoming upset. To me, the woman in The Song was some barbaric queen, beautiful and terrible, and I could imagine her, wearing a long robe of leopard skin and one or two heavy gold bracelets, pacing an alabaster courtyard and keening her unrequited love. (66)

Laurence mentions in her memoir reading selections from the Song of Solomon in her *Pocket Book of Verse* in high school and wondering at "the accompanying comment on that great love poem found in my grandmother's Bible: 'Christ's marriage to the church'" (77). Vanessa's creation is inspired by Solomon's Song, but she romanticizes it in a comically exotic pastiche:

> The heroine in my story (which took place in ancient Egypt—my ignorance of this era did not trouble me) was very like the woman in The Song of Solomon, except that mine had long wavy auburn hair, and when her beloved left her, the only thing she could bring herself to eat was an avocado, which seemed to me considerably more stylish and exotic than apples in lieu of love. Her young man was a gifted carver, who had been sent out into the desert by the cruel pharaoh (pharaohs were always cruel—of this I was positive) in order to carve a giant sphinx for the royal tomb. Should I have her die while he was away? Or would it be better if he perished out in the desert? Which of them did I like the least? With the characters whom I liked best, things always turned out right in the end. (66)

As Vanessa matures, she turns from literature to life for inspiration for her fictions. She confesses, "I was a professional listener" (18), a prerequisite for professional writers, perhaps. She eavesdrops on conversations downstairs from her secret "listening post" upstairs via an air register that visitors to the Margaret Laurence Home in Neepawa can still observe. "If you put your ear to the iron grille, it was almost like a radio" (58), Vanessa explains. Intrigued by Edna's romance with the glamorous Jimmy Lorimer, Vanessa decides to "slip upstairs to my old post, the deserted stove-pipe hole. [But] I could no longer eavesdrop with a clear conscience" (83–84):

> Although I spent so much of my life listening to conversations which I was not meant to overhear, all at once I felt, for the first time, sickened by what I was doing. I left my listening post and tiptoed into Aunt Edna's room. I wondered if someday I would be the one who was doing the talking, while another child would be doing the listening. This gave me an unpleasantly eerie feeling. I tried on Aunt Edna's lipstick and rouge, but my heart was not in it. (77)

Later, when she overhears her aunt crying in her room, her view of true love is drastically revised, as reality explodes romance, teaching Vanessa a valuable but painful lesson about real life:

> Like some terrified poltergeist, I flitted back to the spare room and whipped into bed. I wanted only to forget that I had heard anything, but I knew I would not forget. There arose in my mind, mysteriously, the picture of a barbaric queen, someone who had lived a long time ago. I could not reconcile this image with the known face, nor could I disconnect it. I thought of my aunt, her sturdy laughter, the way she tore into her housework, her hands and feet which she always disparagingly joked about, believing them to be clumsy. I thought of the story in the scribbler at home. I wanted to get home quickly, so I could destroy it. (78)

Vanessa finally realizes that in real life lovers do not always live happily ever after. This epiphany is underlined dramatically by her apocalyptic vision of northern lights, which transform the yard of the Brick House into "a white desert [as] the pale gashing streaks of light pointed up the caverns and the hollowed places where the wind had sculptured the snow" (77).

Vanessa likes to write about death as well as love: "the death scenes had an undeniable appeal, a sombre splendour, with (as it said in Ecclesiastes) the mourners going about the streets and all the daughters of music brought low. Both death and love seemed regrettably far from Manawaka" (66). These are famous last words indeed. When her Grandmother Connor dies, and Vanessa glimpses the grotesque grief of the man behind the mask of the bear, she learns to distinguish reality from romance—the lesson in life that is at the heart of the maturation and creative process. She reflects, "I had not known at all that a death would be like this, not only one's own pain, but the almost unbearable knowledge of that other pain which could not be reached or lessened" (80). As Christian Riegel writes, "the experience of observing grief in others allows her a first-hand experience of how people react to death—an experience that ultimately affects the way she, too, grieves" (72).

Vanessa, "protected from the bizarre cruelty of such rituals" (188) by her youth, does not attend her Grandmother Connor's funeral. Instead, she plans to stage her own memorial service:

> I wanted now to hold my own funeral service for my grandmother, in the presence only of the canary. I went to the bookcase where she kept her Bible, and looked up Ecclesiastes. I intended to read the part about the mourners going about the streets, and the silver cord loosed and the golden bowl broken, and the dust returning to the earth as it was and the spirit unto God who gave it. But I got stuck on the first few lines, because it seemed to me, frighteningly, that they were being spoken in my grandmother's mild voice—*Remember now thy Creator in the days of thy youth, while the evil days come not*—(82).

Vanessa realizes that true art reflects real life, rather than an escape from reality. After her father dies in the title story "A Bird in the House," Vanessa recognizes the facts of death: "*Rest beyond the river.* I knew now what that meant. It meant Nothing. It meant only silence, forever" (105).[2]

But in "The Loons," the story after "A Bird in the House," Vanessa reduces Piquette Tonnerre to a romantic stereotype. Vanessa's vision of Indians is inspired by literature like Longfellow's *Hiawatha*. She asserts, "I was a devoted reader of Pauline Johnson at this age, and sometimes would orate aloud and in an exalted voice, *West Wind, blow from your prairie nest; Blow from the mountains, blow from the west*" (112). Piquette piques her interest when "I realised that the Tonnerre family, whom I had always heard called half-breeds, were actually Indians, or as near as made no difference" (112). Vanessa mythologizes the Métis girl: "my new awareness that Piquette sprang from the people of Big Bear and Poundmaker, of Tecumseh, of the Iroquois who had eaten Father Brébeuf's heart—all this gave her an instant attraction in my eyes" (112). Vanessa romanticizes Piquette: "It seemed to me that Piquette must be in some way a daughter of the forest, a kind of junior prophetess of the wilds, who might impart to me, if I took the right approach, some of the secrets which she undoubtedly knew—where the whippoorwill made her nest, how the coyote reared her young, or whatever it was that it said in Hiawatha" (112).

When Vanessa tries to interest Piquette in the loons, to learn "forest lore" (113), Piquette's rebuff deflates Vanessa's romantic conception: "as an Indian, Piquette was a dead loss" (114). Years later, when Vanessa meets Piquette in the Regal cafe, and Piquette's blank mask slips to reveal a desperate need to belong to a social order she rejected, Vanessa says, "I saw her" (117). Later still, when she learns of Piquette's death in the fire at the Tonnerre shack, Vanessa realizes Piquette "might have been the only one, after all, who had heard the crying of the loons" (120). The adult narrator recreates both Piquette's true poignance and her own childish misconception.

Vanessa learns an important lesson about reality and fantasy from her cousin Chris Connor, who comes to live in the Brick House to attend high school in the story "Horses of the Night." Chris is a dreamer who escapes harsh realities by creating romantic fictions for himself to inhabit. He explains, "I got this theory, see, that anybody can do anything at all, anything, if they really set their minds to it. But you have to... focus on it with your whole mental powers, and not let it slip away by forgetting to hold it in your mind. If you hold it in your mind, like, then it's real, see?" (131). He copes with Grandfather Connor's temper by blithely ignoring it, whereas Vanessa fights. He regales ten-year-old Vanessa with enchanting tales of his Criss-Cross Ranch at Shallow Creek, beyond Galloping Mountain, where he keeps his riding horses Duchess and Firefly. She imagines "the house fashioned of living trees, the lake like a sea where monsters had dwelt, the grass that shone like green wavering light while the horses flew in the splendour of their pride" (135). When Vanessa visits Chris three years later, after her father's death, she is shocked by the reality of the flyblown farmhouse and the work horses Trooper and Floss: "I guess I had known for some years now, without realising it, that the pair had only ever existed in some other dimension" (136).

During the war, Chris, a *traveller* (133), is hospitalized after he suffers a mental breakdown. He writes to Vanessa, "they could force his body to march and even to kill, but what they didn't know was that he'd fooled them. He didn't live inside it any more" (143). Vanessa realizes that this was "only the final heartbreaking extension of that way he'd always had of distancing himself from the absolute unbearability of battle" (143), a way "to make the necessary dream perpetual" (144).

Vanessa holds a private memorial service for Chris, with the miniature saddle he fashioned for her: "I put the saddle away once more, gently and ruthlessly, back into the cardboard box" (144), she recalls, as if burying it in a coffin. The word "gently" reflects affection for Chris, while "ruthlessly" suggests her rejection of the escape fantasy symbolized by the saddle. Whereas Chris uses fiction to escape from reality, Vanessa learns to employ fiction to understand real life. As Bruce Stovel observes, "Unlike the private world of Vanessa's cousin Chris, the imaginary world in Laurence's book is one that many people can walk into and inhabit" (95). In "Revisions and Disagreements"[3] on *A Bird in the House*, Laurence emphasizes how "Chris's dilemma impinged on V's life."

In the next story "The Half-Husky," when paperboy Harvey Shinwell torments Vanessa's puppy Nanuk, Vanessa fantasizes about revenge, but realizes that her fantasies are not realistic:

> Whenever I tried to work out a plan of counter-attack, my rage would spin me into fantasy—Harvey, fallen into the deepest part of the Wachakwa River, unable to swim, and Nanuk, capable of rescue but waiting for a signal from me. Would I speak or not? Sometimes I let Harvey drown. Sometimes at the last minute I spared him—this was more satisfactory than his death, as it enabled me to feel great-hearted while at the same time enjoying a continuing revenge in the form of Harvey's gibbering remorse. But none of this was much use except momentarily, and when the flamboyant theatre of my mind grew empty again, I still did not know what to do in reality. (151–152)

Vanessa is maturing to the point where she is no longer able to escape from reality into fantasy: "I no longer wove intricate dreams in which I either condemned Harvey or magnanimously spared him. What I felt now was not complicated at all. I wanted to injure him in any way available" (154). When she visits Harvey Shinwell's grim home, she realizes he himself is a victim of abuse. So, like Nanuk, "He wasn't safe to go free," although "this was probably not fair, either" (160).

In the final story, "Jericho's Brick Battlements," Vanessa, now twelve, and a would-be escape artist, like many adolescents and most Laurence heroines, is writing a tale of escape. Likewise, Laurence recalls, "I used to write up in my loft, leaving the little door open for light and filling scribblers with stories, one of which I recall took place in a nineteenth-century inn in Quebec, a place and time about which I could scarcely have known less" (*Dance* 68). Vanessa explains:

> The tale was set in Quebec in the early days of the fur trade. The heroine's name was Marie. It had to be a tossup between Marie and Antoinette, owing to a somewhat limited choice on my part, and I had finally rejected Antoinette as being too fancy. Orphaned young, Marie was forced to work at the Inn of the Grey Cat. *La Chat? Le Chat?* And what was Grey? They didn't teach French until high school in Manawaka, and I wasn't there yet. But never mind. These were trivial details. The main thing was that Marie overheard the stealthy conversation of two handsome although shabbily dressed *voyageurs*, who later would turn out to be the great *coureurs-de-bois*, Radisson and Groseilliers. The problem was now plain. How to get Marie out of her unpromising life at the inn and onto the ship which would carry her to

> France? And once in France, then what? Neither Radisson nor Groseilliers would marry her, I was pretty sure of that. They were both too busy with changing back and forth from the side of the French to the side of the English, and besides, they were too old for her.

Vanessa is beginning to become a realist who is no longer satisfied by mere fantasies of escape:

> I lay on the seat of the MacLaughlin-Buick feeling disenchantment begin to set in. Marie would not get out of the grey stone inn. She would stay there all her life. The only thing that would ever happen to her was that she would get older. Probably the *voyageurs* weren't Radisson and Groseilliers at all. Or if they were, they wouldn't give her a second glance. I felt I could not bear it. I no longer wanted to finish the story. What was the use, if she couldn't get out except by ruses which clearly wouldn't happen in real life? (165)

Just as desperate as Marie (or Margaret) to escape, Vanessa is nevertheless becoming a "moral realist," as Rosalie Murphy Baum notes: "Vanessa's progress as a writer, from a very early age, reflects her increasing grasp of 'real' life, her attempts to face reality" (201–202), she concludes.

Teenage Vanessa is "frantic to get away from Manawaka and from the Brick House" (186). The Brick House seems a prison, a "crusader's embattled fortress in a heathen wilderness" (11). Like the ladybird, Vanessa is "unaware that she possessed wings and could have flown up" (60). Morley claims that *A Bird in the House* is Vanessa's *spiritual odyssey*: "its themes are bondage, flight, and freedom" (42). Laurence insists *A Bird in the House* is about "captivity and freedom"; "A BIRD IN THE HOUSE explores aspects of Vanessa's need to free herself" (qtd. in Davies 341, 343). Claustrophobia increases as Vanessa matures, cresting in the concluding story, whose title, "Jericho's Brick Battlements," suggests a walled fortress; indeed, Vanessa's mother, Beth, claims that defying Timothy Connor is just "batting your head against a brick wall" (163). Jericho also suggests Joshua, and Vanessa is the young warrior who defies the stronghold: "I shouted at him, as though if I sounded all my trumpets loudly enough, his walls would quake and crumble" (184). Vanessa must learn that freedom is achieved not by *shouting* but by *singing*, not by war but art. In the words of Keith Richards, "You can build a wall to stop people, but eventually, the music will cross that wall. That's the beautiful thing about music—there's no defense against it. I mean, look at Joshua and fucking Jericho—made mincemeat of that joint. A few trumpets, you know?" (qtd. in Palmer 87). This is the lesson that Vanessa must learn—that language, like music, can liberate.

Vanessa, like Laurence, does eventually escape—to university in Winnipeg—liberated ironically by the sale of the MacLeod silver and Limoges china and her grandfather's old *bonds* (187). But, even though she escapes Manawaka, "I did not feel nearly as free as I had expected to feel" (187). Ultimately, she realizes that escape does not mean freedom. Freedom is achieved by acceptance, not negation. For Vanessa, like Laurence, freedom is realized not by running away from reality but by *writing* about it. Although archrebel James Joyce never returned to Ireland after the death of his mother, he wrote about Dublin obsessively from his exile in Zurich, for art sets one free.

Vanessa returns to Manawaka when her grandfather finally dies. His funeral, her first, is a revelation when the minister claims, "Timothy Connor had been one of Manawaka's pioneers" (188). Bored all her life by his repeated accounts of his epic journey, Vanessa finally realizes its true significance. Ironically, the funeral eulogy, by presenting him as a fictional character, makes him real to Vanessa. In her "Revisions and Disagreements" on *A Bird in the House*, Laurence emphasizes Vanessa's epiphany: "The pioneer bit now means something different to V than it did when she heard it from the old man, and was bored. Now she sees what it really meant."

After the funeral, Vanessa holds her own memorial service for her grandfather. She visits the stable-garage and his coffin-like chariot, the MacLaughlin-Buick, observing, "Rust grew on it like patches of lichen on a gravestone" (189). She recalls a "memory of a memory" of her childhood vision of her hero: "I remembered myself remembering driving in it with him, in the ancient days when he seemed as large and admirable as God" (190). She recalls "gazing with love and glory at my giant grandfather as he drove his valiant chariot through all the streets of this world" (166). She is surprised by his death: "Perhaps I had really imagined that he was immortal. Perhaps he even was immortal, in ways which it would take me half a lifetime to comprehend" (189).

Margaret Laurence experienced the same epiphany Vanessa MacLeod does. In "A Place to Stand On," the first in her collection of travel essays *Heart of a Stranger* (1976), she explains:

> The final exploration of this aspect of my background came when I wrote—over the past six or seven years—*A Bird in the House*, a number of short stories set in Manawaka and based upon my childhood and my childhood family, the only semi-autobiographical fiction I have ever written. I did not realize until I had finished the final story in the series how much all these stories are dominated by the figure of my maternal grandfather, who came of Irish Protestant stock. Perhaps it was through writing these stories that I

finally came to see my grandfather not only as the repressive authoritarian figure from my childhood, but also as a boy who had to leave school in Ontario when he was about twelve, after his father's death, and who as a young man went to Manitoba by sternwheeler and walked the fifty miles from Winnipeg to Portage la Prairie, where he settled for some years before moving to Neepawa. He was a very hard man in many ways, but he had had a very hard life. I don't think I knew any of this, really knew it, until I had finished those stories. I don't think I ever knew, either, until that moment how much I owed to him. One sentence, near the end of the final story, may show what I mean. "I had feared and fought the old man, yet he proclaimed himself in my veins." (5)

Twenty years later, after the death of her mother, Vanessa revisits Manawaka for the last time, visiting the family graves to grieve. But she says, "I did not go to look at Grandfather Connor's grave. There was no need. It was not his monument" (191). Instead, she visits the Brick House, called a "massive monument" to Timothy Connor on the first page of *A Bird in the House* (11). In *That House in Manawaka* Jon Kertzer demonstrates that the Brick House is Connor's monument. But I suggest that Vanessa's narrative is his real memorial, just as Laurence's Canadian stories constitute John Simpson's true monument. Perhaps Vanessa does compose her pioneer story, "The Pillars of the Nation," after all, but its title is *A Bird in the House*—just as Del Jordan does complete Uncle Craig's history of Wawanash County in Alice Munro's *Lives of Girls and Women*. The narrators, like their creators, have learned to free themselves for the future through fiction. In "Cages and Escapes in Margaret Laurence's *A Bird in the House*," Arnold Davidson concludes:

> Beyond the narrator who delimits her life's story, is the fictionalist who frees it. If in one sense the author is the exhibitor of cages, the proponent of the human condition, with all its limitation, then she is also the master of escapes. For Laurence, the last escape is art, the achievement of an extra dimension. The young Vanessa is an aspiring writer who composes imitation conventional romances. As an adult, she is a promising writer who explores the partly fictitious reality of her past. (100)

Kertzer claims Vanessa "wants to perfect the power of imaginative recall until it can roam freely through the past and forge an over-arching vision, which is sympathetic, creative, and human" (34). In *A Bird in the House* Margaret Laurence recreates in the character of Vanessa MacLeod the development of an artist who learns about life through the painful experiences of love and death and who progresses from romance to realism, freeing herself from the past through writing.

NOTES

1. Helen Buss examines the "identity theme" in "Margaret Laurence and the Autobiographical Impulse," and Peter Easingwood explores it in "Semi-Autobiographical Fiction and Revisionary Realism in *A Bird in the House*," with particular emphasis on metanarrative in "The Loons."
2. Laurence explains the autobiographical source of this: "On January 13, 1935, our father Robert Wemyss died of pneumonia. I have written about this in a story called 'A Bird in the House.' The story is fiction, but in that particular story, fiction follows facts pretty closely" (*Dance* 55).
3. Laurence's "Revisions and Disagreements" in the Special Collections at McMaster University catalogue her responses to her Knopf editor Judith Jones's requests for changes and deletions to the manuscript of *A Bird in the House*, which Jones urged Laurence to turn into a novel.

WORKS CITED

Abrams, M. H. *A Glossary of Literary Terms*. New York: Holt, Rinehart & Winston, 1993.

Baum, Rosalie Murphy. "Artist and Woman: Young Lives in Laurence and Munro." *North Dakota Quarterly* 52 (1984): 196–211.

Buss, Helen. "Margaret Laurence and the Autobiographical Impulse." *Crossing the River: Essays in Honour of Margaret Laurence*. Ed. K. Gunnars. Winnipeg: Turnstone Press, 1988. 147–168.

Capone, Giovanna. "*A Bird in the House*: Margaret Laurence on Order and the Artist." *Gaining Ground: European Critics on Canadian Literature*. Eds. Robert Kroetsch and Reingard M. Nischik. Edmonton: NeWest Press, 1988. 161–169.

Davidson, Arnold E. "Cages and Escapes in Margaret Laurence's *A Bird in the House*." University of Windsor Review 16 (1981): 92–101.

Davies, Richard A. "Half War/Half Peace: Margaret Laurence and the Publishing of *A Bird in the House*." *English Studies in Canada* 17 (1991): 337–346.

Easingwood, Peter. "Semi-Autobiographical Fiction and Revisionary Realism in *A Bird in the House*." *Critical Approaches to the Fiction of Margaret Laurence*. Ed. Colin Nicholson. Vancouver: U of British Columbia P, 1990. 119–132.

Fabre, Michel. "From *The Stone Angel* to *The Diviners*: An Interview with Margaret Laurence." *A Place to Stand On: Essays by and about Margaret Laurence*. Ed. George Woodcock. Edmonton: NeWest Press, 1983. 193–209.

Kertzer, Jon. *"That House in Manawaka": Margaret Laurence's A BIRD IN THE HOUSE*. Ed. Robert Lecker. Canadian Fiction Studies. Toronto: ECW Press, 1992.

Laurence, Margaret. *A Bird in the House*. Toronto: McClelland and Stewart, 1970.

———. "Books That Mattered to Me." *Margaret Laurence: An Appreciation*. Ed. Christl Verduyn. *Journal of Canadian Studies*. Peterborough: Broadview Press, 1988. 239-249.

———. *Dance on the Earth: A Memoir*. Toronto: McClelland and Stewart, 1989.

———. *Heart of a Stranger*. Toronto: McClelland and Stewart, 1970.

———. "On 'The Loons.'" *The Art of Short Fiction: An International Anthology*. Ed. Gary Geddes. Toronto: HarperCollins, 1993. 805–806.

———. *The Diviners*. Toronto: McClelland and Stewart, 1974.

Morley, Patricia. "The Long Trek Home: Margaret Laurence's Stories." *Margaret Laurence: An Appreciation*. Ed. Christl Verduyn. *Journal of Canadian Studies*. Peterborough: Broadview Press, 1988. 38–51.

Palmer, Robert. *The Rolling Stones*. London: Sphere Books, 1984.

Riegel, Christian. "'Rest Beyond the River': Mourning in *A Bird in the House*." *Challenging Territory: The Writing of Margaret Laurence*. Ed. Christian Riegel. Edmonton: U of Alberta P, 1997. 67–80.

Stovel, Bruce. "Coherence in *A Bird in the House*." *New Perspectives on Margaret Laurence*. Ed. Greta M. K. McCormick Coger. Westport: Greenwood Press, 1996. 81–96.

Oedipus and Anti-Oedipus, Myth and Counter-Myth: Sheila Watson's Short Fiction

DEAN IRVINE

THE OPENING PANORAMIC SHOT of the National Film Board documentary on Sheila Watson would (if one existed) likely capture the institution surrounded by gardens where her father, Dr. Charles Edward Doherty, was superintendent of the Provincial Mental Hospital in New Westminster, British Columbia (Bessai and Jackel, "Sheila Watson" 3). On the cover of Watson's collection *Five Stories* the reader is presented with the reproduction of the mental hospital, the *simulacrum* of a psychiatric institution to hold her five (formerly four) stories. Of her *Five Stories*, "Brother Oedipus," "The Black Farm," "Antigone," and "The Rumble Seat" collectively inscribe what Watson calls in her essay "Myth and Counter-Myth" a "mythic cycle" (125)—that is, a story cycle analogous to the Sophoclean myth of Oedipus recorded in his Theban cycle, *Oedipus Rex, Oedipus at Colonus,* and *Antigone*. Watson's Oedipal story cycle is inhabited by characters bearing the names of figures from classical Greek myth, but cast in the roles of the modern bourgeoisie and enacting what Roland Barthes describes as a "bourgeois myth" (147). Through the bourgeois figure of Oedipus, the keystone of Freudian psychoanalysis, Watson re-enters the psychiatric institution—the institution symbolizing "the massive structures of bourgeois society and its values" (Foucault 274)—and deconstructs its structures from the inside: "As you know," Watson's Oedipus says in "The Rumble Seat," "I was born and raised inside the walls of a madhouse" (*Five* 62).

The same hypothetical documentary film would probably pan the grounds of the University of Toronto, where Watson worked on her doctoral thesis, "Wyndham Lewis and Expressionism," under the supervision of Marshall McLuhan from 1957 to 1965. During this seminal period, Watson would emerge on the scene of Canadian modernism not only with her novel *The Double Hook* (1959), but also with her Oedipal story cycle and her critical essays, first published in Canadian periodicals in the 1950s and 1960s and later in the winter 1974–1975 special issue of *Open Letter, Sheila Watson: A Collection*. Taken together, the publication of her Oedipal story cycle and her critical essays in *Sheila Watson: A Collection* importantly represents Watson's dual capacity as a writer-critic through a composite fictional and critical text, as well as retrospectively recontextualizes the coincident compositional histories of her criticism and short fiction from the mid-1950s through the early 1970s. Of equal importance, given both his academic relationship to Watson and his concurrent theorization of social myths within this same historical frame, McLuhan's approach to cultural and social semiotics inevitably subtends the critical theory and method Watson employs in her essays, especially in "Myth and Counter-Myth." In his 1951 cultural critique *The Mechanical Bride: Folklore of Industrial Man*, McLuhan exhibits the objects of mass culture which, he claims, "represent a world of social myths or forms and speak a language we both know and do not know" (v). In "Myth and Counter-Myth," Watson historically contextualizes McLuhan's structuralist analysis of myth as a semiotic system in relation to Roland Barthes's *Mythologies*, published in 1957, and thus interpolates his interpretation of "'collective representations' of so-called mass culture as 'sign systems'" (119). Like McLuhan's *The Mechanical Bride*, Barthes's *Mythologies* deploys a structuralist reading of mass cultural semiotics and, by extension, of contemporary "social myths or forms." So given the genealogy of Watson's critical interpolation of both McLuhan and Barthes in "Myth and Counter-Myth," and given the contemporaneous composition of her Oedipal story cycle from the 1950s through the early 1970s, it is necessary to any historical recontextualization of Watson as a writer-critic to project a metacritical reading of her "mythic cycle" through her own structuralist analysis of social myths and forms.

Although absent from Watson's critique of Barthes's "structuralist activity" in "Myth and Counter-Myth" (qtd. in Watson 136), Jacques Lacan's lecture "Subversion of the Subject and the Dialectic of Desire in the Freudian Unconscious" neatly problematizes and historicizes the Oedipal complex in the context of a critique of Freudian psychoanalysis:

> [T]he Oedipus complex cannot run indefinitely in forms of society that are more and more losing their sense of tragedy. ... [A] myth is not enough to support a rite, and psychoanalysis is not the rite of the Oedipus complex. ... [E]ven if we did not have Freud's express, and sorrowful avowal, the fact would remain that the myth Freud gave us—the latest born myth in history—is no more than that of the forbidden apple, except for the fact, and

this has nothing to do with its power as myth, that, though more succinct, it is distinctly less oppressive. (316-317)

In his lectures conducted in the 1950s and 1960s, Lacan calls into question the Oedipal complex: for him, it is no longer the Oedipal myth, but the Freudian myth, "the latest born myth in history." For Gilles Deleuze and Félix Guattari in their extensive critique of the Oedipus complex, *Anti-Oedipus: Capitalism and Schizophrenia*, the Freudian myth of Oedipus has been reduced to the "familial complex" (58), the familial myth. For Barthes, again, the prevailing myth then and today is the bourgeois myth. Obviously we can no longer think about myth as an ancient and eternal story. Recognizing the historicity of myth, Barthes therefore problematizes the ahistorical concepts of the myth of origin and the origin of myth: "Ancient or not, mythology can only have an historical foundation, for myth is a type of speech chosen by history: it cannot possibly evolve from the 'nature' of things" (118). Deleuze and Guattari are particularly shrewd on this point of historical contention: "Oedipus is literary before being psychoanalytic" (134); in other words, the Freudian myth of Oedipus is inextricably linked to a literary history and a historical type of speech. (Hence Freud himself cites the Sophoclean myth of Oedipus [*circa* fifth century B.C.] as his literary source.) Yet myth, as a semiological system, is always anterior to a mythic form of literature; so a Sophoclean Oedipus is always already a second-order Oedipus; a Freudian Oedipus a third-order Oedipus; and so on, down the semiological chain of Oedipal signifiers. Clearly, then, there is no master Oedipus myth for Freud or, in our case, Watson to cite as origin. Barthes is therefore right to ask of the reader of contemporary social myths: "What is a myth, today?" (117).

According to Deleuze and Guattari, the Oedipal myth, today, has become its own "autocritique" (299). In *Mythologies*, Barthes also theorizes the autocritical function of myth: "the best weapon against myth is perhaps to mythify it in its turn, and to produce an *artificial myth*: and this reconstituted myth will in fact be mythology" (147). Barthes's joint examples of Saussurean linguistics and Freudian psychoanalysis as semiological systems illustrate the elements basic to the production of an artificial myth: "A signified can have several signifiers: this is indeed the case in linguistics and psycho-analysis. It is also the case in the mythical concept [as a signified]: it has at its disposal an unlimited mass of signifiers" (129). Watson's Oedipal story cycle thus constitutes what Barthes calls an artificial myth, an autocritique that takes the Freudian myth of Oedipus as its point of departure: it too has at its disposal a multiplicity of mythical signifiers. The constitutive Freudian myth is, to follow Barthes's semiological chain, "a second order semiological system" (123). For her Oedipal story cycle, therefore, Watson takes the second-order Freudian myth as a departure point for a third semiological chain. Applying Barthes's construction of an artificial myth to Watson's Oedipal story cycle, her "mythical form" (the mythical signifier) empties out the history of the Freudian myth of Oedipus only to reconstitute a whole new history through the "mythical concept" of Oedipus (the mythical signified) (126–129). The result is an artificial myth, a counter-myth. As an artificial, bourgeois myth, her Oedipal story cycle becomes—to cite Watson herself who, in turn, cites Barthes—"counter-mythical" (Barthes 149).

Watson's earliest story in her Oedipal cycle, "Brother Oedipus," immediately signifies as an artificial myth insofar as its title breaks with the literary referent of classical myth: Oedipus neither *has* a brother nor *is* he a brother in either the classical or Freudian myths. However, Oedipus does have a brother-in-law, Creon, Jocasta's brother (who becomes Watson's unnamed fraternal narrator); hence the foregrounding of a familial genealogy in the title as well as the presence of Oedipus's nameless wife and mother in "Brother Oedipus" signal the production of a familial myth and, ultimately, a bourgeois myth of Oedipus.

Moreover, to engage Watson's autocritique of bourgeois myth in "Myth and Counter-Myth," the Oedipal family in "Brother Oedipus" fictionally represents what she calls "a mythic middle class" (122). Furthermore, to transpose Deleuze and Guattari's dual critique of Freudian psychoanalytic and capitalist economic structures in *Anti-Oedipus*, Watson's "oedipalization" of "a mythic middle class" in the form of short fiction produces what they denominate an "Oedipal form" or "commodity form" of representation (134). According to Deleuze and Guattari's theory of literary consumption, "oedipalization is one of the most important factors in the reduction of literature to an object of consumption conforming to the established order… the *Oedipal form*" (133). "Brother Oedipus," however, strategically generates an autocritique of its own "Oedipal form" as an object of consumption through the "counter-mythical" form of Watson's artificial, bourgeois myth.

The Oedipus myth, today, exists as a commodity form and an object of conspicuous consumption. In their historical survey of commodity fetishism, *Female Fetishism: A New Look*, Lorraine Gamman and Merja Makinen claim that the concepts of "conspicuous leisure and conspicuous consumption" in Thorstein Veblen's *The Theory of the Leisure Class* (1899) have since characterized twentieth-century Western bourgeois society in that fetishism is a consequence not of the production of commodities (in a Marxian sense) but rather of their consumption (30). In producing a narrative of typical bourgeois "conspicuous leisure and conspicuous consumption," Watson's narrator, Brother Oedipus, relates: "Puss [Oedipus] and I had read Veblen together. We had hidden the book under the mattress and read it in the toilet behind locked doors.... We foreswore our heritage, played commuters, hobnobbed with the gardener and the cook, and damned the family dog as one of the symbols of our class. I thought the story might amuse Puss" (*Five* 11–12). Brother Oedipus recollects this anecdote about reading Veblen just after he is reminded of another anecdote about one of the so-called symbols of the "leisure class"—a story about a friend of a friend's dead dog, which he thinks might amuse Puss. The intervening Veblen anecdote becomes an object of "conspicuous consumption," a "non-productive consumption of time" afforded by the leisure class (Veblen 46). The Veblen book itself is regarded by Oedipus and Brother Oedipus as a fetish object, yet another symbol of the leisure class. In fact, Oedipus and Brother Oedipus reading Veblen itself represents a "conspicuous consumption," a way of exercising their "conspicuous leisure" and conferring their status as members of the leisure class, an act which Veblen defines as "immaterial evidences of past leisure" such as "quasi-scholarly or quasi-artistic accomplishments and a knowledge of processes and incidents which do not conduce directly to the furtherance of human life" (47). Even reading "Brother Oedipus" itself then becomes a kind of "conspicuous consumption." Watson's reader is therefore implicitly and complicitly a conspicuous consumer of Oedipal form: either the reader becomes what Barthes calls a "mythologist" who deciphers and demystifies the bourgeois myth, or becomes "a reader of myths" who responds to "the constituting mechanism of myth, to its own dynamics" and "consumes the myth according to the very ends built into its structure: the reader lives the myth as a story at once true and untrue" (139).

If "Brother Oedipus" represents a social myth or form subject to demystification, then it seems appropriate to ask what kind of society Watson represents. Through their critique of the Freudian myth of Oedipus, Deleuze and Guattari would describe the fraternal relation between Oedipus and Brother Oedipus as "a resurgence of the 'society without the father'" (80):

> This becomes even more clear when Freud elaborates the entire mythico-historical series: at one end the Oedipal bond is established by the murderous identification [of the father in form of neurosis], at the other end it is reinforced by the restoration and internalization of paternal authority [of becoming the father in the form of normalcy]. (81)

Deleuze and Guattari thus articulate the double bind of the society without the father, the double impasse of the Oedipal complex, where the individual unconscious is tied off by neurosis at one end and normalcy at the other. Oedipus's wife submits the same alternatives of normalcy versus neurosis to Brother Oedipus: "You sound like Oedipus. ... Perhaps you aren't normal like me, but mad like Oedipus" (14).

Deleuze and Guattari offer further insight into "Brother Oedipus" as society without the father, that is, as "the society of brothers who forbid themselves the fruit of the crime, and spend all of their time internalizing" (81). As such, we encounter Oedipus and Brother Oedipus fantasizing about symbols of the individual unconscious, the symbols of their class: "I have," Oedipus says while idly cultivating his rose garden and conspicuously consuming gin, "superannuated social consciousness and sent it to hook mats for senior citizens. I concentrate on growing things. The individual unconscious is in tune with these" (12). Echoing Oedipus, Brother Oedipus speaks symbolically of the willow tree, which literally has taken root in and damaged the drains of their mother's house next door: "And the individual unconscious scorns insurance. It is insured by the great vegetation myth which promises more than the insurance company can offer" (14). Both Oedipus and Brother Oedipus spend their time internalizing, mystifying, individualizing, even privatizing "social consciousness" in terms of the "individual unconscious." The individual unconscious takes stock of the contents of a bourgeois myth that is occupied by private property—that is, commodity fetishes encoded with archaic and mythical values. Oedipus and Brother Oedipus treat their roses and their willow tree as commodity fetishes; these fetishes are, in a Marxian sense, commodities attributed with use-value (in terms of property value) and invested with special "mystical" qualities. Furthermore, their mythification and mystification of the social in terms of the natural constitutes in Barthes's terms "bourgeois *pseudo-physis*" (170), which is, according to Watson's interpretation, "the variously masked and ambiguous structures which appear to operate in men like nature" ("Myth" 120). Neither the rose nor the willow tree is rooted in nature, but in false nature (*pseudo-physis*); their historical and social significance has been emptied out "so as to make them signify a human insignificance" (Barthes 155). Oedipus and Brother Oedipus only recognize themselves within the limits of these fetishistic and eternalized images of an individual, familial, bourgeois unconscious. Their bourgeois myth takes root, like the willow tree, in the "great" symbol of the bourgeois, the mother's house.

In contrast to what I identified earlier as the "Oedipal form" or "commodity form" of "Brother Oedipus," Deleuze and Guattari imagine an "Anti-Oedipal form" of writing freed from catholic signifier of Oedipus; that is, a form of writing which is "asyntactic, agrammatical, the moment when language is no longer defined by what it says, even less by what makes it a signifying thing, but what causes it to move, to flow, and to explode—

desire. For literature is like schizophrenia: a process and not a goal, a production and not an expression" (133). It is a kind of "schizophrenic" writing that resists "conspicuous consumption" and therefore signifies a continual production rather than a representation, a process instead of a product.

In opposition to the structuralist theory of Saussurean and post-Saussurean semiotics, Deleuze and Guattari's Anti-Oedipal theory of language generates a poststructuralist semiotics that extrapolates from Louis Hjelmslev's *Prolegomena to a Theory of Language*. Hjelmslev's theory and analysis of semiotic systems sets in motion the processual and reciprocal relation between the form as well as the purport of content and expression manifested in the sign, rather than the subordinated relation between signifier and signified. "Far from being an overdetermination of structuralism and of its fondness of the signifier," Deleuze and Guattari implore, "Hjelmslev's linguistics implies the concerted destruction of the signifier, and constitutes a decoded theory of language" (243). Extending from Saussure's discipline of semiology, however, Hjelmslev's linguistics also calls attention to sign systems other than language. Among the analogous semiotic systems that course through a decoded theory of language—an Anti-Oedipal theory which Deleuze and Guattari specify as "a linguistics of flows" (241)—are electric currents, molecular chains, and cloverleaf interchanges.

A linguistics of flows analyzes the decoded flows in semiotic systems that break through the structural limit of the signifier; it follows the flows of a "schizophrenic" form of writing, an Anti-Oedipal form. The task engaged by what Deleuze and Guattari call the practice of "schizoanalysis" (273) proposes to "de-oedipalize," "de-familialize," and "de-individualize" the unconscious through a process of decoding signifying chains of Oedipal codes. Applied to a textual system where, as Hjelmslev puts it, "[t]he text is a chain, and all the parts (for example, clauses, words, syllables, and so on) are likewise chains" (105), "schizoanalysis" decodes the chains of signifiers in a text. To risk vast oversimplification, the process of "schizoanalysis" thus involves decoding already encoded flows of linguistic information in a given textual semiotic. In short, to import the electronic semiotic of a television transmission, the signals are scrambled.

Given the medium of television circulating through Watson's fourth and final story in her Oedipal cycle, "The Rumble Seat," I will extend the metaphor of scrambling codes into a textual semiotic. The story itself stages a fictional television interview between Oedipus and Pierre Berton, which is watched on television by "our uncle," who is unnamed but presumably Brother Oedipus (or Creon), and narrated by one of Oedipus's children. The story begins with a scrambling of linguistic codes, causing in Deleuze and Guattari's terms "flows to circulate... to overcome a limit" of Oedipal or commodity form of representation (133). If the process "schizoanalysis" intends to "de-oedipalize" the unconscious, to scramble its codes, then the process of "The Rumble Seat" serves to "de-oedipalize" the Freudian myth of Oedipus, to scramble its Oedipal form. The process commences, as mentioned, with the scrambling of linguistic codes and proceeds to cross and transverse as many lines of communication as possible: television transmission, polylingualism, dialogue and trialogue (between interviewer, Pierre Berton, interviewee, Oedipus, and viewer, Creon), familial genealogies, highways, railroads, stairways, and institutional passageways. Moving Watson's short fiction through a linguistics of flows, for example, Pierre scrambles linguistic and mythic flows: "Panta rei, he said. Everything flows. But not fast enough. Nel mezzo del camin, on the throughway, we still find the Volkswagen with Laius behind the wheel" (58–59). Here the constitutive codes of the Oedipal myth circulate through an asyntactic, agrammatical, even "schizophrenic" textual system of flows. As an Anti-Oedipal form of writing, "The Rumble Seat" processes "a violence against syntax, a concerted destruction of the signifier, non-sense erected as a flow, polyvocity that returns to haunt all relations," called for by Deleuze and Guattari (133).

Such a radical break with and scrambling of conventional codes and lines of communication, however, is bound to provoke a counter-reaction. So threatened by Pierre's mechanistic analogies for human existence, Brother Oedipus first explodes at the television screen, "Are we a mechanized sequence, an organized seriality" (63), and later cries out against the "servomotor" (65), an automatic device that controls great amounts of power through a small input of power, thus maintaining constant performance of a mechanism, as an automatic pilot. In the circuit of electric currents that mobilize a linguistics of flows, Brother Oedipus thereby interjects as a kind of resistor, even as an autocritique, of the textual system of "The Rumble Seat." Yet Brother Oedipus is, of course, also subject to the same textual system, so that the purport of his linguistic content and expression is scrambled, and the form of his bilingual messages erratic (likely symptomatic of a generalized Canadian television viewer):

> Réflexes verbaux de la conversation française, our uncle remarked categorically from his place in front of the set. Provocation and instant retort. The confessionals are empty but the listening posts are crowded. Allons, du calme! Cela passera. Play it cool. Mufle! Abruti! Espèce de menteur! No need to translate. C'est vous qui nous avez trahis! You lied. Jamais. I too was deceived. Un livre de pain par jour ne me suffit pas! I can't live on that. Qu'est-ce qu'il vous fait? The walkout's out. Invade. Il gronde son père maintenant. The father-figure is an anachronism. Il n'y a plus d'enfants. We must open the freezers. La vie nous réserve bien des désillusions. The pack-

aging obscures the content. I was deceived by spinsters. Ce n'est que justice! That's the way the belly buttons. (60)

The textual semiotic of "The Rumble Seat" accommodates what Hjelmslev describes as the situation in which "any text that is not of so small extension that it fails to yield a sufficient basis for deducing a system generalizable to other texts usually contains derivates that rest on different systems," so that different stylistic forms, media, tones, idioms, vernaculars, regional languages, and national languages converge in the production of the text (115). "Given unrestrictedness (productivity) of the text, there will always be 'translatability'" (117), Hjelmslev writes of the production of a textual system such as "The Rumble Seat," a system which translates and incorporates into the form of short fiction a heterostructural as well as a heteroglossic semiotic.

The question of "translatability" leads into one of the most contentious issues concerning myth (especially in the 1950s and 1960s), which is confronted in "The Rumble Seat," namely, the theological debate over "demythologizing." In his book *The Comfortable Pew: A Critical Look at Christianity and the Religious Establishment in the New Age,* the subject of Watson's fictional interview, Pierre Berton writes: "If Christianity is to survive, it must, to use Bultman's [sic] term, 'demythologize.' Unless it cuts itself free from the clinging undergrowth of myth, it will be strangled" (120). Watson briefly entertains the concept of "demythologizing" in "Myth and Counter-Myth," "in the sense in which the word has been used in certain theological circles," but then cautions, "how much this demythologizing is strategic, only those who have given sufficient attention to Bultmann's polemic are competent to judge" (120). Bultmann's coinage of the term "demythologizing" in his essay "The New Testament and Mythology," as well as in others' subsequent volumes of arguments *against* and *for* the term, ultimately boil down to the question of whether there is "No need to translate," as Brother Oedipus says, or a need to translate the symbols and images of myth out of a mythological world view, though not into a modern scientific world view, but into a language "freed from any world view produced by man's thought, whether mythological or scientific" (Bultmann, *Jesus* 83). In "The Rumble Seat," Watson points to the present difficulty in constituting a "demythologized" Oedipus, which is to say, neither a historical-mythological Oedipus of the ancient world, nor a psychoanalytic Oedipus of the modern world, nor a literary-mythological motif of "myth today":

Dwellers in our native Thebes, he said, I am Oedipus who knew the famed riddle.

He seemed to be trying out a role.

> This is Toronto, Pierre said. Riddles are beside the point. Here we have obstruction, obscuritantism, and worse.
>
> We must, he said turning to Oedipus, demythologize.
>
> > For me it is too late, Oedipus answered, although since Protestantism has not yet fully acknowledged Freud there might still be time. For some I have already become a complex, for others a thematic design like the sphere, the cylinder, and the cube. (61)

After the abrupt failure of his own demythologization, his failure to translate himself from a mythological world into the modern world, Oedipus falls back upon his familial myth, recounting to Berton, his interviewer-analyst, the history of his childhood: "I was born and raised inside the walls of a madhouse..." (62). Oedipus himself becomes "oedipalized," re-encoded by the mythic signifier of Oedipus. He becomes a psychoanalytic Oedipus in dialogue with his analyst, a Freudian Oedipus, an Oedipus complex, playing a role in the sound-set of the unconscious.

In a circuitous way, so to speak, I have arrived at a conclusion to Watson's "mythic cycle." Rather than spin in the structuralist dialectic of Oedipal myth and counter-myth, the poststructural activity of decoding the Oedipal myth in "The Rumble Seat" marks the dramatic turn in Watson's story cycle away from her structuralist activity in "Brother Oedipus." "The difficulty of vanquishing myth," Watson writes of Barthes's counter-mythical strategy, "is that the very effort one makes in order to escape its stranglehold becomes in turn the prey of myth" (130). Through the example of Oedipus in "The Rumble Seat," Watson suggests, also, that Bultmann's demythologizing strategy is as vexed as Barthes's counter-mythical activity. Even when writing of Lewis, and simultaneously anticipating the implications of her own Oedipal story cycle and of her own literary-myth criticism, Watson also "would have been the first to challenge any claims of the structuralists to set up an absolute myth of their own" (136). From structuralism to poststructuralism, from myth to counter-myth, from Oedipus to Anti-Oedipus, Watson's engagements with myth cycle through the transitional phases of theory and fiction, the ever-changing territories and histories of her own and our own critical and creative activities.

WORKS CITED

Barthes, Roland. *Mythologies.* 1957. Abr. ed. Trans. Annette Lavers. London: J. Cape, 1972.

Berton, Pierre. *The Comfortable Pew: A Critical Look at Christianity and the Religious Establishment in the New Age.* Toronto: McClelland and Stewart, 1965.

Bessai, Diane, and David Jackel, eds. "Sheila Watson: A Biography." *Figures in a Ground: Canadian Essays on Modern Literature Collected in Honour of Sheila Watson*. Saskatoon: Western Producer Prairie Books, 1978.

Bultmann, Rudolf. *Jesus Christ and Mythology*. New York: Scribners, 1958.

Deleuze, Gilles, and Félix Guattari. *Anti-Oedipus: Capitalism and Schizophrenia*. 1972. Trans. Robert Hurley, Mark Seem, and Helen R. Lane. Minneapolis: U of Minnesota P, 1983.

Foucault, Michel. *Madness and Civilization: A History of Insanity in the Age of Reason*. 1961. Abr. ed. Trans. Richard Howard. New York: Random House, 1971.

Gamman, Lorraine, and Merja Makinen. *Female Fetishism: A New Look*. London: Lawrence and Wishart, 1994.

Hjelmslev, Louis. *Prolegomena to a Theory of Language*. 1943. Trans. Francis J. Whitfield. Madison: U of Wisconsin P, 1961.

Lacan, Jacques. "Subversion of the Subject and the Dialectic of Desire in the Freudian Unconscious." *Écrits: A Selection*. Trans. Alan Sheridan. New York: Norton, 1977. 292–324.

McLuhan, Marshall. *The Mechanical Bride: Folklore of Industrial Man*. New York: Vanguard, 1951.

Veblen, Thorstein. *The Theory of the Middle Class: An Economic Study in the Evolution of Institutions*. New York: Macmillan, 1899. Rpt. as *The Theory of the Middle Class*. Intro. by C. Wright Mills. New Brunswick, N. J.: Transaction, 1992.

Watson, Sheila. *Five Stories*. Toronto: Coach House, 1984.

———. "Myth and Counter-Myth." *Sheila Watson: A Collection. Open Letter* 3:1 (1974–75): 119–136.

Mapping Munro: Reading the "Clues"

ROBERT THACKER

> My connection was in danger—that was all. Sometimes our connection is frayed, it is in danger, it seems almost lost. Views and streets deny knowledge of us, the air grows thin. Wouldn't we rather have destiny to submit to, then, something that claims us, anything, instead of such flimsy choices, arbitrary days?
>
> —Alice Munro, *Open Secrets* (1994)

THIS QUOTATION IS FROM "The Albanian Virgin" (1994)—a story in which, perhaps, Alice Munro has strayed as far as she yet has (at least culturally if not geographically) from her "home place," Huron County, Ontario. In that straying, we seem both to have left Munro country and, at the same time, not: here is a narrator's voice, caught in the quintessential Munrovian act: divining, wondering over, articulating, and defining "connection"—connection to the world, connection to various parts of—what she has called "wooing"—the self, connection to others. "Connection. That was what it was all about," Munro wrote in "Chaddeleys and Flemings 1. Connection" (*Moons* 6). As I have been arguing for some time, for Munro *the* most urgent connection has been to her rural southwestern Ontario birthplace in Huron County, Wingham—the "home place," her cultural map, her profound talisman. Flowing through the town, we know, is a mystical and mythic river, the Maitland—called "The Meneseteung" by the Natives, as Munro noted in a brief 1974 essay:

> I am still partly convinced that this river—not even the whole river—but this little stretch of it—will provide whatever myths you want, whatever adventures. I name the plants, I name the fish, and every name seems to me triumphant, every leaf and quick fish remarkably valuable. This ordinary place is sufficient, everything here touchable and mysterious. ("Everything" 33)

Yes. "Everything [t]here is touchable and mysterious," as Munro has demonstrated, again and again. But our understanding of those demonstrations falters yet.

Last summer, I was asked to write an extended review essay focussed on the Munro criticism published since 1990; it will follow another essay on work published during the 1980s that appeared in the *Journal of Canadian Studies* in 1991. Munro has had, already, eleven single-author volumes published on her work, and her work comprises eight volumes plus the *Selected Stories* (1996). Among the books I looked at, most spectacularly, is James Carscallen's almost 600-page tome *The Other Country: Patterns in the Writing of Alice Munro* (1993). Ironically, given Munro's unwavering attachment to the short story as a form, most of these have posited—in effect—master narratives of putative discursive patterns, à la Carscallen. Equally, too, the journal-article count (via the *MLA International Bibliography*) is now approaching 200.

Another reviewer of two of these recent titles begins her comments by asserting that the books "belong to the 'second generation' of Munro criticism, one that is no longer in awe of the mimetic qualities detected by first-phase Munro critics but brings sophisticated theoretical frameworks to bear on her work" (Canitz 247). The notion of "'second generation'" seems a good point of departure for this brief examination of other ways of mapping Munro's writing, especially since some of the recent books are of doubtful worth; they establish their authors' presence and fulfill academic career needs—probably their most urgent function—but do very little for Munro studies. Indeed, much of this reviewer's vaunted "second generation" criticism merely reiterates the first using other terms.

Given this, I want to suggest another way of "Mapping Munro," one which seems to me most needed. First, I am struck by several things having to do with the relation of Munro's work to its critics. Foremost among these are the ways by which Munro's writing creates what amounts almost to an empathetic union among readers, critics most apparent among them. We are drawn to her writing not so much by its verisimilitude but rather by the feeling of being itself or, as I have said elsewhere in a review of *The Progress of Love* (1986), of just being a human being. Thus what seems to drive critics who have taken up Munro's work—and this is especially so of those who have embarked on book-length studies, I think—is a desire to articulate some personal relation to the work, to replicate in the criticism our feelings upon reading Munro's work. I certainly feel this myself.

What is more, a passage from "Circle of Prayer" (1986), which I quoted in that review, is relevant here: "What are those times that stand out, clear patches in your life—what do they have to do with it? They aren't exactly promises. Breathing spaces. Is that all?" (*Progress* 273). The beginnings of this passage are found in a draft holograph fragment of "Dulse" (*Munro Papers* 38.11.7), by the way, and that relation encapsulates a quality in Munro that seems ever to beckon reader and critic alike. The "progress" of insight, from momentary vision to larger understanding, fleeting, tentative, illusory, yet powerful. Standing back from this recent body of Munro criticism, I am struck by this same quality, the desire of the critic to, as Magdalene Redekop has written, identify "the story that I hear Munro telling *me*" (x). Each critic does this, of course, according to her or his lights—however bright or dim—seizing Munro's work most often at these very "clear patches"; that is, at those points of story at which her art is most evident, and most pointed. There is real consensus that it is never transparent, always elusive, with points of view and meanings compounding, patterns emerging out of other patterns. Katherine J. Mayberry has stated the matter succinctly:

> Munro's understanding of the function of narrative is mordantly paradoxical. Throughout her career, she has insisted on the existence of pre-linguistic experience, of a truth that originates outside of, independent of language. This truth is wholly experiential and wholly personal, never going beyond the bounds of individual perception. Particular and circumscribed, it would seem a simple truth, though as Munro's vision matures, its constitution grows increasingly intricate, its excision from the surrounding web of falsehoods, uncertainties, silence, and alternative perceptions increasingly difficult. But simple or complex, this truth admits little access. The approaches attempted by most of Munro's characters are memory and narrative—virtually equivalent faculties in that they both order past experience, re-collect lived moments within a chronological frame.

She concludes that in Munro "Narrative is finally not the province of truth; to tell is at best to revise, but never to perfectly revive" (540). What Mayberry calls "lived moments" here are Munro's "clear patches," "Breathing spaces"—insights based on moments or incidents that appear briefly in a draft or earlier story only to emerge as central in a later one. These need to be mapped, triangulated—not explained and paraphrased as they have been thus far.

Take as but one instance Munro's early story "The Peace of Utrecht" (1960). There, the narrator, Helen, returns to Jubilee, enters her childhood home and looks in the hallway mirror; in it, she sees

> the reflection of a thin, tanned, habitually watchful woman, recognizably a Young Mother, whose hair, pulled into a knot on top of her head, exposed a jawline no longer softly fleshed, a brown neck rising with a look of tension from the little sharp knobs of collarbone—this in the hall mirror that had shown me, last time I looked, a commonplace pretty girl, with a face as smooth and insensitive as an apple, no matter what panic and disorder lay behind it. (*Dance* 197–198)

The processes of self-analysis and self-understanding evident here are symbiotically conjoined in the relation of each author's narrator to her home place, and that textual trail is, as Mayberry suggests, intricate.

The importance of "The Peace of Utrecht" to Munro's *oeuvre* is evident, as is its demonstration of the fundamentally autobiographical connection the author has to her home place (see Thacker, "Connection"; and Weaver). Munro has called this her "first really painful autobiographical story" and, more to the point, she has returned to its circumstances again and again (Metcalf 58). The story meditates on the mother/daughter relation and that relation, as any reader of Munro knows, is central to her work: "The Peace of Utrecht," "Red Dress—1946," "Images," *Lives of Girls and Women*, "Winter Wind," "The Ottawa Valley," "Chaddeleys and Flemings: 1. Connection," "The Progress of Love," "Friend of My Youth." As Munro writes parenthetically in the uncollected story "Home" (1974), commenting metafictionally in her own voice on the opening pages of the story: "*Also the bit about Mother, who probably doesn't belong in this at all but I can't come in reach of her without being invaded by her*" (137). The mother's presence is but a single autobiographical instance in Munro's work, but it is one redolent with meaning, one that confirms the ongoing critique of being human—"being a human being"—that Munro continues. And mainly because she works through the short story, Munro offers what amounts to a persistent, recurrent, and multilayered attempt to articulate the mysteries of being—one that has left multiple traces, multiple "clues" for the critic.

This latter point needs to be asserted because of what is in the Munro archives at the University of Calgary. The materials there reveal numerous instances in which Munro may be seen trying to find a suitable place for this or that detail or story from her own past and, most often, out of her own home place. The multiple pieces in the archive demonstrate, too, in connection with various single texts, the need for better maps of Munro's work. These resources have been left largely untouched by critics—the most recent group as much as those who published books and articles in the 1980s.

An example. During the mid-1970s, after her first marriage had broken up and she had moved back to Ontario, Munro worked on the text for a book of photographs of Ontario scenes by Peter D'Angelo, which was to have been published by Macmillan. For reasons that are unclear, it never appeared—judging from the archival material, however, Munro spent a good deal of time working on her text. It is made up of short, Sherwood Anderson-like vignettes, few of which are more than a page or so; they are anecdotal, descriptive, and reminiscent. They are also haunting, looming. Among them is one entitled "Clues"; it goes like this:

CLUES

In a little glassed in side-porch, from which people can look out at the street, but not be seen themselves, very easily, the following things can be found, on window-sills or tacked up on the wall:

A calendar picture of a kitten asleep between the legs of a Great Dane, the dates torn off.

A photograph of Princess Anne as a child.

A Blue Mountain pottery vase with three yellow plastic roses.

Six shells from the Pacific coast.

The Lord is My Shepherd, in black cut-out scroll sprinkled with glitter.

An amber glass cream jug, from Woolworth's, with a bunch of wildflowers, drooping. White and orange daisies, white and purple money-musk.

Newspaper photograph of seven coffins in a row. Father, mother, five children. All shot by the father a few years ago in a house about five miles out of town (hard to find but most people have persisted, asking directions at the gas station on the highway and then at a crossroads store; most people have driven past).

[Typed, struck out] A mobile of blue and yellow paper birds, crude and lovely, made by a seven-year-old child at school, bobbing and dancing on undetectable currents of air.

[Replaced with, in Munro's hand] Some blue and yellow paper birds, cut by the wobbly hand of a seven year old child, strung from sticks so they bob delicately on undetectable currents of air.
(*Munro Papers* 37.13.11.f27–28)

Starkly, it is with material images such as this that the author of "Material" (1973) begins and, indeed, has always begun. During this period, certainly, Huron county material was prominent since her next book was to be *Who*

Do You Think You Are? (1978), but such home-place material is never far distant, though Munro's characters may be themselves.

A particularly good example of such a crux is "Miles City, Montana" (1985). It ends in book version with the parents, back in the front seat of their car heading east toward Ontario from B. C. yet again, the story's central excitement over and their younger daughter, Meg, now quite fine after her near brush with drowning in Miles City, Montana. As it ends, Munro refers once more to the image with which she began the story—the remembered drowning of eight-year-old Steve Gauley, his body carried across the field in her memory by the narrator's father, though the narrator doubts the veracity of that memory. Munro also develops a complicity between the parents and this child's drowning—only Steve's father, who never pretends that life is anything other than random, is exempt. The book version ends: "So we went on, with the two in the back seat trusting us, because of no choice, and we ourselves trusting to be forgiven, in time, for everything that had first to be seen and condemned by those children: whatever was flippant, arbitrary, careless, callous—all our natural, and particular, mistakes" (*Progress* 105). Passages like this stand out in Munro's work—they are, in fact, "Breathing spaces" (*Progress* 273), and they frequently end her stories without really concluding them. Most often, what is valued in Munro's stories is the precision and exactitude of emotion such passages communicate while, equally, articulating the utter uncertainty and ambivalence of being. Thus among the most interesting—and vexing—questions revealed by the Munro archives have to do with how she got to passages of the sort just quoted. Submerged beneath that paragraph are a welter of emotions, most seemingly contradictory, which are made the more identifiable by comparing them to, if you will, their earlier selves—reading the "clues"—a word redolent with meaning within the contexts of mapping Munro. Thus a paragraph from the end of a holograph draft of "Miles City, Montana": Munro has the main action of the story pretty much as it is in the published versions as she works toward an ending:

> Why wasn't it enough for me, just to have escaped? I didn't believe in escape, that was it. Andrew believed in luck, his luck, would celebrate it like a virtue. If something not lucky happened, he would shove that out of mind, ashamed. That was why he never mentioned the dead baby. And my mentioning it would seem a kind of sickening parade of misfortune, a dishonesty. I understood, I too hated fiercely that reply clinging onto miseries the gloating voices of women saying "a tragedy["] so how could we understand what we were doing. Who is ready to be a father, a mother, who is fit? I always hated to hear the names of my children called in the streets, I had hated when my own mother called me, in public, as I had hated the name she had chosen: Le-on-a. The names proclaimed the mother's ownership,

> her creation. I didn't want my own children burdened like that. What was more, I didn't want them to be crowning products of my life, so I was trying out this less definite, humourous, even tentative, statement of motherhood, thinking we would all be the better for it. (*Munro Papers* 7.3)

Though this passage appears to be an early version of the paragraph that now ends the story, it also contains elements of the paragraph that now immediately precedes Munro's return to her narrator's memory of Steve Gauley's funeral (103). The dead baby—an autobiographical detail—has also been dropped in the published versions. Yet the question asked here—"Who is ready to be a father, a mother, who is fit?"—and indeed the whole mystery of the narrator's wondering over her "escape" envelopes "Miles City, Montana" and, arguably, the whole of Munro's work. In what is perhaps her first perfect story, "Thanks for the Ride" (1957), Munro describes such moments with the phrase "*That headlong journey*"; they pose questions of wonder, unanswerable: "To find our same selves, chilled and shaken, who had gone that headlong journey and were here still" (*Dance* 56–57).

Implied within such passages too are the narrator's recollection of Steve Gauley's drowning and her recalled ambivalences over his death, her ambivalences toward her former husband, and her feelings for her then-about-to-be-visited relatives, both her father and her in-laws. Each of these invocations ties the narrator to Munro's home place, to the rural Ontario of her youth, to the British Columbia years of her twenties and thirties and to the circumstances of her first marriage. They are offered, too, from the perspective of the native returned to Ontario—though this perspective is largely mute.

The archives also reveal what might be called Munro's recurrences; that is, repeated returnings to an image or incident. From the late-1970s on, for example, she repeatedly tried to find a place for the threatened hanging now at the centre of "The Progress of Love" (1985). A most graphic instance of this, and perhaps more interesting, is the recurrence of an industrial decapitation that first appeared briefly in "Thanks for the Ride" (1957)—a story Munro submitted to Robert Weaver at the CBC in 1955—as the cause of Lois's father's death. There the incident is a brief description offered to Dick by Lois's mother (*Dance* 51). It has become a major focus in "Carried Away" (1991), where Louisa's imagined suitor, Jack Agnew, is killed in the same accident—and described in much more detail—his severed head being "carried away" by the factory owner, Arthur Doud, whom Louisa eventually marries. Such recurrent incidents seem more worth analysis than many, if not most, of the patterns Carscallen elaborates (Carrington).

These processes—revealed in their beginnings by the Calgary archives—have resulted in the emergence of a group of Munro stories that might themselves be seen as particularly indicative of her work's complexity. That is, owing to what seems their centrality to Munro's work—and one of the functions of this is the extent to which they attract critical attention—these most often serve as paradigmatic. "Walker Brothers Cowboy" (1968), "Images" (1968), "Thanks for the Ride," "The Peace of Utrecht," and "Dance of the Happy Shades" (1961) are arguably among this group in *Dance of the Happy Shades*. "The Flats Road," "Changes and Ceremonies," "Baptizing," and "Epilogue: The Photographer" from *Lives of Girls and Women* (1971). In *Something I've Been Meaning to Tell You* (1974), three stand out: the title story, "Material," and most especially "The Ottawa Valley" (1974). Most recently, "Meneseteung" (1988) and "Carried Away" (1991) appear to be qualifying and, though its authority is by no means clear, the *Selected Stories* both confirm and complicate this view. This is not the place to elaborate a theory of such selection; it is sufficient, however, to see such stories as embodying Munro's most urgent concerns and displaying her most artful effects—the very moments of being during which each of us, as readers more than as critics, recognize as resonant.

Such instances demand attention, as readers and as critics. Carscallen has this pointedly and well articulated: "In a way opaque to ordinary logic, though implicit in it, we know that the one and the many, like truth and reality, do not ultimately shut each other out. We are our fully individual selves; we are also members of one another—participants in a humanity that is no bare abstraction" (88). What this has meant to Munro criticism, and especially in the instance that is Carscallen's *The Other Country*, is that beyond moments of epiphany—"clear patches"—Munro's art remains about "Connection" (*Moons* 6). Human connections, perceptual connections, echoes of other stories, other incidents, other characters, other scenes, other. ... Alice Munro's art is shaped by a sensibility that ever sees, ever feels, the press of her own separateness, her own connection, her own being. And ours. And because of this, and especially because Munro's work is in the short story form, it is an art that demands mapping in ways not yet done. To my mind, all such maps begin in Calgary.

WORKS CITED

The Alice Munro Papers: First Accession. Comp. Jean M. Moore and Jean F. Tener. Eds. Apollonia Steele and Jean F. Tener. Calgary: U of Calgary P, 1986.

The Alice Munro Papers: Second Accession. Comp. Jean M. Moore and Jean T. Tener. Eds. Apollonia Steele and Jean F. Tener. Calgary: U of Calgary P, 1987.

The Alice Munro Papers: Third Accession. Comp. Jean M. Moore and Jean F. Tener. Eds. Apollonia Steele and Jean F. Tener. Calgary: U of Calgary P, n.d.

Canitz, A. E. Christa. Rev. of *The Other Country* by James Carscallen and *The Tumble of Reason* by Ajay Heble. *University of Toronto Quarterly* 65 (1995–96): 247–250.

Carrington, Ildikó de Papp. "What's in a Title?: Alice Munro's 'Carried Away.'" *Studies in Short Fiction* 30 (1993): 555–564.

Carscallen, James. *The Other Country: Patterns in the Writing of Alice Munro.* Toronto: ECW, 1993.

Mayberry, Katherine J. "'Every Last Thing… Everlasting': Alice Munro and the Limits of Narrative." *Studies in Short Fiction* 29 (1992): 531–541.

Metcalf, John. "A Conversation with Alice Munro." *Journal of Canadian Fiction* 1:4 (1972): 54–62.

Munro, Alice. *Dance of the Happy Shades.* Fore. Hugh Garner. Toronto: McGraw-Hill Ryerson, 1968.

———. "Everything Here Is Touchable and Mysterious." *Weekend Magazine* [*Toronto Star*] May 11, 1974: [33].

———. *Friend of My Youth.* Toronto: McClelland and Stewart, 1990.

———. "Home." *New Canadian Stories: 74.* Eds. David Helwig and Joan Harcourt. Ottawa: Oberon, 1974. 133–153.

———. *Lives of Girls and Women.* New York: McGraw-Hill, 1971.

———. *The Moons of Jupiter.* Toronto: Macmillan, 1982.

———. *Open Secrets.* Toronto: McClelland and Stewart, 1994.

———. *The Progress of Love.* Toronto: McClelland and Stewart, 1986.

———. *Selected Stories.* Toronto: McClelland and Stewart, 1996.

———. *Something I've Been Meaning to Tell You: Thirteen Stories.* Toronto: McGraw-Hill Ryerson, 1974.

———. *Who Do You Think You Are?* Toronto: Macmillan, 1978.

Redekop, Magdalene. *Mothers and Other Clowns: The Stories of Alice Munro.* London and New York: Routledge, 1992.

Thacker, Robert. "Connection: Alice Munro and Ontario." *The American Review of Canadian Studies* 14 (Summer 1984): 213–226.

———. "Go Ask Alice: The Progress of Munro Criticism." *Journal of Canadian Studies* 26 (Summer 1991): 156–169.

———. "Munro's Progress." Rev. of *The Progress of Love* by Alice Munro. *Canadian Literature* 115 (1987): 239–242.

Weaver, John. "Society and Culture in Rural and Small-Town Ontario: Alice Munro's Testimony on the Last Forty Years." *Patterns of the Past: Interpreting Ontario's History.* Eds. Roger Hall, William Westfall, and Laura Sefton MacDowell. Toronto: Dundurn, 1988. 381–402.

Hands and Mirrors: Gender Reflections in the Short Stories of Alistair MacLeod and Timothy Findley

LAURIE KRUK

WHAT DO THE SHORT STORIES of Alistair MacLeod and Timothy Findley have in common, and how do they "reflect" and "reflect on" gender? Seemingly old-fashioned MacLeod, his roots in the oral tradition and Cape Breton's Celtic culture, described by Michael Ondaatje as "one of the best short story writers in Canada"[1]... and Findley, a publicly gay or homosexual writer,[2] whose critically popular work has been described as both "postmodernist" in form and "feminist" in outlook? While Findley has been noted for creating "remarkable women" possessing "hyper-realistic sight," as one critic puts it (Murray 217), the heterosexual MacLeod's work is presented from a distinctively masculine (though not masculin*ist*) perspective. Aside from the excellence of the stories in question, initially, their differences are more apparent than any similarities. Yet I propose to argue that the visually-oriented Findley and the verbally-oriented MacLeod travel over some of the same territory. Both writers, for instance—whether comfortable or not with the increasingly fuzzy term "realist writer"—believe strongly in getting at the "real." In interview, MacLeod described realist writing simply as "telling the truth as I happen to see it" ("Exiles" 159); Findley redefined "realism" as placing "the anchor in the *real* heart, the *real* spirit and the *real* turmoil of *real* life" ("Edge" 18).[3] At the same time, Findley added—not surprisingly, given his earlier acting career—that "theatricality" is a "very positive thing" and "writing is a performance art" ("Edge" 19, 3). Consequently, Findley appears to approach the issue of gender identity from the view endorsed by Judith Butler in *Gender Trouble*, one described as "performative—that is, constituting the identity it is purported to be. In this sense, gender is always a doing, though not a doing by a subject who might be said to preexist the deed" (24–25). Obviously, neither writer presents the rigorously deconstructive philosophy Butler advocates; both men, it must be acknowledged, may be characterized as adhering to "a metaphysics of substance that confirms the normative model of humanism as the framework for feminism" (20). Indeed, that is the framework within which I am operating. I take a largely social psychology approach to the discussion of gender and treat these male authors' "gender reflections" as aspects of this (largely) realist fiction's ability—for this (female) reader, at least—to be a compelling "representation" of certain aspects of our lives as men and women, lives which are both emphatically embodied and culturally constructed.[4]

Yet Findley's emphasis on the *performative* aspects of writing does point to a significant divergence in outlook from MacLeod. And this divergence will be revealed through my focus on their "reflection" of gender relations and identities in their short stories. That is to say, while MacLeod's treatment of men and women returns us, powerfully, to our physical and sensual existence, Findley probes the performative aspects of our social and sexual roles as gendered beings. In her review of *Dinner Along the Amazon*, Barbara Gabriel writes, "Findley's most radical politics are the politics of gender" (89). He utilizes his admittedly "other" perspective, as a gay man, to reflect on the ways that gender roles entrap both sexes. In *Headhunter*, his heroine Fabiana declares, "It's a drag act—men pretending to be men—women pretending to be women"(341). Alternatively, MacLeod's short stories frequently draw our attention to his characters' work-marked *hands*. This repeated detail creates a synecdochic effect that reinforces the presentation of his very physical characters as not only shapers of, but also shaped by, the surrounding natural world. Meanwhile, one of Findley's guiding metaphors appears to be the *mirror*, linked in turn to his recurring theatrical motif of masks in particular and performance in general. Having established their difference in approach to gender identities and relations, by means of an overview of this contrasting imagery, I will analyze a story by each author that addresses similar concerns about masculine identity. The stories to be discussed offer moving variations on the shared theme of the lost, sacrificed father: MacLeod's acclaimed "The Boat" (*Gift*) and Findley's "Stones" (*Stones*).[5]

Short stories are often neglected by literary critics, viewed as drafts for novels, or as supplements to that legitimate project. Certainly MacLeod, who has built his career writing only short stories, thus far,[6] disproves this view. His stories owe much to the oral tradition, and as Janice Kulyk Keefer notes, "Often he seems to sing rather than tell his stories" (182). By incorporating into his prose sonorous Gaelic rhythms and folkloric repetition, MacLeod enters the company of bards and storytellers. Except for two ("The Tuning of Perfection" [*Birds*] "The Golden Gift of Grey" [*Gift*]), all of MacLeod's stories take advantage of the intensity of a first-person narrator. More importantly, all of them focus on a male protagonist, heightening their "autobiographical," and masculine, quality.[7] By contrast, Findley's short stories are more varied in form and style, and may be described as exploring the "experimental" aspect of the modern short story in its more self-consciously literary development. The first things Findley wrote were short stories, just as his earliest reading experiences involved "the self-contained entity, [the story] that is taken at one dose" ("Edge" 1). The fact that several of his stories were related to plays he wanted to write ("Daybreak at Pisa," "Out of the Silence"[*Dinner*]; see also "Edge" 116), or novels such as *The Last of the Crazy People* (1967) ("Lemonade" [*Dinner*]) and *Headhunter* (1993) ("Dinner Along the Amazon" [*Dinner*]) does not diminish them as separate entries in this genre. But it does suggest that his stories may be more justly seen as experiments in narrative and subject matter. Mary Louise Pratt has suggested that the short story is the place "to introduce new (and possibly stigmatized) subject matters into the literary arena" (187). If that is true, then the exploration of such matters would appear here first. For instance, in Findley's "Minna and Bragg" and "A Gift of Mercy" (*Stones*), he introduces, for the first time, an explicitly homosexual protagonist; two later Minna and Bragg stories tackle issues of gay identity and its contradictions ("A Bag of Bones," "Come as You Are" [*Dust to Dust*]; see also the collection's "Dust"). While homosexuality was either hinted at (or the heterosexuality of his characters subtly questioned) in other places within the Findley canon, Bragg is the first male protagonist whose homosexuality is not only evident but also central to the story. At the same time, while increasingly open about his own homosexuality, Findley defies narrow categorization. He notes that "I'm not turning my back on [homosexuality], and I'm perfectly happy to have it said, 'He is a homosexual' in any biographical material. But I just don't think I want to be collected exclusively in gay anthologies. ... I want my world to be wider than my sexuality" ("Edge" 9–10).

In making "The Case for Men's Studies," Harry Brod has said, "While women have been obscured from our vision by being too much in the background, men have been obscured from our vision by being too much in the foreground" (41). This intriguing insight has motivated my exploration of the two authors' portrayal of men. If MacLeod's tendency is to focus on the totality of the individual's freedoms and limitations, Findley's stories highlight the contradictions and burdens of what social psychologists call the "sex or gender role" (Pleck). There is ample evidence within his fiction that Findley's distinctive perspective as a gay man leads him to treat sympathetically women trapped or exploited by sexual stereotyping, as well as to probe deeply into traditional social or cultural expectations of men. Don Murray has delineated Findley's "optical imagery," and its relationship to themes of physical and psychic survival. He includes among it the use of sight "to locate oneself, especially in stories where mirrors are prominent, in order to confirm one's existence" (201). Thus, Findley's use of the mirror in his stories aptly "reflects" his special consciousness not simply of problems of psychological identity, but of the constructedness of gender identity.[8] For instance, in "Lemonade" (*Dinner*), Renalda Dewey's descent into alcoholism and rejection of her son appears to be facilitated by her own entrapment by a gender role that has outlived its usefulness. The woman described as formerly "one of the most beautiful... you could see anywhere in the world," loses her main audience after her husband is killed in the Second World War. Her main activity within the home consists of her morning "performance" as wealthy lady and adored mother. She must reconstruct her feminine identity, with the aid of cosmetics, before her lonely son can enter the sanctuary of her bedroom. Looking in the mirror, for her, becomes a confirmation of the success of her role-playing, yet, increasingly, this image is no longer sufficient: "She looked into the mirror. It was as though she couldn't find herself there. She had to go very close to it and lean one hand against the table to steady herself and she had to almost close her eyes before she found what she was looking for" (15). Her eventual suicide is foreshadowed by her stagnation in a kind of role-playing that lacks the appropriate audience, trapping her in a static, silent image like the "floating figure in a Japanese print... the mime" she resembles as she prepares her toilette.

Similarly, the poet Annie Bogan, in "The Book of Pins" (*Dinner*), neurotically obsessed with controlling or "pinning" her environment, focusses on her image in a mirror across the room, which is once again described as "Japanese" (237).[9] She seeks the mirror's confirmation that she is not only "dressed" and "erect" but "immensely real" (248). The story draws attention to her obsession with mirrors by starting and finishing, in a kind of chiasmus, with the same description of the same old women reflected in the mirrors in the hotel lobby. Her fascination with "fixing" or "pinning" the world around her into artistic figures gives Annie a kind of sterile self-absorption that would be dangerous to others if it were not ample evidence of the (suicidal) fragility of her own psyche.

Vivien Eliot, in "Out of the Silence" (*Dinner*) also stares into her mirror for long periods of time, as if questioning not only her sanity, but the contribution of male-dominated society (represented by both husband and doctor), to the undermining of that sanity. This use of the mirror reflection to offer reassurance regarding the achievement of a proper social or sexual image reappears in several places in Findley's short stories. "Dinner Along the Amazon"'s Fabiana summarizes her acceptance of a passive role as the woman "chosen" by the desiring suitor with her reference to her younger self as always "sitting in the front seat, watching in the mirror" (290). "Almeyer's Mother" (*Stones*) finds comfort in watching herself—in the mirror—lunching with her son and daughter-in-law in the stately Royal Ontario Museum cafeteria. The image freezes them in their appropriate social and gender roles as a family. "*This is us*, the picture informed her, *sitting where we belong*" (177). In "Losers, Finders, Strangers at the Door" (*Dinner*), Daisy McCabe, struggling to maintain her ladylike role as "Mrs. Arnold McCabe" against her despairing rage at the situation her husband's unusual sexual desires have placed her in, refers bitterly to the confirmation of her mirror that "the loveliness—the innocence" is gone. In her case, the innocence may really be the ignorance of people's true complexity: a knowledge that is stifled by rigid gender identities, Findley suggests.

Men, too, are presented gazing into mirrors in Findley's stories, but often in a dramatization of a questioning, rather than a confirmation, of their various roles or personae, including gender roles. Bragg, in "A Gift of Mercy" (*Stones*), glances in the mirror "the way most people do who don't want to see themselves" (36); Ishmael, in "Hello Cheeverland, Goodbye" (*Dinner*) briefly regards "his whole self" with horror in the bathroom mirror before turning away (185). And in "Masks" (*Stones*), the reclusive Professor Glendenning catches a glimpse in the mirror of the "unmasked" self that he discovers later when trying on the Japanese fox masks at the Royal Ontario Museum (66). In a more explicit example of the imprisoning potential of gender roles, Bud, in "Real Life Writes Real Bad" (*Stones*), is obsessed with the monstrous form his male body appears to present: "Every time he looked [in a mirror], you might have thought he'd never seen himself in mirrors or photographs before. ... He always cringed while peering at himself through narrowed eyes—a voyeur watching through a window. 'Look at his hands!' he would say, *as if the person in the mirror wasn't him*, 'Look at the size of his bloody hands, Neil!'" (156, emphasis added). Bud's alienation from his (reflected) body underscores his own emotional imbalance, while symbolizing men's equal entrapment in gender roles or identities that may not fit their needs or personalities.

Alistair MacLeod, on the other hand, draws our attention precisely to *that* other: the life of the body, male or female, within the larger, natural environment. This dynamic is frequently figured by the *hand*. Gender roles in his fictional world appear to follow the age-old prescription of men's and women's separate spheres: the woman ruling the household and the man providing for his family by means of physically demanding, dangerous work. However, in the harsh, maritime environment of the stories, these roles are equally important. So while this segregation of the sexes into traditional roles clearly has a restrictive aspect—often forcing the next generation away from the community, to escape rigid gender roles through formal education and greater opportunities—it also strengthens, grounds and ennobles those who stay. While Findley directs our attention to seeing, and, more politically, to *being* seen, MacLeod reminds us, with his focus on the hand, of *doing*: shaping, but also being shaped by, one's environment. MacLeod's stories evoke a time and place where people do not pay, as many urban professionals now do, for "the pleasures of perspiration" ("The Closing Down of Summer," *Birds* 23) and one's physical nature is an integral factor in determining success, or even survival. The body in MacLeod's world serves an important purpose, in its capability and endurance, and is not simply a token in the social games that Findley's more privileged, urbanized people have leisure to play. Indeed, in the same way that memories are often experienced as being carried by the physical body, these stories might be described as "embodied" narratives. For at the beginning of "Vision" (*Birds*), MacLeod describes not "the time around scars," as Michael Ondaatje did in the poem of that name, but the psychic scar, "medallion of... emotion," that forms around a powerfully told story. The scarring wound that MacLeod introduces to make his storytelling analogy is, not surprisingly, inflicted on the hand ("Vision," *Birds* 128).

Just as the hands are scarred, but also strengthened, by their labour, so MacLeod's people are moulded into roles that, if narrow, still carry deep satisfactions for some. MacLeod's stories are deemed by Colin Nicholson "elemental fictions" (90) and Janice Kulyk Keefer also uses the word "elemental" to describe the embrace between husband and wife that occurs at the end of "In the Fall" (*Gift*). There, the wife's long hair is associated with "the wind and snow whirling round them," as well as the mane of the loyal horse the husband agrees to sell for slaughter. It at first appears that MacLeod is propagating the familiar (and in much feminist analysis) patriarchal linking of women with nature. Yet his descriptive focus on the detail of the hand, and the animal and natural world surrounding his characters, is applied to both men and women. It reinforces MacLeod's vision of humanity as inevitable participants within the cycle of nature, however foolishly we ignore and defy or disrupt it.

Nicholson observes that in MacLeod's stories "identity and relationships are very much prefigured in imagery associated with the human hand" (93). But hands themselves feature as key indices in MacLeod's stories, not just of choice of work but of character, and of gender role, with its mixture of limitations and opportunities. Returning to "In the Fall," Janice Kulyk Keefer remarks on the correlation of gender role with hand description: "The narrator tells us how, whenever his mother does speak, 'She does something with her hands. It is as if the private voice in her can only be liberated by some kind of physical action'" (184). Although this detail does suggest an entrapment in the daily domestic work of the traditional, rural woman's role, elsewhere MacLeod's heroines are described, along with their hands, as strong and independent and decidedly practical, in the face of their men's tendency toward impetuous schemes and sentimental loyalties. Hands, those most subtle and supple of tools, are more often described as defined by their labour in these stories. The father's left hand and arm are enlarged by his work as a stevedore in "In the Fall" (*Gift*), while the miner father of "The Vastness of the Dark" (*Gift*) has lost "the first two fingers from his right hand" (25) in an accident with dynamite. Violence flows from the paternal hand in this story as well, as the narrator describes his father inadvertently injuring him by flailing out in his sleep and once, in a drunken rage, putting his hand through a window. This defiantly self-destructive act suggests the father's wordless protest at his entrapment by both economic circumstances and gender role. The damage done to the father's hand is more than symbolic of latent frustration, however, as mother and son together pray "that no tendons were damaged and that no infection would set in because it was the only good hand that he had and all of us rode upon it as perilous passengers on an unpredictably violent sea" (33). As if emphasizing all that rides on the work of the hand, the hands of MacLeod's people are almost always large, even "gigantic" ("The Vastness of the Dark," *Gift* 28) or "massive" ("The Golden Gift of Grey," *Gift* 101), as are the people. Even the women share in this characteristic, having "powerful, almost masculine hands" ("Vastness," *Gift* 37) or "strong brown hands" ("Vision," *Birds* 142).

As well, the divided state within a family is represented, in "The Return" (*Gift*), by means of a division of hands: Alex's right hand is squeezed almost painfully by his nostalgic father as they arrive by train in his home village. All the while, he is aware of his left hand lying peacefully, painlessly, beside his urban, unimpressed mother's right, "on the green upholstered cushion" (72). Alex's grandmother has "powerful hands," while his grandfather's are described as "very big" (76); the strength with which they each swing Alex up into the air when they greet him reveals a life of—and their pride in—hard physical work. The grandfather's grimy hugging of Alex after his shift at the mine, a hug which tests the boy's endurance and covers him in coal dust—marking him with the traces of a masculine gendered economy—expresses the ambivalence many of MacLeod's protagonists feel toward their birthplaces, and the traditional gender roles associated with them. Like the hug, these places comfort but also constrict. It is no accident that the callous and vulgar salesman, heading back to Toronto, who offers the hero a ride in "The Vastness of the Dark" (*Gift*) is described as having "very white and disproportionately small" hands (42). If hands in

MacLeod are an index of character as well as lifestyle, then his "very white" hands reflect not simply his class, but also his personal inferiority to the local people he so easily dismisses, including the widowed women whose loneliness he exploits. MacLeod's stories present an elegiac treatment of a passing way of life, not simply an economic one, but also a philosophical or spiritual one. If his characters share certain traits, as suggested by the detail of the hand, this is in the interest of impressing on the reader, by the folktale technique of repetition, the image of a community of men and women who were not simply strong, but big—a bigness which clearly has a spiritual or emotional quality. As he says of the doomed animal breeder in "As Birds Bring Forth the Sun" (*Birds*), "He was a man used to working with the breeding of animals, with the guiding of rams and bulls and stallions and often with the funky smell of animal semen heavy on his *large and gentle hands*" (120, emphasis added). The conjunction of largeness and gentleness is significant, as it suggests not the stereotypical male role of aggressor, but a controlled, channelled strength. And the detail of the smell of animal semen reinforces the stories' presentation of human and animal world not as separate spheres, but linked and interacting. MacLeod's love for his people brings into being stories that, in their solemn beauty and widespread appeal (translated into languages as diverse as Russian and Urdu [Pakistani]: "Exiles" 3), testify to the life-giving power of fiction.

Despite their different interests, Findley and MacLeod have each written a story that presents, from a first-person perspective, the son's relationship with a father whose end defines a conflict between the individual man and his society's vision of "Manhood." But here, Findley puts aside the image of the mirror to address the male gender role, and how it is "reflected" from father to son, through a pattern of natural imagery—flowers, stones, hands, the sea—more common in MacLeod's work. David Max, father of Ben Max, the narrator of "Stones," contentedly runs a flower shop along with his wife and three children on the outskirts of Rosedale until the Second World War comes along. When it does, he is among the first to sign up. His theatrical announcement, "Children... I am going to be a soldier" (200), suggests a certain pride in putting on a role that is still rewarded in the theatre of our society. Ben is frightened, but his older brother, Cy, "crowed with delight and yelled with excitement. He wanted to know if the war would last until *he was a man* and could join his father at the front" (200, emphasis added).

This contrast between the two brothers is exploited by the father when he returns, four years later, discharged from duty for deserting his men at the disastrous battle of Dieppe. In a grim ceremony that seems to parody the theatrical moment in which David Max announced his decision to join in the war, he is paraded in the Exhibition grounds before his family with other discharged, wounded men. Already seen as a "failure" as a male, Ben now bears the brunt of his disturbed father's wrath. For as if recognizing in his younger son his own weakness, the alcoholic father, stigmatized by his "dishonourable discharge," turns on Ben. When Ben obeys his terse orders unquestioningly, the father taunts him with the notion of rebellion, which would threaten the filial bond but strengthen Ben's presumed masculinity through a display of defiance. The crisis occurs when David Max drunkenly assaults his younger son: "One night, he came into the bedroom where I slept in the bunk-bed over Cy and he shouted at me *why don't you fight back?* Then he dragged my covers off and threw me onto the floor against the bureau" (212). This attack reveals the savagery released in a shame-filled man who failed to "do his duty" and die with his men. Before the battle of Dieppe, Ben learns, his father, a Captain, was considered a "natural leader" and it was asserted that his men "would have followed him anywhere" (215).[10] Once David's dream of upholding the law of honour, based upon the stoical aspect of the male gender role,[11] is shattered, all he can do is take out his frustrations on his too-obedient son, in the guise of instilling in him the more useful, as it now appears, law of the jungle.

David Max's self-hatred next leads him to assault his wife viciously. This attack is precipitated by a humiliating confrontation with a survivor of Dieppe determined to pronounce publicly Max's cowardice. That evening, the children find their mother "lying on the sofa... *her hands* broken because she had used them trying to fend off the blows" of the hammer he attacked her with (214, emphasis added). David is then institutionalized in the Asylum for the Insane on Queen Street. Turning away from his family, he joins other outcasts of society—gender rebels: "whores and derelicts"— and dies unmourned by his children. Only Ben, the "failure" at masculinity, cares enough to carry out his father's last request. David Max asked if his ashes might be put with the blood of the men who died at Dieppe: among the stones.

The stones of the title first suggest coldness or hard-heartedness, as in Ben's lament that, despite his father's behaviour, "I would have loved a stone" (218). This makes the placement of his ashes among the "treacherous" stones ironically apt to his son: "*Why not*, I thought. *A stone among stones.*" A stone can also be a weapon; in the story "War" (*Dinner*) which Lorraine York has linked to this one, the young boy Neil throws stones at his father in anger at his imminent desertion of the family for service in the war. As a fact of the landscape, the stones of the beach also played a role in thwarting the attack, since they "jammed the tank tracks" (216). And of course, as a title, "Stones" recalls the biblical proverb which Findley brings to mind here, generally paraphrased as "Let he who is without sin, cast the first stone" (John 8:7).[12]

"Fathers cannot be cowards," Ben insists (217). Which term excludes the other? If Max remains accepted and loved as Ben's father, despite everything, then what meaning does "coward" hold for him? Surely, Findley implies, fathers endure, despite the labels society may apply to their actions. In mingling his father's ashes with those of his obedient men, the "heroes" at Dieppe, Ben finally challenges the distinction between "heroes" and "cowards" that so burdened his father.

If David Max's dilemma is that he fails to live up to an ideal of masculinity that his son comes to question, the unnamed father in "The Boat" lives up to his gender role all too well.[13] With the help of "the boat," the father supports his large family of six daughters and one son—the narrator, now looking back as an adult—through the summer season of lobster and trawl fishing.

The father, forty when he married, is described by his son as an old man when he is born, lending mystery to their relationship. Within the son's memory-map of the family home, the father's bedroom represents his silent protest against the harsh outdoor labour of his life. Radio and reading lamp always on, it also appears as a masculine refuge from the feminine order of the household. The unmade bed he lies on top of, the fact that "he never seemed to sleep, only to doze" implies an intellectual restlessness which his simple, seasonal life will not satisfy. The mythically described "daughters of the house," after a brief apprenticeship at home, are led by reading their father's books into a similar restlessness. Tempted by the money and excitement offered by working in the American-owned Sea Food Restaurant, they allow themselves to be wooed, won and taken away by visiting American men. And the father, MacLeod implies, appears to sympathize with his daughters, for he himself is wooed by the outside world. After he takes a group of tourists out for a ride in the *Jenny Lynn*, he succumbs to their flattery and alcohol, and entertains them with Gaelic songs dating back three hundred years. The father who has moved uncomplainingly between his life in the boat, and the life of his books, acts also as a guileless prophet of the past, amazing and shaming his listening son.

Consequently, it is with a sense of guilty duty that the son, when he turns fifteen, steps into the role that his mother's family had envisioned for him. His father wants him to continue with his studies. But the mother here reinforces "manly behaviour" to the extent that she remains loyal to the traditional ways and gender roles of the village, including an obligation that is also the son's birthright.

MacLeod has stressed the importance form plays in shaping his fiction, saying "[v]ery often, when I write stories, I write the concluding paragraph about half-way through. And I find that this more or less helps me because I think of it as, 'This is the last thing I'm going to say to the reader, this will be the last statement that I'll make—the last paragraph or the last sentence'" ("Exiles" 151). Whether or not this was the case with "The Boat," its final paragraph is almost a story—or a poem—in itself. The son has promised to "remain with [his father] as long as he lived and... [to] fish the sea together" (122). Yet this promise perhaps serves to shorten the father's life, as his disappearance from the boat in a November squall releases the son from his noble vow. Whether by active suicide or passive exhaustion, the father appears to have sacrificed himself. The story concludes with the son's terrifying encounter with the body of the father, consumed by the sea the mother still loves:

> His hands were shredded ribbons as were his feet which had lost their boots to the suction of the sea, and his shoulders came apart in our hands when we tried to move him from the rocks. And the fish had eaten his testicles and the gulls had pecked out his eyes and the white-green stubble of his whiskers had continued to grow in death, like the grass on graves, upon the purple bloated mass that was his face. There was not much left of my father, physically, as he lay there with the brass chains on his wrists and the seaweed in his hair. (125)

The father's body has been both transformed and absorbed, the consumption of eyes and testicles recalling the ways in which his life was consumed by others. The lyrical parallelling of "brass chains on his wrists" and "seaweed in his hair" suggests an unconscious garlanding. Numerous figures of paradoxical, inverted paternal authority are here suggested, such as Lear, garlanded with weeds and wild flowers on the heath, or the royal father in Ariel's song in *The Tempest* (I.ii.398–406). But perhaps the most important word in the description is the adverb "physically," qualifying the father's disintegration. Unlike the pronouncement by Ben Max upon *his* father's absorption by the sea, that "He is dead and he is gone" (220), the narrator's statement here implies that his father remains more alive in death. Both fathers are imaged as absorbed by the sea; both may also be described as enacting a sacrifice. In "The Boat," the sacrifice is made to free the son from an unwanted social, as well as gender, role; in "Stones," "sacrifice" may be exactly what David Max failed to achieve. However, by mentally walking with his lost men, "all through hell... to do them honour" (218), during the bitter remainder of his life, he has absolved his son of the necessity of enacting a rigid gender role that, tightened by the demands of war, left his father "pummelled and broken" (219).

As I have shown, Timothy Findley and Alistair MacLeod are in many ways very different writers. Frequently utilizing the image of the mirror, which reinforces the overarching theme of social life as theatre, Findley emphasizes the "performative" quality of gender relations. Yet his sensitivity to our ongoing social "theatre" is based upon an underlying awareness of our original, if estranged, participation in an elemental, sacred order, seen in the natural imagery deployed in "Stones." MacLeod, drawing his artistic authority from the timeless act of storytelling, reminds us of our human rootedness... in a landscape, a community, a body. MacLeod's recurring focus on hands—a focus which links the two stories—connects his men and women to the natural order. By doing so, he reclaims an ancient relationship that today is urged by many, from feminists, to native healers, to environmentalists. Each male author reflects gender from an angle unique to his interests and experiences, yet the men and women their equally moving, magical stories offer us are well worth reflecting on.[14]

NOTES

1. Personal communication made to me by Prof. Stan Dragland of the University of Western Ontario. Ondaatje's selection of *two* MacLeod stories, "As Birds Bring Forth the Sun" and "The Closing Down of Summer" for his anthology of Canadian stories *From Ink Lake*—they hold the significant position, respectively, of "opening" and "closing" story—clearly demonstrates his admiration.

2. On this vexed question of "identity politics," Carol Roberts notes: "Findley refuses to be called a homosexual writer and opposes the labelling of any group in society, whether based on gender, colour, nationality, or sexual orientation. He told Peter Buitenhuis in 1988, 'I'm opposed to the ghettoization of homosexuals. "Gay" is a word I loathe and detest. As a homosexual, it offends me deeply and it offends me twice deeply when other homosexuals choose that as an appellation—as an "us against them" word. It's so confining. The point is to join the human race, as my mother would say'" (Roberts 105–106). However, in our 1993 interview, Findley used *both* terms freely. I will follow his more recent practice in this essay.

3. In this paper, I will be drawing on my published interviews with both writers: "'I Want Edge': An Interview with Timothy Findley" (abbreviated to "Edge," *Canadian Literature* 148 [Spring 1996] 115–129) and "Alistair MacLeod: 'The World is Full of Exiles'" (abbreviated to "Exiles," *Studies in Canadian Literature* 20:1 [1995]: 150–159).

4. I am using representation in the sense of being "an image brought clearly to mind," although it may also include "a dramatic production or performance" (*Collins English Dictionary* 1979).

5. The following abbreviations are being used to represent the two authors' story collection titles: *Birds* for *As Birds Bring Forth the Sun and Other Stories*, *Gift* for *The Lost Salt Gift of Blood* and *Dinner* for *Dinner Along the Amazon*.

6. As he told me in our interview, he is presently working on a novel about Highland soldiers at the siege of Quebec, entitled *No Great Mischief If They Fall* ("Exiles" 150).

7. This bias in favour of masculine speakers or protagonists has finally been challenged in the long short story / novella (a vexed distinction) "Island," which has recently been published, by Thistledown Press (Saskatoon, 1989), in a specialty edition. Written in the third person, the story narrates the life of the last of a line of lighthouse keepers, Agnes MacPhedran.

8. The use of a mirror as a trope for identity or self-knowledge, and the quest for that identity, is a familiar one; see M. H. Abrams's *The Mirror and the Lamp*. In Findley's case, however, the questioning is frequently specifically related to *gender* roles and identities; a questioning that is perhaps more commonly seen in the writing of women.

9. Cf. her discussion of *The Butterfly Plague*, where Barbara Gabriel makes the following observation about the "Orientalist" description of the sexually ambiguous Octavius: "Associated throughout the novel with the aesthetics of the Japanese, Octavius's coding as oriental ephebe is made clearer in the first version of the novel, where he suggests these 'small, delicate Japanese faces carved in ivory and teakwood—dark Buddhas and russet warriors—golden daughters of the Mikado' (Findley 1969, 33). Yet his framing also anticipates the Lucy figure of Findley's *Not Wanted on the Voyage*, who is even more explicitly drawn as the *Onna gata* of the Japanese Kabuki theatre, that ideal stylization of the feminine, which is always performed by a man" (233).

10. "Manliness during the [Second World] War encompassed the traditional attributes of courage, endurance, toughness and a lack of squeamishness when confronted by the dangers of a raging battle. ... An additional fear was that a solider might be thought of as less than a man and unsuitable for soldiering if he did not perform well" (Dubbert 231).

11. In *The Forty-Nine Percent Majority*, four stereotypical attitudes associated with masculinity are said to define "the male sex role": 1. No Sissy Stuff. 2. The Big Wheel. 3. The Sturdy Oak. 4. Give 'Em Hell! The attitude David Max has *most* failed to express, out of the four, is that of being "The Sturdy Oak" in a situation in which no amount of violence or aggression could have protected him.

12. Prof. Louis MacKendrick of University of Windsor has pointed out that "stones" is also male slang for the testicles, and associated traits like bravery or daring. Gender *does* affect reading, it seems.

13. Significantly, none of the characters is given a name in "The Boat." By deliberating omitting names, MacLeod underscores the universal quality of the story's conflicts.

14. I gratefully acknowledge the assistance of the Social Sciences and Humanities Research Council of Canada, who provided funding for this research in the form of a Post-Doctoral Fellowship.

WORKS CITED

Abrams, M. H. *The Mirror and the Lamp: Romantic Theory and the Critical Tradition.* London: Oxford UP, 1953.
Brod, Harry. "The Case for Men's Studies." *The Making of Masculinities: The New Men's Studies.* Ed. Harry Brod. Boston: Allen and Unwin, 1987. 39–62.
Butler, Judith. *Gender Trouble: Feminism and the Subversion of Identity.* New York; London: Routledge, 1990.
David, Deborah S., and Robert Brannon, eds. *The Forty-Nine Percent Majority: The Male Sex Role.* Reading, Mass.: Addison-Wesley, 1976.
Dubbert, Joe L. *A Man's Place: Masculinity in Transition.* Englewood Cliffs, N. J.: Prentice-Hall, 1979.
Findley, Timothy. *Dinner Along the Amazon.* Markham, Ont.: Penguin, 1984.
——— . *Dust to Dust: Stories.* Toronto: HarperCollins, 1997.
——— . *Headhunter.* Toronto: HarperCollins, 1993.
——— . *Stones.* Markham, Ont.: Penguin, 1988.
——— . *The Last of the Crazy People.* Markham, Ont.: Penguin, 1967.
Gabriel, Barbara. Rev. of *Dinner Along the Amazon,* by Timothy Findley. *Canadian Fiction Magazine* (1985): 87–89.
——— . "Performing the Bent Text: Fascism and the Regulation of Sexualities in Timothy Findley's *The Butterfly Plague.*" *English Studies in Canada* 20:2 (June 1995): 227–250.
Kruk, Laurie. "Alistair MacLeod: 'The World Is Full of Exiles.' " *Studies in Canadian Literature* 20:1 (1995): 150–159.
——— . " 'I Want Edge': An Interview with Timothy Findley." *Canadian Literature* 148 (Spring 1996): 115–129.
Kulyk Keefer, Janice. *Under Eastern Eyes: A Critical Reading of Maritime Fiction.* Toronto: U of Toronto P, 1987.
MacLeod, Alistair. *As Birds Bring Forth the Sun and Other Stories.* Toronto: McClelland and Stewart, 1976.
——— . *Island.* Saskatoon, Sask.: Thistledown, 1989.
——— . *The Lost Salt Gift of Blood.* Toronto: McClelland and Stewart, 1976.
Murray, Don. "Seeing and Surviving in Timothy Findley's Short Stories." *Studies in Canadian Literature* 13:2 (1988): 200–222.
Nicholson, Colin. "Signatures of Time: Alistair MacLeod and His Short Stories." *Canadian Literature* 107 (Winter 1985): 90–101.
Ondaatje, Michael, ed. *From Ink Lake: Canadian Stories Selected by Michael Ondaatje.* Toronto: Lester and Orpen Dennys, 1990.
——— . "The Time Around Scars." *There's a Trick with a Knife I'm Learning to Do: Poems 1963–78.* New York: Norton, 1979. 19.
Pleck, Joseph. *The Myth of Masculinity.* Cambridge, Mass.; London: MIT Press, 1981.
Pratt, Mary Louise. "The Short Story: The Long and the Short of It." *The New Short Story Theories.* Ed. Charles E. May. Athens, Ohio: Ohio UP, 1994. 91–113.
Roberts, Carol. *Timothy Findley: Stories from a Life.* Toronto: ECW Press, 1994.
York, Lorraine M. *Front Lines: The Fiction of Timothy Findley.* Toronto: ECW, 1991.

"To make the necessary dream perpetual": Postrealist Heroes in Canadian Short Fiction

DEBORAH BOWEN

TEN YEARS AGO at an international conference in Rome, Robert Kroetsch presented a paper entitled "Learning the Hero from Northrop Frye." Though liberally sprinkled with what Kroetsch himself calls "wilful misprisions" in the manner we have come to expect of him, his paper is nevertheless a delightfully wilful tribute to Frye. Kroetsch applauds Frye's dictum that, in the process of creating literary myth out of the disconnected elements of romance, "the real hero becomes the poet, not the agent of force or cunning whom the poet may celebrate" (*Secular* 178, qtd. in "Learning" 160); Kroetsch concludes that the most thoroughgoing heroic poet in Canadian literature is Frye himself, because his work is "an extended commentary on the great Canadian epic poem... whose text we do not have," and he himself therefore becomes the voice of that epic (161).

Kroetsch celebrates the text that we do not have because, he argues, it is not any "inherited... meaning" of heroic myth that matters, but rather "its narrative reliance," its "narrative necessity," which provides "a *potential* for meaning, a potential that locates me and loses me, a potential that is present in my telling of a story, yet beyond that telling" (158–159). The narrative that Kroetsch weaves around Frye-as-hero is a response to this potential in myth for escape from conformity with its meaning: "Frye, in his offering of 'myth as a shaping principle,' offers a place to locate and to release [the] imaginative energy" (159) of resistance against the powerful centre—in this case, Frye himself. "Simply put, by the act of retelling we can tell ourselves both out of and into story" (159). Kroetsch's retelling of Frye is such a resistance; it is an inscription of *reader*-as-hero of that romance genre to which Frye and Kroetsch concur in ascribing an "inherently revolutionary quality" because of its recreativeness (160).

Two years earlier, Kroetsch had written that "Canadians, uncertain of their meta-narratives, are more than uncertain of their heroes" ("Disunity" 28). Would-be heroes in literature turn out to be faltering, weak, multiple personalities, like Philip Bentley in *As for Me and My House*; successful heroes resist the traditional metanarratives and refuse the norms, like Wiebe's Big Bear. But "[i]n this near-hopeless separation of hero from communal behavior, the Canadian psyche, once again, both survives and flourishes" (29). In fact it was back in 1977 that Ronald Sutherland suggested that Canadian literature was seeing the birth of a new kind of hero: in place of the stolid, God-fearing pillar of society was emerging the somewhat unwillingly respected but not respectable individualist, like Doc Hunter in Ross's *Sawbones Memorial*; in place of the self-effacing, confused and guilt-ridden citizen appeared the independent, unconventional outsider who knew his or her own mind and challenged accepted values, like Hoda in Wiseman's *Crackpot* (*New Hero* 10–16).

> What has happened in Canadian fiction is that the erstwhile outcasts have suddenly become the heroes. Now that the Old Order and the conventions of society have faded away, those who managed to live outside the pale have become the subjects of intense examination. We always knew that they were there, despised them, marvelled at them and pitied them, but now we would like to know their secret, their vital truths. (*New Hero* 10–11)

In his Conclusion to *A Literary History of Canada* (1965), Frye described how, in the twentieth century, Canadian popular romantic fiction had become the social mythology of a conservative society, and realism had become the mode for unsettling stock responses, the realistic having "a moral dignity that the [romantic] lacks" (35). But there has been a further sea change since 1965: the realism on which Canadian prose fiction as we knew it was largely dependent has finally floundered into the nets of poststructuralism, and belief in an easily mimetic language is no longer possible—if, indeed, such a belief ever really existed. *Realism* is now perceived as the mythology of a bourgeois materialist culture, and something *beyond* realism is needed to unsettle its assumptions of transparency and normalcy.

Recently the magic real has been in the ascendant, especially in literature understood as socially or thematically marginalized, because magic realism offers a particularly potent "imagining otherwise." But in this paper I want to argue for the generativity of a postrealist kind of *romance*, where the hero (like Kroetsch, like Kroetsch's Frye) is resistant, subversive, retold. A fresh interest in definitions of the heroic, the larger-than-(whose?)-life, is another response to the felt need for "vital truths" in what

I am calling postrealist fiction. It has often been argued that short fiction is in any case still closely allied to its pre-realist origins in fable, fairy story, folk-tale, and myth (see Shaw vii, May xviii). These genres already signal a developed awareness of audience. And what is of particular interest in the stories I want to discuss is the degree to which the recognition of a new, culturally-resistant type of heroism depends on the sophistication of that audience—depends, in fact, on a culturally resistant reader.

The three stories I'd like to focus on are all stories from the Prentice-Hall collection *Canadian Short Fiction: From Myth to Modern*. They are from three different decades and (at least) three different geographical and cultural settings: Margaret Laurence's "Horses of the Night" (1967), Alistair MacLeod's "The Boat" (1974), and David Adams Richards's "Dane" (1982). It is possible to describe all three as conventional realist fiction—indeed, this is the primary reading offered by the editor of the collection, W. H. New. But a realist reading elides the cultural resistance that is spoken through the postrealist heroes of these stories. Foregrounding the psychology of the storytelling process itself, each of these stories is written in the first person, and in each case the narrator is using story as a means of overcoming trauma: all three stories are narratives of loss.

Writing in the first person provides a layered method of reaching back into the past. Like Kroetsch's story about Frye, all three of these stories narrate events over a long time period, of some ten years or more, and are recounted from a distance of as much as thirty years after that; thus they cannot easily be contained within that characterization of the short story which sees as definitive the notion of one connected episode, nor do they offer a single climactic action or a simple epiphanic moment. Because the first-person narrator can "frame" difficult earlier experiences with the hindsight of maturity, such narration offers a particular challenge to the reader, who is invited to decode the framed narrative through the frame, but also to recognize the frame as device. Thus in this type of postrealist narration the short story's traditional emphasis on closure is undermined by the possibility of a subversively epiphanic moment for the reader, which is embedded within or even concealed by the narrative.

Such a gesture has a precedent in the technique of, for instance, the Anglo-Irish writer Elizabeth Bowen, when she talks of her stories as "questions asked: many end with a shrug, a query, or, to the reader, a sort of over-to-you" ("Preface"). One might register such modernist open-endedness as precursor to the simultaneous inscription and subversion of meaning that I am proposing in these postrealist fictions. That is to say, it is possible for a reader of Laurence or MacLeod or Richards to accept the status quo that the story describes; but such a reading is uninflected by the resistance of the heroic that can equally well be found here.

One way to deal with loss is to narrate it into gain—to rewrite the outsider as the hero, especially when that outsider has disappeared or died, and this experience of loss has been traumatic for the narrator. Narrative inevitably restructures and reorganizes the empirically real; it is a contemporary cliché that the notion of true story is oxymoronic. But this cliché can provide a palimpsestic supplement of meaning for the writer. If storytelling by definition creates as much as it reveals truth, then for both narrator and reader the victim can become the hero, and trauma can become romance. As Kroetsch has both argued and demonstrated, writers can demythologize the systems that threaten to define them ("Unhiding" 58). Once the heroic itself is disclosed as a socially defined construct, it can be "uninvented" and rewritten otherwise. "By the act of retelling we can tell ourselves both out of and into story" ("Learning" 159).

Margaret Laurence's "Horses of the Night" has often been read as New presents it, as one story of several in *A Bird in the House* that offer a "graphic account of Depression pressures on thwarted women and displaced men" (New 271). Chris grows up on a subsistence farm with a rough-and-tumble family; his engineering ambitions are dashed by lack of funds for continuing his education; he suffers humiliations as a travelling salesman and psychological trauma in military service in World War II; he ends as a permanent patient in a mental institution. But I want to suggest that the narrative voice enables a doubled reading of the main character's loss.

From the opening of the story it is clear that Chris's cousin Vanessa, who is the narrator, sees him as a figure from myth. In childhood she thinks of Shallow Creek, where Chris comes from, as "a legendary winter country" inhabited by Eskimos (289). Chris's own imaginative escapes from the harsh realities of life—the house made out of trees, the stories of his sleek riding horses and his ranch, the miniature saddle he stitches for Vanessa, and later the "brave and useless strokes of fantasy" of his schemes and plans for his future (302)—all these are escapes that Vanessa relishes and, at least as a child, embellishes in her own imagination. Chris treats her as an equal, even when she is a young child, and a girl at that; when leaving Manawaka at the end of high school, he tells her that "anybody can do anything at all, anything, if they really set their minds to it. ... If you hold it in your mind, like, then it's real, see?" (295) Thus when, much later, Chris writes from the horrors of army service that he does not live inside his body any more, we may recognize in this, his final "unreal solution" (302), a perpetual mental reality made out of a dream that is necessary for him.

So it is that, at the end of the story, when Chris is shut up in his own mind in the institution, Vanessa muses, "I could not know whether the land he journeyed through was inhabited by terrors... or whether he had discovered at last a way for himself to make the necessary dream perpetual" (302). Laurence's challenge to the reader seems to me to be to allow *either* of these possibilities to be true. Commentators (and students) usually assume the tragedy of the first; but if the second, then Chris continues to be a figure of romantic myth even in the institution, beyond the reach of the real, larger and not smaller than life. Is it possible to read this ending as positive, in any sense? That depends on the salvific power we are willing to allow to the world of imagination, as opposed here to the world of the body—a power that Vanessa herself understands. Whether Chris is read as victim or hero depends vitally, then, on the social values of the reader, who is presented with an unresolved crux, and with an epiphanic possibility that remains resolutely indeterminate.

The drowned father of Alistair MacLeod's "The Boat" is also presented as a legendary figure. This story is described by New as "a characteristic initiation or coming-of-age story, realistic in its detail, straightforward in form, and elegiac in tone" (398). I disagree on all counts but the last—which has, indeed, led another critic, Colin Nicholson, to say that MacLeod writes "as if the style itself were keening" ("Signatures" 98). I read this story as being about the power of narrative to create myth from the real, and the psychological necessity of so doing in order to come to terms with the traumatic loss of a deeply significant person. Joyce Carol Oates, in the "Afterword" to McClelland and Stewart's 1989 edition of *The Lost Salt Gift of Blood*, writes, "If I were to name a single underlying motive for MacLeod's fiction, I would say that it is the urge to memorialize, the urge to sanctify" (159). The narrator's urge turns his family into figures of legend, combining elements of the Celtic past and the all-American Hemingwayesque. Rather than presenting the reader with a "moment of insight," this story creates a whole cast of mind that is conscious of making story, and the narrator tacitly requests the reader's complicity in the myth-making process.

The narrator opens the story by telling us of his present-day nocturnal awakenings in which he expects to find his father waiting for him beneath the window, and the fishing boat waiting at the pier. But ten years have gone by and these haunting memories are "only shadows and echoes" of the past (399). Several times during the story the narrator reminds us that his narration is with the power and also the faultiness of hindsight: "I say this now as if I knew it all then. ... But of course it was not that way at all" (400). Both the tall dark mother and the beautiful willowy daughters are described as characters from romance. The huge dishevelled fisherman-father is a lover of books, despite his wife's disapproval, so that it seems quite appropriate when the tourists call him "*Our Ernest Hemingway*," more particularly since after taking them out in his boat he has drunk a great deal, and sung old sea shanties and Gaelic drinking songs and war songs for three hours while they taped him: "When his voice ceased, the savage melancholy of three hundred years seemed to hang over the peaceful harbour and the quiet boats and the men leaning in the doorways of their shanties with their cigarettes glowing in the dusk and the women looking to the sea from their open windows with their children in their arms" (405).

There is another and definitive way in which for the son this father establishes his status as a heroic, mythical character. During the last season of fishing with him, the son realizes that his father has chosen the sea out of the need to support his family, and not out of any love for the ocean; that his first love would have been books, and a university education; and the son recognizes in the father great bravery. The father's final gesture is his jump—or fall—to his death from the back of the boat on the last day of the fishing season, into the huge Atlantic waves. This liberates his son from a bond of loyalty to the boat, but also binds him to go on with his studies as his father had wanted. A week later the father's battered body is found wedged between boulders below cliffs miles up the coast: the last sentence of the story reads, "There was not much left of my father, physically, as he lay there with the brass chains on his wrists and the seaweed in his hair" (411). Earlier when the son had felt that he must abandon his education, *The Tempest* was one of the books that he named as a dearly loved friend: in his death in a literal tempest, the father becomes a sea-changed creature. And, as with all figures from myth, his power is not in what remains physically, but in the life he has lived, caught between the two cultures of boats and books, and the moving forces of that life: his books, his songs, his spirit. The son becomes a university professor who sleeps badly. The son writes the story because he needs to: "by the act of retelling we can tell ourselves both out of and into story" ("Learning" 159).

Nicholson writes of another of MacLeod's stories that "genre discriminations between realism and romance and hitherto assumed boundaries between memory and myth are sufficiently blurred for the reader to be in some doubt" about which way to take the story ("Regions" 136). This "unsettling effect" is also present in David Adams Richards's story "Dane," though the difference in tone is such that readers have often been hoodwinked into one interpretation only. New introduces the story in the Prentice-Hall anthology by saying that "[t]ypically, Richards's characters slide from failure to failure" (505); he sees this story as an example of characters who are "reduced" and experience "lack" in profound ways. I want to argue, rather, that this story too is enacting the creation of a legend. What may initially appear to be a depressing realist portrait slides into a postrealist romance mode, through the irony of the framing device and the admiration of the narrator for this young man whose death he reads as a last laugh on middle-class society.

Again, the narrator tells his story with the wisdom of some years of hindsight; again, the layering of the narrative offers to the reader the opportunity for a subversive epiphany, in which, in this case, the "decent" society of Dane's town is itself judged as "lacking" something. At the opening of the story, a man "who may have been a Chartered Accountant" comes out of the apartment building that stands where the winos' huts and Dane's house used to be: he represents protected well-to-do middle-class life as he "wraps the heavy fur-lined coat about him, and wipes his mouth with a handkerchief" (506). At the end of the story, the alcoholic Dane is killed in a car accident, "[a]nd people said that was for the best, because he'd made quite a mess of his life" (509). The town did what they could: when Dane went on a trip with the school's all-star hockey squad, he was billetted with "'one of the better families' so he could see how they lived, and could be given, for those 3 or 4 days, anything he wanted" (508). But somehow this kindness was ill-conceived: after his trip Dane quits the hockey squad, becomes even less socially acceptable, even more of a "failure," and during his bouts in jail for stealing or drunkenness he takes delight in escaping to filch boxes of chocolates "and other things that look absolutely absurd to be caught with" (509).

All through the story Dane is described with a kind of envy, as someone who marches to a different drummer. Even as a five-year-old he spent his days among winos on the back streets, taking bottles back to the liquor store for a few cents apiece; whatever dark things he may have witnessed, "he was as quick as a monkey and funny and alive and none bothered him" (506). His clothes were ragged and he was a latchkey kid from a tumble-down house, but "he was a fine and agile sports enthusiast at a young age, and a leader in most things he did" (506). When he was in his teens "he excelled in everything he wished to"—hockey, swimming, baseball, cricket, academics at school, and even bingo; and he was fiercely loyal to his family. He was a fine shot, but never shot at animals like the other kids, settling for windows and street lights instead: "Consequently he became known to police as a vandal while those who slaughtered squirrels and birds were considered good mannered" (506). When Dane sneaks into the movie theatre that Jess's father owns, even though Jess had invited him "for free," the clash of value-systems is stark: Jess is hurt that his conventional capitalism has been rejected, but of course cannot articulate why; and Dane cannot understand why, if Jess did not want him to pay in the first place, he has done anything wrong in bucking the system by his wits.

Even as a wino Dane has style. With a wink and a laugh he steals everything he can lay his hands on, and then works out a system for getting out of jail: "there was a hilariousness in all of this that he couldn't help—as if he sought after and needed, however briefly, the great universal laugh" (508). His half-smile the last time Jess sees him, two days before his death, is "somewhere between a savage and a saint" (509). Once we have noticed all this, as readers, we cannot simply identify with the people who said he'd "made quite a mess of his life." As with Chris in the mental institution, as with the drowned father who frees his son from the grip of tradition, so with Dane—by whose value system are they weighed and found wanting? Could there be other values at work that demand a hearing too?

In 1972, five years before Sutherland's book on *The New Hero*, Margaret Atwood had pointed to "a superabundance of victims in Canadian literature"—she suggested that "the Canadian gloom is more unrelieved than most and the death and failure toll out of proportion" (*Survival* 39, 35). What is less often remembered is that her argument for the "creative non-victim" as antidote to this situation was in fact an argument for storytelling; she defined the *author* as creative non-victim at the moment of writing, and the *reader* as creative non-victim at the moment of insight (40). In place of Atwood's hero-as-victim, the stories I am discussing allow for the social subversion of victim-as-hero. The use of first-person narrators signals the configuration of a doubleness in the narrative: not only is there a story to be told by the narrator, but there is the telling of a story to be decoded by the reader; moreover, each telling is of more than a *single* story. Which way to jump? Each story implies that heroism is a social construct dependent on a shared value-system about what is worthwhile and socially laudable; these heroes will neither change nor save their own societies, but they do offer a critique of their societies in their tacit appeal to the reader to resist the power of the accepted cultural centre and to actualize in reading just that kind of retelling and self-redefinition that Kroetsch describes as the narrative necessity of myth. In these stories the social outsider, the character who marches to a different drummer, can be read as the hero, exactly because the narrator of his story, who stands in the "between," inscribes the possibility that he has appropriated the "vital truth" of making "the necessary dream perpetual" (Laurence 302). And this unspoken invitation to the reader to valorize a social mythology other than the conventional one creates the potential for the reader too, by the act of retelling, to become—sired by Frye, out of Atwood, racing the track with Kroetsch—a creative non-victim, a postrealist hero.

BIBLIOGRAPHY AND WORKS CITED

Atwood, Margaret. *Survival: A Thematic Guide to Canadian Literature.* Toronto: Anansi, 1972.

Bowen, Elizabeth. "Preface." *Early Stories.* New York: Knopf, 1951.

Frye, Northrop. *The Secular Scripture: A Study of the Structure of Romance.* Cambridge, Mass.; London: Harvard UP, 1976.

——. "Silence in the Sea." 1968. *The Bush Garden: Essays on the Canadian Imagination.* Toronto: Anansi, 1971. 181–197.

——. "Conclusion" to *A Literary History of Canada.* 1965. *The Bush Garden* 213–251.

Kroetsch, Robert. "Disunity as Unity: A Canadian Strategy." 1985. *The Lovely Treachery of Words: Essays Selected and New.* Toronto; New York; Oxford: Oxford UP, 1989. 21–33.

——. "Learning the Hero from Northrop Frye." 1987. *The Lovely Treachery of Words: Essays Selected and New.* Toronto; New York, Oxford: Oxford UP, 1989. 151–162.

——. "Unhiding the Hidden." *The Lovely Treachery of Words: Essays Selected and New.* Toronto; New York; Oxford: Oxford UP, 1989. 58–63.

Laurence, Margaret. "Horses of the Night." 1967. *Canadian Short Fiction: From Myth to Modern.* Ed. W. H. New. Scarborough: Prentice-Hall, 1986. 288–302.

MacLeod, Alistair. "The Boat." 1974. *Canadian Short Fiction: From Myth to Modern.* Ed. W. H. New. Scarborough: Prentice-Hall, 1986. 398–411.

May, Charles E., ed. "Introduction." *The New Short Story Theories.* Athens: Ohio UP, 1994. xv–xxvi.

Middlebro', Tom. "Imitatio Inanitatis: Literary Madness and the Canadian Short Story." *Canadian Literature* 107 (Winter 1985): 189–193.

New, W. H., ed. *Canadian Short Fiction: From Myth to Modern.* Scarborough: Prentice-Hall, 1986.

Nicholson, Colin. "Regions of Memory: Alistair MacLeod's Fiction." *British Journal of Canadian Studies* 7:1 (1992): 128–137.

——. "Signatures of Time: Alistair MacLeod and His Short Stories." *Canadian Literature* 107 (Winter 1985): 90–101.

Oates, Joyce Carol. "Afterword." *The Lost Salt Gift of Blood,* by Alistair MacLeod. 1976. Toronto: McClelland and Stewart, 1989. 157–160.

Richards, David Adams. "Dane." 1982. *Canadian Short Fiction: From Myth to Modern.* Ed. W. H. New. Scarborough: Prentice-Hall, 1986. 505–509.

Shaw, Valerie. "'Only Short Stories': Estimates and Explanations." *The Short Story: A Critical Introduction.* London; New York: Longman, 1983. 1–28.

Sutherland, Ronald. *The New Hero: Essays in Comparative Quebec/Canadian Literature.* Toronto: Macmillan, 1977.

The Canadian Short Story

ALISTAIR MACLEOD

I WOULD LIKE TO BEGIN BY STATING that everything that is to follow is, in the words of Alice Munro, "an offering." In other words "you the listeners" may take from these remarks whatever might prove helpful. It is very difficult to be truly objective in dealing with literary matters and even the most "objective" of views may, in the end, veer dangerously close to personal opinion.

We must first of all remember that writing Canadian short stories is a quite recent phenomenon. All of Canadian literature, in terms of the larger world, is relatively recent. In Pelham Edgar's chapter on "English Canadian Literature" in the *Cambridge History of English Literature* (1916), he describes the problems associated with a "colonial literature," the product, as he says, of "a young country born into the old age of the world." Nineteen-twenty-eight is the date of Raymond Knister's *Canadian Short Stories*, the first anthology of Canadian short stories, commissioned by Macmillan publishers. What might we say, then, about a genre that, if we consider anthologized publication, is only some seventy years old? We might ask larger questions about a "total literature" that has journeyed only one hundred and fifty years from its time of birth.

The question often asked is, "Who writes literature anyway?" The answers may often spin off into all those myriad issues regarding appropriation of voice and so forth, but it seems safe to say that literature is written by literate people—people who can read and write. I believe that to create literature one has to have "language and leisure" and for many years there were not many people in this country who had both. (I am not talking about "oral story telling" or "orature," which is a subject in which I am very interested.) If one looks to the U.S. during the period of slavery, one finds that there was a population of some 12 million who were enslaved; but one does not find the great slavery novel rising from such ranks. These were people who had neither language (because they were denied it through lack of education) nor the "leisure" required for composition. It was not because they had *nothing to say*. The great slavery/anti-slavery novel is probably *Uncle Tom's Cabin* written by an upper-class white woman who had *both* language and leisure, and indeed, "something to say."

The early literature in Canada was written by individuals who had both language and leisure and there were not very many of them. Outside the boundaries of Quebec, the first authors were generally British and they brought with them the attitudes often associated with their birthplace. Many of them were simply afraid of the country: the winters were long, the forests were vast, the animals were strange and sometimes dangerous, the aboriginal peoples distinctly "different." Often there were few people with whom to associate and they often missed the opera, the theatre and the music they had enjoyed during their formative years. This is the beginning of the much talked about "garrison mentality" and the introduction of authors who might be described as "permanent tourists" in the phraseology of P. K. Page.

Almost immediately the question of "audience" surfaces. Early writers were concerned by the fact that they often had to send their work to Britain or the United States and this situation could not help but influence what was happening at their desks (writing in one country for publication in another). Also, almost immediately, arguments arose concerning the nature and purpose of the literature. Early criticism suggests a "Canadian literature" that might foster a Canadian identity albeit one that maintained the values and standards of nineteenth-century Britain. There were others who felt that the growth of an indigenous literature was hampered by too much dependence on the British tradition resulting in our unfortunate "colonial position."

There is also, almost from the beginning, the argument concerning the local, the regional, and the national. One might debate these labels within the country itself but one must remember that in the "big picture" of the Commonwealth, to write of *anything* Canadian might be considered "local" or "regional" or *quaint* to an English audience residing in London. Almost anything written from Canada would be considered on the periphery of literature written in English rather than at the core. This has led to a particular schizophrenia, which until recent years has caused Canadian authors to debate such issues as whether their characters should be more

British or more American or whether individual authors should use British or American spelling. Hopefully we are beyond that now, although some pressures still exist. I would like to introduce two quotations that I find particularly relevant. Northrop Frye, in *Divisions on a Ground*, states that "We study Canadian Literature as we might study Canadian geography, not because it is better geography or worse geography than someone else's but because it is our own." The second quotation is from the "Afterword" to Margaret Atwood's sequence of poems *The Journals of Susanna Moodie*: "We are all immigrants to this place even if we were born here: the country is too big for anyone to inhabit completely, and in the parts unknown to us we move in fear, exiles and invaders."

The points made in the above quotations are obvious: we should study (and create?) Canadian literature because, first, it is our own, and, second, in "the parts unknown to us," we may not feel a high degree of cultural comfort. An exchange between a unilingual student from Quebec and a unilingual student from Calgary may, at first, result in a high degree of stress and perhaps actual "fear." Especially if the individual is "alone" and cut off from other members of his/her cultural group. The hitherto simple act of ordering a cup of coffee may be fraught with uncertainty accompanied by an increased heart rate and undue perspiration. A young person from the outports of Newfoundland or from one of the Cree settlements near James Bay may find nothing in their previous life experiences that has prepared them for the Toronto subway system or the general busyness of a large metropolitan centre. The student from the large metropolitan centre may be similarly ill-prepared for the experience of the trapline or the open boat; and the howling of the huskies or the wolves or the crying of the baby seals on the Atlantic ice floes may be uncomfortable substitutes for the urban sound of twenty-four-hour traffic. I imagine that all of these young people are computer-literate and quite capable of doing calculus. At the conclusion of their visits they will have learned something that they did not know before but each will probably say, "I am glad to be home." "Home" being not only those whom they love but a conglomeration of familiar sights seen through their windows, familiar food, familiar accents, familiar music on the radio, perhaps familiar political and religious attitudes, perhaps an opportunity to converse with unilingual grandparents who have never been where they have recently journeyed. Yet Canada is home to all.

The theory has been advanced that people write about "what worries them." If "worry" seems too strong a word we might substitute "concern" or even "thought." We write about what we think about. The more we think about it the more we are apt to write about it. In Canada, for example, we think a lot about winter. Winter can kill us if we are not careful! If one has no shelter in mid-February, unless one is in Vancouver or Victoria, the experience could be fatal anywhere in Canada. Each fall there is a flurry of people checking their furnaces, applying weather-stripping, buying winter tires, checking anti-freeze, buying mittens, gloves, window-scrapers, shovels, coats, scarves, and so on. No one in Florida does any of these things. This does not mean that people in Florida do not die; but they do not die "from winter" and hence they do not think about it or worry about it very much and they certainly don't write many stories about it. Of course there are other things that might serve as subjects. My point is that winter affects the majority of Canadians in a very basic manner. Other "worries" are more regional but nonetheless quite real. At the time of this conference the residents of southern Manitoba, who are seeing their livelihoods swept away by the rampaging floods, have worries that differ considerably from those individuals who live in downtown Regina or Vancouver or Halifax. It is difficult for Manitobans to think of much else when they go to bed at night—if they go to bed at all. The worries of the Newfoundland fishers are different than those of the Saskatchewan farmers or the B. C. loggers. All of these people worry, however, about the universal subjects. They worry about love and death and betrayal and the welfare of their children. They do it, however, in different landscapes and in different weather. Canada in its vastness is not a country like Switzerland or Belgium, although individuals in those countries have their worries as well.

In addition to the vast geographical differences there are also cultural, linguistic, and historical differences that affect most Canadians whether they have been here for a short or a long period of time. Some Québécois are by now twelfth or thirteenth generation residents of that province. Some writers with Quebec roots are the literal descendants of Abraham Martin (1589–1664), who came to New France as Champlain's ship's pilot and who gave his name to the Plains of Abraham. Some are descendants of Hélène Langlois Des Portes, who was the first white child born in Canada. It is not surprising that some of these people look at Canada and the world through certain sets of eyes. The population of Newfoundland is also, comparatively, very old. Ninety-six percent of Newfoundland's population trace their ancestry back to either Ireland or the British Isles. They have endured, over the centuries, very different lives than, let us say, many of the citizens of Toronto. Toronto as Canada's largest city consists of a population in which close to fifty percent of its citizens were not born *in Canada*. It has become a region in itself in all of its uniqueness followed closely, perhaps, by Vancouver.

I believe that the above explains to some extent why the strongest literature has seemed to come from the regions. The country is too vast and varied for it to be any other way. In a 1980 interview with Robert Fulford in *Aurora*, Northrop Frye stated, "I think that as a culture matures it becomes more regional." It seems we, as Canadians, find ourselves most vividly in the different sections of the Canadian mosaic rather than in the larger, more bubbling melting pot of the United States.

We find ourselves in Howard O'Hagan's stories, which could only have been written of and from the mountains that are their source. We find ourselves in the Vancouver Island created by Jack Hodgins. And we find ourselves in the prairies of Sinclair Ross and W. O. Mitchell and Margaret Laurence; in Rudy Wiebe and Robert Kroetsch and W. D. Valgoadson and Sandra Birdsell. In Ontario we encounter not only the older Toronto world of Morley Callaghan but also a more recent vision shared by a variety of younger and often emigrant writers. We find ourselves also in the small town world so well described by George Elliott in *The Kissing Man* or in Alice Munro's "Jubilee." In Quebec, which is the most obvious of the regions, we may find ourselves not only in the "correct" French of Marie Claire Blais or Anne Hébert but also in those writers who choose to use the much maligned *joual*. Michel Tremblay and Claude Jasmin are two writers who come to mind. In the Maritimes the voices of David Adams Richards, Ernest Buckler, and Alden Nowlan loom the largest, followed perhaps by Milton Acorn, Harold Horwood, Fred Cogswell, Percy Janes, and the young black Loyalist poet George Elliot Clark.

Perhaps it is because most Canadians are relative newcomers to the urban experience that the above (with the exception of Toronto) is so. Most Canadians are not yet "masters" of the city nor do they feel particularly at ease there as far as the development of their artistic perceptions is concerned. The exceptional group that comes most obviously to mind is the Jewish segment of the population. Coming directly, for the most part, into the North American experience from the cities of Europe, they have proven to be "of the city" in a most unique and distinctive way. This of course is reflected in the excellence of their art. Yet even here we find that that which is most brilliant and enduring often reflects not the world of the larger city but rather that of the smaller ghetto within the vast metropolis. A sort of small town containing hundreds of recognizable faces, familiar shops and sounds and boundaries that are recognizably real and that tend to contain as well as to exclude. The world of Winnipeg's North End so well described by Adele Wiseman and Mordecai Richler's St. Urbain St. seem to fall within this category. Finding the vastness of the universal in the apparently small and comparatively isolated is, of course, nothing tremendously new. It has been the practice of such diverse authors as Jane Austen carefully polishing her "small square two inches of ivory," D. H. Lawrence with his Nottinghamshire, the Brontes with their Yorkshire moors, Thomas Hardy with his Wessex. It has been the strength of Joseph

Conrad to show us to ourselves through the medium of the small ship upon the tremendous ocean.

Shortly before his death, George Ryga said to me, "All of the best literature comes from all of the worst places." I did not realize he was so close to death at the time and I am not sure if his subsequent death has caused me to "think" or "worry" about his comment more than I might have otherwise. I am not sure how (or if) it applies to the above other than to indicate that the rural outport and the large city may simultaneously be "the best place" for some and "the worst place" for others. But I think it is fair to say that the best writers know their region extremely well. They know it not only with their heads but deep within their hearts. They know what they want to say and how they are to say it. They are writing of Canada and they go at their task with the single-mindedness of the Ancient Mariner encountering the wedding guest. "Look," he says, "no wedding for you today because I am going to tell you a story. And I am going to hold you here not with my hand nor with my glittering eye but by the very power of what I have to tell you and how I choose to tell it. I am going to show you what I saw and heard and smelled and tasted and felt. And I am going to tell you what it is like to be abandoned by God and by man and of the true nature of loneliness and of the preciousness of life. And I am going to do it in such a way that your life will never ever again be the same."

To recognize the awesomeness of the great in the dazzling brilliance of the small requires that that which is small must first be perfectly rendered and understood. And then all things are possible.

We, as Canadians, often inhabit individual rooms within the larger house called Canada. We do not sleep twenty-four hours within our room nor necessarily barricade ourselves behind locked doors. We are free to be social and to be free in the sharing of both our gifts and responsibilities. Therein lies our strength. In our writing and in our lives.

REAPPRAISALS: CANADIAN WRITERS

Reappraisals: Canadian Writers was begun in 1973 in response to a need for single volumes of essays on Canadian authors who had not received the critical attention they deserved or who warranted extensive and intensive reconsideration. It is the longest running series dedicated to the study of Canadian literary subjects. The annual symposium hosted by the Department of English at the University of Ottawa began in 1972 and the following year University of Ottawa Press published the first title in the series, *The Grove Symposium*. Since then our editorial policy has remained straightforward: each year to make permanently available in a single volume the best of the criticism and evaluation presented at our symposia on Canadian literature, thereby creating a body of work on, and a critical base for the study of, Canadian writers and literary subjects.

Gerald Lynch
General Editor

Titles in the series:

THE GROVE SYMPOSIUM, edited and with an introduction by John Nause

THE A. M. KLEIN SYMPOSIUM, edited and with an introduction by Seymour Mayne

THE LAMPMAN SYMPOSIUM, edited and with an introduction by Lorraine McMullen

The E. J. PRATT SYMPOSIUM, edited and with an introduction by Glenn Clever

THE ISABELLA VALANCY CRAWFORD SYMPOSIUM, edited and with an introduction by Frank M. Tierney

THE DUNCAN CAMPBELL SCOTT SYMPOSIUM, edited and with an introduction by K. P. Stich

THE CALLAGHAN SYMPOSIUM, edited and with an introduction by David Staines

THE ETHEL WILSON SYMPOSIUM, edited and with an introduction by Lorraine McMullen

TRANSLATION IN CANADIAN LITERATURE, edited and with an introduction by Camille R. La Bossière

THE SIR CHARLES G. D. ROBERTS SYMPOSIUM, edited and with an introduction by Glenn Clever

THE THOMAS CHANDLER HALIBURTON SYMPOSIUM, edited and with an introduction by Frank M. Tierney

STEPHEN LEACOCK: A REAPPRAISAL, edited and with an introduction by David Staines

FUTURE INDICATIVE: LITERARY THEORY AND CANADIAN LITERATURE, edited and with an introduction by John Moss

REFLECTIONS: AUTOBIOGRAPHY AND CANADIAN LITERATURE, edited and with an introduction by K. P. Stich

RE(DIS)COVERING OUR FOREMOTHERS: NINETEENTH-CENTURY CANADIAN WOMEN WRITERS, edited and with an introduction by Lorraine McMullen

BLISS CARMAN: A REAPPRAISAL, edited and with an introduction by Gerald Lynch

FROM THE HEART OF THE HEARTLAND: THE FICTION OF SINCLAIR ROSS, edited by John Moss

CONTEXT NORTH AMERICA: CANADIAN/U.S. LITERARY RELATIONS, edited by Camille R. La Bossière

HUGH MACLENNAN, edited by Frank M. Tierney

ECHOING SILENCE: ESSAYS ON ARCTIC NARRATIVE, edited and with a preface by John Moss

BOLDER FLIGHTS: ESSAYS ON THE CANADIAN LONG POEM, edited and with a preface by Frank M. Tierney and Angela Robbeson

Printed and bound
in Boucherville, Quebec, Canada by
MARC VEILLEUX IMPRIMEUR INC.
in October, 1999